Mesdames
of
Mayhem

13 O'Clock

Edited by
Donna Carrick

**CARRICK
PUBLISHING**

13 O'Clock

An anthology of crime stories

by the Mesdames of Mayhem

Edited by Donna Carrick

Copy-edited by Ed Piwowarczyk

Cover Art by Sara Carrick

CARRICK
PUBLISHING

Carrick Publishing

ISBN 13: 978-1-77242-025-8

Print Edition 2015

TABLE OF CONTENTS

FOREWORD

By M. H. Callway

15 twisted tales of time and crime…

Time stops for no man – or woman. Time spares no one, nor does crime as you, dear reader, will discover in these twisted tales penned by 13 fabulous Mesdames of Mayhem and an equally fabulous friend.

The clock strikes one, echoing the dastardly deeds of the past where to be a learned woman could mean losing one's life. The early hours pass slowly, as though the past refuses to release its grip on the present: a troubled young woman finds danger in her decayed family cottage, a feisty senior refuses to give up on her ex-husband and an older man seeks his lost love at – what could be more appropriate?- a crime writers' conference.

The clock strikes six, heralding the daylight hours, the hours of business. Planning is everything, as a clever marketing consultant or a seemingly faithful husband will tell you. Yet some of us take time for reflection: a respectable matron is preoccupied by puzzles and a retired judge revisits his courtroom and old battles. We scurry to serve time - and our timepieces - though they may lead us to commit disturbing crimes and to acts of violence and revenge.

Daylight fades, the hours grow long. Dedicated financial managers and hardworking librarians move swiftly to beat the clock and save lives. Sadly, some victims pass out of time while others do deadly battle with time, with equally deadly consequences.

The hands meet at midnight, but what is this? The clock strikes not 12, but 13, marking our passage to a land out of time. And yet this land, too, is beset with crime fought by a unique duo.

The Mesdames of Mayhem are 16 friends who are established Canadian crime authors. Most of the Mesdames have won or been short-listed for major crime writing awards, including the Arthur Ellis, Bony Blithe, Bony Pete, CWA's Debut Dagger, Derringer, MWA's Edgar, Indie and Polar Expressions.

To learn more about our novels and stories, follow the links in these pages and visit our website at http://mesdamesofmayhem.com/ .

PERFECT TIMING

By Melodie Campbell

Dave laughed and offered me the morning paper. "It finally happened," he said. "Take a look at this."

I took the paper from him and looked down at the headline: Board Chair Killed by Gavel.

The photo said a thousand words. Dead guy, head smashed in, wooden gavel resting in a pool of blood next to the teak boardroom table.

Oh yeah. I could believe it.

"Probably deserved it," I said. "Coming onto the board with an agenda. Manipulating everyone. Making life hell for the staff."

Dave grinned and nodded. "Apparently the executive director just picked up the thing and whacked the guy. They were in the middle of a committee meeting. There were eight witnesses."

"Not smart." I shook my head.

"But effective. He got in four whacks before someone could grab his arm. Obviously it was a crime of passion." He laughed again. "Maybe the jury will go lenient."

"Poor sod," I murmured. "I expect he was an accountant. They deal in the here and now. Obviously didn't have a marketing background."

Dave, who was a college prof, turned his gaze to me. "Interesting. Why do you say that?"

I placed the newspaper down on the kitchen table. "It's our training. Marketers are planners. We're all about timing. Everything we do—every campaign we launch—involves a three- to six-month plan. We may seem like risk-takers, but in actuality, we are the world's most meticulous planners."

"So you're saying…"

"A marketer would have planned this murder to the minute. Examined all possible choices. Considered the risks. Gone with the most logical strategy. Allowed for a defense plan. Then executed the thing—or rather the person" (I giggled here) "with timed precision."

I took a sip of steaming Kenyan AA from the mug, savoring it before continuing. "He wouldn't strike in the heat of the moment like this guy in the paper here. It's against character."

Dave looked at me funny. "I would hate to be on your hit list."

I laughed. "No worries for you, my man. I adore you. You know that." I reached over to ruffle his blond-gray hair.

Now he grinned.

I smiled back. I do adore him. He treats me well. Which is more than I can say for my first husband—the manipulative, lying bastard—who at this moment is lying at the bottom of Lake Ontario.

I executed that plan with perfect timing.

About Melodie Campbell

The *Toronto Sun* called her Canada's "Queen of Comedy." *Library Journal* compared her to Janet Evanovich. Melodie Campbell got her start writing standup.

Winner of nine awards, including the 2014 Derringer (US) and the 2014 Arthur Ellis (Canada) for the crime caper, *The Goddaughter's Revenge*, Melodie has over 200 publications, including 40 short stories and eight novels.

Her humorous time travel series, the *Land's End Trilogy*, was an Amazon Top 50 Bestseller in January 2015, putting her ahead of Diana Gabaldon and Nora Roberts.

Melodie has been a bank manager, college instructor, marketing director, comedy writer and possibly the worst runway model ever. These days, she is the Executive Director of Crime Writers of Canada.

http://funnygirlmelodie.blogspot.ca/

Amazon Author Page

Facebook

Twitter

Mesdames of Mayhem

PULLING A RABBIT

By Catherine Astolfo

The whole affair started with a solid idea. Despite her effort and planning, however, things went seriously wrong. Ethel had no idea how the weekend got so messy.

The plan was right there on her calendar: Get the stuff for The Visit.

After coffee, Ethel felt invigorated and healthy, especially after the strong java jolt and the seeds, raisins, nuts and fat of the morning glory muffin.

"Well," she said to Grandfather Clock, "isn't this a magnificent day? I believe I'll *walk* to BuyALot and back. Yes, I think that is just what the doctor ordered."

Grandfather simply ticked and tocked as usual.

Ethel set off at a brisk pace, bolstered by the warmth of an early spring sun.

"It's Bunny Rabbit time! Chocolate eggs and jelly beans!" she thought to herself, picturing the fun they would have.

She was determined to make this holiday utterly glorious, unlike the memories she had of this time of year. Her very religious family believed the occasion was a solemn one—time to spend on bended knee repenting for sins Ethel didn't remember committing.

When she wasn't very old, Ethel proclaimed religion was crap and began a life of excitement. After all, her name was Ethel, which meant "noble." People with her moniker, she read, were "dynamic, energetic, optimistic and fought convention." That described her to a T, as she told Grandfather (Clock).

She'd lost touch with most of her family because of her hippie nature. For the first 50 years, Ethel lived a life filled with a career and one baby. Her love child, raised by his cheerfully single mother, had become a lawyer, a husband, a dad. Not a bad accomplishment.

This Easter, Stephen and his family were coming all the way from Los Angeles, where he and his wife were legal consultants for the film industry. Ethel could not for the life of her picture what they did all day. Apparently there was a world of trouble those moviemakers could get into, even at the script stage. It was beyond Ethel.

She'd visited Los Angeles many times, enjoyed the warm climate, the crazy busy-ness of it all, the potential of glamor. Once in a while, she even got to attend a film premiere where she glimpsed some star or other. But she always headed back to good old Toronto and her independence.

Ethel was astounded by the goodies on display at BuyALot. Everything was glittering, pink, fluffy or yummy. Chocolate in all kinds of shapes. Trinkets and playthings.

"Oh, yes, let's get fun things to do outside! It *is* spring, after all. And after this walk, I'm sure I can manage a little child's play, ha, ha. Oh, this thing is cool..." She placed a net and a ball that stuck to its middle into her cart.

Great long lines snaked through the aisles to reach the checkout.

"Bloody BuyALot doesn't have enough cashiers," the woman in front of her confided, as though Ethel hadn't noticed.

"That's how they save money. Hire so few workers. Costing us time, but they don't give a hoot," said the man behind her.

When Ethel finally got to the cash, she was initially shocked by the price. After all, every single thing she'd bought was BuyALot Cheap. Bag after bag churned out across the checkout.

"It's worth it though," she told herself. "Think of the loads of fun we're going to have."

At the exit she suddenly remembered that she didn't have her car. She wondered if she could push the cart home and bring it back. However, narrowly spaced bright yellow posts laughed at her from the front walk. Another BuyALot cost saving.

Fortunately, at that moment she spied some (BuyALot Cheap price again) shopping carts hanging on the wall. The kind old ladies who lived in apartments used.

She looked back at the lines. They were even longer now.

This was where Ethel's spontaneous adventurous spirit superseded all that fine planning. She really couldn't explain why she did it, other than a sense that, after the enormous bill and an hour's wait in line, BuyALot owed her a way to get home.

Ethel reached up and took one of the shopping carts down. In the little hallway that led to the bathroom (surely there were no cameras here), Ethel tore off the price tags and bar codes.

No one seemed to notice her as she limped along like a bag lady with her packages over her back and the cart clutched under her arm.

Out in the parking lot, she hid in one of those sheds that promised a new windshield instantly. Currently, no one's glass was broken.

She took the wheelie out of the packaging. It was hard enough just doing that. Teeth and the one fingernail she had left were involved.

The cart was far bigger than she'd expected. Tall and rectangular, it was practically an entire shopping buggy with canvas sides. Ethel tried to read the instruction page about how to put the wheels on.

There were three sets of them. The back ones were big and solid, but the middle and front were small. Since she didn't have a wrench, she decided to tie the back wheels on with a piece of plastic from the wrapping.

"The other sets will probably sit in place once we're on the ground," she thought.

When the container was stretched out and ready, Ethel stuffed all her Easter treasures inside. There was plenty of room. She rolled out of the shed, a changed woman, a superhero who walked to and from the store.

"I'll be right back with this cart," she announced aloud in the direction of BuyALot.

"I am being decidedly un-Ethe-cal," she chuckled to herself as she dragged the cart toward home.

That was when she saw the security guard.

He was one of those tiny men that big women like Ethel often coveted but were afraid they might squash. Slim, gray-haired, his skin had an olive tone, but his eyes were a startling blue. He was astonishingly handsome. Ethel sucked in her breath and curled her toes.

His countenance was friendly, but she *had* just borrowed—technically stolen—a cart. Ethel's heart began to drum. The guard grinned at her and remained leaning against the BuyALot wall, making no move to arrest her.

Sweat trickled down Ethel's face and arms. The day was unseasonably warm, but she didn't want to stop to remove her coat. She also didn't want to rejig anything. The items in the cart were perfectly balanced.

Halfway through the lot, the front wheels fell off for the first time.

The second time, the jolting halt caused the cart to tip slightly sideways. Several bags of candy and chocolate flew out. Ethel bent over to fetch them, forgetting to use her knees. But she managed to balance all the bags without pulling her back.

The third time the wheels fell off, Ethel swore.

"Okay you blankety-blank thing, how about we just use these big back ones?"

She stuck the smaller wheels in her coat pocket and tilted the cart toward her hip. Pulling it and walking with her ample hip stuck out sideways worked extremely well. She got up the hill, down the sidewalk, and to the intersection before one of the remaining two wheels fell off. The plastic that she had tied to the end of the post was gone.

Ethel put the wheel back in its place with nothing but gravity and the weight above to keep it there.

"Please," she pleaded with it out loud, "please just make it across the intersection."

Luckily, it listened. She got all the way across the four-lane highway onto the sidewalk. Then she took the bags out and dug up the instruction sheet. Lo and behold, there was a little bag with a tiny wrench, screws and other thingies taped to the bottom. Ethel hadn't noticed it before.

She put a screw in the post and tightened it with her fingers. Perhaps that would do the trick until she reached home.

"When we get home, I'll fix you up properly before I take you back," Ethel promised the buggy (again out loud).

Sweating profusely now, she took off her coat and laid it across the cart. The other wheel and its plastic thingy, as well as the precarious screw, flew off all at once. The sudden jolt pitched a number of the bags onto the sidewalk.

One of them was filled with those bright plastic balls that she had pictured the grandkids playing with up and down the driveway. Easter Bunny-inscribed as they were, they hopped across the road, glanced harmlessly off car wheels and floated into water-filled ditches. Bunny faces grinned all the way.

That was when Ethel saw the security guard again.

He dodged the cars in the road, bent over to peer into the ditches, and snatched up Easter Bunny balls.

"Be careful!" she hollered at him.

He looked up and grinned, covered in muddy water, arms full of plastic rabbit heads. He waved with one free hand.

"I'm okay!"

"A little overly chummy, aren't ya?" Ethel muttered to herself while waving cheerfully back. Especially since he might be calling the cops next.

When he stood in front of her, puffing, she felt gigantic. Not that he was as short as she had thought. In fact, they were eye to eye, which was disconcerting. His eyes were mesmerizing.

Ethel felt a tingle in places she thought had shriveled and died. Suddenly, she decided he wasn't being chummy enough.

If only she hadn't stolen the damn cart. She scowled at it as though the buggy had done the deed all by itself. Ethel hadn't felt this flustered since the 1960s. Rather than have him arrest her, she wanted him to kiss her.

"I think I got them all," he said, plopping them into the wheelie. "Looks like you're planning a great Easter holiday."

"My son and his family are coming," Ethel said. "I don't usually celebrate. I mean, I'm not a religious person or anything. Well, obviously not, since bunnies and chocolates aren't exactly part of the whole died-for-our-sins thing."

She was babbling and aghast at what had come out of her mouth.

But he laughed and when he did, he was even more attractive. He reminded her of that Trivago guy on the TV ad, Latino version.

"I'm not religious, either," he confided. "But I don't have any kids or grandkids, so no excuse for buying chocolate. Or believe me, I would."

He gestured down at the wheels.

"May I?"

With a sheepish nod, she handed him the little wrench.

"Sure, I'd be very grateful."

With a couple of twists and a yank, he had the wheels fastened.

"There we go," he said. "That wheelie will carry all kinds of things."

They automatically began to stroll down the sidewalk toward her house.

"My name's Peter, by the way," he said.

He pointed to his name tag, one of those generic things without the fancy store logo. He must work for an agency and not BuyALot. Peter Boehner, Ethel read. But he didn't pronounce it the way she expected.

"Peter Bayner," he added.

"I'm Ethel. Why is your name so familiar?"

He dipped his head in a gesture that was somehow humble.

"I'm the one who developed Twig."

"Huh?"

"You know, that online social media thing where you can send out a short message which then gets onto a branch and forms a tree of…"

He saw her blank look and stopped, laughing.

"Okay, I guess you just read my name in the paper."

"So you're famous?"

"Yup. And rich."

"And you work as a security guard."

"Just for fun. I sold the company, and now I'm bored."

"Really? Isn't being a security guard boring too?"

"Not at all. You wouldn't believe the things people get up to. Even respectable women like yourself."

Ethel looked directly into his eyes. He didn't seem the least bit unfriendly or suspicious. It was just her guilty conscience, she decided.

"I want to be a writer, so I'm gathering some good anecdotes," he continued. "It's my dream to complete a crime novel. I'd love to get a publisher and…"

Before Ethel had time to think about what to do when they reached her house, they were there.

Peter stopped talking as she slowed to a halt. They both looked up at her Toronto version of a New York brownstone. Two narrow stories, a fenced front yard, a long thin driveway squished between other houses that looked exactly the same.

Normally Ethel rented out the two-bedroom apartment at the top, but right now it was empty. Students wouldn't come back until September, and that was okay with her. Stephen and his family planned to stay up there during their visit.

"Why rent it at all, Mom?" Stephen had asked. "I don't really like the idea of strangers coming and going in your house. If you need money, I've got plenty."

"I don't need the money," she had told him. "I like the company. The buzz of young people's energy."

Despite its sketchy location, Ethel loved this house. Her main floor apartment was big and airy and open. She even loved the spooky unfinished basement with all its spidery nooks and crannies.

"Nice place," Peter said.

Ethel liked the way he stood there, legs slightly apart, hands on hips. He looked delicious.

"Even though it is across from a crack house."

That threw her a bit.

"You know this area then?"

"Oh, for sure. I grew up around here. Can I help you get the buggy into the house, or is that too weird for someone you just met?"

She didn't want to admit that it *was* a bit weird. Yet she didn't really want him to leave. He'd have to go before Stephen and his family arrived, but that gave them hours to...talk.

Ethel smiled her most seductive smile.

"Please, do come in. I feel as though we've known each other for a while."

"That's great! Me too."

Luckily, the act of moving the wheelie into her house wasn't onerous because there were only three steps to climb. Ethel unlocked the outer door as well as the one to her apartment. She directed Peter to stash the cart in the hallway.

Once inside, he gazed around appreciatively.

"I love when the old wood is restored like this. Love the open concept, too."

"So do I. Two walls had to come down and a steel beam added, but it was worth it."

He went to stand beside the grandfather clock. It seemed to tick a bit louder, as though it purred under his touch.

"This is a beauty. I must get one of these. Do the chimes bother you?"

"You get used to it," she said. "Would you like a tour of the house?"

"I'd love that! You don't mind?"

"No, like we said, I feel as though we're friends."

Privately, Ethel hoped that being friends meant he wouldn't turn her in. Maybe they could be friends the same way many of her renters were with one another. With benefits. She almost giggled out loud. Her libido was turning her into a wild woman.

"Would you like a drink first? We can take it with us on the tour."

Armed with a glass of wine each, they went out her apartment door and climbed the stairs to the upper level. Peter was an excellent tourist, asking questions and making complimentary comments. Back downstairs, she showed him her two bedrooms and the bath and a half.

Ethel couldn't meet his eyes when they stood by her bed. She was afraid he'd see the X-rated pictures hidden there.

When they passed the basement door, she knocked on the wood.

"You probably don't want to see the spooky level," she said.

"Are you kidding? I love those old basements. I spent my childhood playing hide-and-seek in one that I bet was just like it."

"A man after my own heart."

They finished off their wine and she put the glasses on the table.

"We'll need more after the scary bit," she laughed.

Ethel pulled the door open and flicked on the light. "Be careful going down. You'll see what I mean in a second."

He followed her down the steep, narrow steps to the landing and stood close beside her. She flipped on the main switch. Crumbling cement, half walls and a couple of wooden storage bins met their gaze from below.

"See what I mean? This basement is so deep. I have no idea why they dug so far. Look where the windows are."

Peter followed her finger as she pointed at the small casement windows above them.

"They even had to construct a landing for the staircase. The walls are so high I can never get the damn spider webs down."

"I hate spiders," he said.

He was so close to her that his breath, slightly boozy and warm, tickled her ear. Ethel felt a tremor go through her.

"So do I."

"You're very clever." It was a whisper this time.

"What?"

"I saw what you did."

Now his breath felt hot and dangerous.

"What do you mean?"

"I saw you steal that cart."

There was a beat of silence during which Ethel didn't think or breathe. He placed a heavy hand on her shoulder.

She hip-checked him down the rest of the stairs.

Ethel hadn't meant to do that. It had been an automatic response. She had been afraid.

She stared down at his still form. He was curled up at the bottom like an enormous fetus.

"Peter?"

As she crept down the steps, she was met by silence. When she reached his side, she carefully turned him over. His face was scraped and bruised, and his right knee was twisted out of place.

His eyelids fluttered, and his lips moved.

She had to lean close to hear him.

"Bitch," he said.

Ethel went to her tool stand and searched. When she found the cable ties, she rolled him back onto his side. It wasn't easy to bind his hands, but she did it. Next she fetched the duct tape and wound it around his ankles.

The whole time, Peter's eyes remained shut, as though glued together. He kept muttering in a dreamlike fashion. Did he have a concussion or something?

When she stood over him, trussed up and helpless, Ethel wondered why on earth she had done any of this.

"You were going to turn me in, weren't you?" she asked him, as though he might have the answer.

To her surprise, he replied in a whiny tone that grated on her nerves.

"I just wanted my money."

She squatted down to hear him better. "Your money?"

This time he forced his eyes open and looked at her. The pupils were a bit dilated. Whoops.

He continued to speak like a little boy who was used to bullying and couldn't stand having the tables turned.

"I'm not really a security guard."

"I bet you're not Peter Boner either."

"Bay-ner. It's pronounced Bayner. And I am so. I hid my money in your basement."

"How in hell did you get into my house?"

"Those stupid renters were always leaving the front door open."

He sounded accusatory as though it was her fault that her tenants had been so careless.

"I spent quite a lot of time across the road, you see. I watched you. I actually *liked* you."

As though she had just stupidly ruined a big romantic chance.

"You really should be more careful, in this neighborhood especially. One time you went down the driveway to talk to your neighbor and left your own door unlocked. I slipped right in. I knew these old basements had lots of hiding places."

"I thought you were rich and famous. If you're that rich, wouldn't your money be in the bank?"

He shut his eyes again.

"It's not my fault that most of the money I made is gone. Those crack dealers across the street..."

"Got a little habit, have we?"

"Not anymore. I cleaned up. But I can't help it if I have an addictive personality. I started gambling just to take my mind off the coke, but pretty soon...well, everything's gone except what I stashed here. And you've kept the house locked up tight as a vestal virgin since the students left, or I wouldn't have had to follow you and bother you."

Bother must be the definition for frighten and who knows what else, she thought. Her knees hurt so she stood up again.

"But my *basement*? Why the hell did you put your money *here*?"

"I was going to give my dealer what I owed him eventually, but he wanted everything, just to be vindictive. So I stood on the sidewalk looking at his place, which just happened to be the day he got raided. That's when you left your door open and went to talk to your neighbor. You were both staring at what was going on across the street…and I just…well, I had the idea to put the money where no one would ever look. Plus, I *liked* you. Once I introduced myself and we became friends, I figured I could get the cash back any time. Or just go in when the doors were open. Which they were—a *lot*—when those students were here."

"That was a pretty stupid idea."

"Remember I told you I grew up around here? Well, this was my house! I grew up right here. It was a sentimental idea, I guess."

"Still a stupid one."

"I thought the idea of pretending to be a security guard was a good one, though."

As if she ought to agree with him on that score.

"I figured I'd pretend I represented BuyALot and offer to walk you home, but you played right into my hands when you…"

"Where is the money?"

"Inside the old coal bin. Right-hand side, under the biggest pile. You really should have that stuff removed. It might be bad for your health."

Ethel scrambled over the crumpled bits of coal and pulled out a canvas bag filled with bills. She leafed through them.

"There's hundreds of thousands of dollars here!" she squealed. "How much do you *owe* those dealers?"

She set the bag down beside him, where he could see but not touch his stash.

"Oh, I wasn't going to pay them. I hid that so they'd think I was completely broke. They hacked into my bank accounts. They followed me around. They're really bad people."

"Like you're not."

"I'm not. Honest. I just have this addiction problem."

"What the hell am I going to do now?"

"Let me go. I'll give you some of the cash and—"

"Shut up," Ethel said.

She turned around and started for the stairs. Peter's yell made her jump. She reversed her steps and placed a nice fat piece of duct tape across his mouth. Blessedly, it cut off the sound of his whining, self-absorbed complaints and any hollering for help.

It was silent upstairs. Grandfather Clock smiled at her and ticked contentedly. Ethel looked beyond him to the cart filled with goodies. Time had raced past. Stephen and his family would be here in a few hours.

What was she going to do? Had she gone crazy since she started out for BuyALot?

There wasn't enough time to get rid of Peter. She was certain he wouldn't just leave. He'd try to hurt her. He might threaten her family. Ethel made her decision.

First, she threaded an old towel through his legs and around his groin. No sense in having to clean piss—or worse—off the floor. Then she padded his head with a pillow and covered him with a blanket.

"I'll be back with water," she assured him. "You won't die."

He blinked and moaned.

When she went back upstairs, Ethel padlocked the door. She always did that when children were here. No one was allowed down those rickety steps.

Next she hid the Easter eggs and bunnies and trinkets all over her apartment as well as upstairs. She folded the wheelie and placed it in the hall closet.

When Ethel brought Peter a cup of water, there was a spider sitting contentedly on his blanket, right where the poor man could see it. His eyes were open as wide as possible, as though he could freeze it with his stare. At least he wouldn't sleep, Ethel thought, which you're not supposed to do if you have a concussion. He was barely able to take a gulp of water; most of it ended up on his chin.

Later, she sat upstairs with another glass of wine and rested her head against the sofa cushion. Grandfather Clock soothed her with his precise measuring.

"The grandfather clock was too large for the shelf, so it stood 90 years on the floor," she sang. "Ninety years without slumbering. Tick tock, tick tock."

By the time Ethel's family arrived, bringing their tanned L.A. faces, their boundless energy and chatter, she had almost forgotten about Peter. She was able to chat, make dinner, participate in the Easter hunt, and laugh out loud. It was only after Stephen and his gang had gone upstairs that she remembered she had a prisoner in the basement.

Dear Lord, she thought, even though she didn't believe in Him.

When everything was quiet upstairs, Ethel went down to the basement with another cup of water and a bent straw. The kids always liked those bendy straws. When she turned on the light, she saw Peter rocking back and forth. He moaned and complained under the tape.

She bent over and brushed the big spider off his nose. "Gross."

Tears rolled down his cheeks. She almost felt sorry for him. He sipped the water and took great big gulps until it was gone.

"Listen," she said. "Sorry I can't let you go right now. I'll think of something."

Ethel was quite sure he was sobbing when she left.

Out in the great room, she poured yet another glass of wine and began a search on her laptop.

His life seconds numbering, tick tock, tick tock...

When she typed in Peter Boehner, his picture popped up immediately. Those mesmerizing eyes, that lovely tanned skin, the trim figure. Ethel fervently wished this day had turned out differently.

Except for the Easter hunt. At least that had been fun.

Peter had definitely been a silly rabbit. All the gossip sites had the "facts" on his cocaine and gambling addictions. One enterprising reporter had even taken a picture of the house across the street.

"Suspected home—or perhaps we should say office—of dealer Ricardo Montenegro," the accompanying column stated, "has a famous frequent visitor by the name of Peter Boehner, creator of Twig. Why would Mr. Boehner be there so often, inquiring minds want to know?"

Ethel went to bed wondering how on earth she would make it through the next two days.

When Stephen came downstairs the next morning, he hugged her and grinned as though he had a present behind his back.

"Mom, I forgot to tell you. We've taken more time off work. We want to stay for two weeks!"

Her face must have looked odd.

"Isn't that okay?"

"Oh, yes, of course, of course it is. It's wonderful news."

It was. It truly was.

Except for Peter Bo-ner.

Ethel was somewhat distracted throughout all the activities that day, but by evening she had a plan.

Once Stephen and his family had settled upstairs, she went back to the basement armed with water. Peter drank it down like a camel.

"How much do you owe those guys across the street? Nod when I get to the number."

He moved his head up and down when she reached $50,000.

"Good Lord," she said once again. She was becoming quite religious.

Ethel got the wheelie out of the closet and took it downstairs.

Dumping Peter into it was not easy. He fought her, tried to roll away, moaned and pitched like a seal. Folded in half, his head and feet didn't even peep over the edge.

The next part was even more difficult.

She was big and strong and he weighed very little, but the cart was unwieldy. BuyALot should rethink this design. Even worse, she had to be as quiet as possible.

Up one step, rest. Drag, gentle clump, stop. Breathe.

Tick tock, tick tock. It took so long to get to the top that she half expected to see the sunrise when she opened the basement door.

But all was dark and quiet. She listened for a moment. No sounds from above.

Peter tried to rock, but his awkward position made his efforts useless. Still, she hurriedly opened her door, the outer one, and the gate, and pushed him through.

The house across the street still had lights on. She dragged him along the driveway and knocked on the side door. A sneering twenty-something answered the door.

"Yeah?"

"I want to see Mr. Montenegro."

"Huh?"

She bared her teeth.

"Get Montenegro now or I'll scream."

He twisted his head and hollered.

"Rick, some crazy old lady's at the door."

When the man in the Internet picture slouched before her, she handed him an envelope.

"Here's the money Peter Boehner owes you. And—" she pointed to the cart "—*that* is Peter."

Montenegro stepped out onto the driveway and looked into the cart. He gazed at her from hooded eyes but said nothing.

"I would appreciate it if you would make sure he never comes back here. I don't want you to hurt him or anything, but I'm sure you can get him out of the city. Forever."

The dealer didn't move a muscle.

"The money was my neighborly gesture. This favor could be yours."

Finally, Ricardo nodded.

"Okay, neighbor," he said. "I'll take care of him. Don't you worry. You'll never see him again."

"Thanks. Just a hint, Mr. Montenegro. Whatever you do to him should involve spiders. Bye, Peter. Too bad it didn't work out the way either of us planned."

She ambled back to her house and locked both doors.

Grandfather Clock smiled and hummed. *It stopped short, never to go again, when the old man died...*

"Now we have time with Stephen and the kids," she whispered to him. "Lots of glorious time."

Plus her son would never discover that she had lied to him, because now she did have money.

She had pulled a rabbit out of her hat. One named Peter, to boot.

About Catherine Astolfo

Catherine Astolfo is the author of The Emily Taylor Mysteries (*The Bridgeman, Victim, Legacy* and *Seventh Fire*), a standalone *Sweet Karoline*, and a novella, *Up Chit Creek*, all published by Imajin Books. *Sweet Karoline* was an Eric Hoffer Award Category Finalist and is recommended by Kirkus Reviews and US Review of Books.

Her short stories are included in several anthologies. "What Kelly Did", first published in *NorthWord Literary Magazine*, won the Arthur Ellis Short Crime Story Award in 2012. She's a Derrick Murdoch Award winner for service to Crime Writers of Canada. All Catherine's books and links can be found right here:

http://www.catherineastolfo.com/
Amazon Author Page
Facebook
Twitter
Mesdames of Mayhem

Mesdames of Mayhem

THRICE THE BRINDED CAT

By Joan O'Callaghan

Thrice the brinded cat hath mew'd.

—Macbeth, *Act 4, Scene 1*

A full moon again. The white light poured in through the small window. Anna tossed restlessly. She sat up and pushed her tangled heavy black hair over her shoulders. With a start, she realized she was alone. Gudrun wasn't in the cottage. Gathering her nightdress around her, she opened the door and peered out, calling softly, "Gudrun, Gudrun...where are you?"

As her eyes became accustomed to the play of moonlight and shadow, she saw the older woman, her fingers pressed to her lips, standing under a large oak tree. Anna ran silently to her, her feet damp from the heavy dew. "What is it? Are you not well?"

"Hush! Do you not sense it?" Gudrun's lips moved almost soundlessly and Anna had to strain to hear her. Gudrun shook her head. "No good can come." She looked at Anna as if seeing her for the first time. "Child, you'll catch your death. No wrap, nothing on your feet. Come. Back to bed. Pay no attention to the musings of an old woman."

Inside the cottage, Anna pulled tight the cords on her wooden frame bed, and gathered the cloak that served as a coverlet around her. Soon she heard the even rhythm of Gudrun's breathing. The old woman was asleep. But sleep would not come to Anna. She lay awake, staring at the thatched cottage roof, wondering what had wakened Gudrun and what she meant, what she had sensed.

The morning dawned bright and sunny. Anna awoke to the sounds of Gudrun setting their simple breakfast on the table. She stepped outside to wash her face and hands in the brook that rippled through the woods around Gudrun's cottage. Ambrose, Gudrun's large black-and-white tomcat, perched above her in his favorite spot among the leaves of the oak, licking one white paw and watching her.

Inside the cottage, Gudrun silently passed Anna coarse black bread and cheese, then poured ale into two tankards. Anna waited, knowing the old woman would speak when she was ready. At last, Gudrun stood abruptly and began clearing the table. Anna helped. Overhead, drying herbs swayed back and forth in the light summer breeze.

"There's trouble at the castle," Gudrun said. Anna knew better than to ask how she knew. Gudrun just *knew* things. "And there will be trouble here. Prepare yourself, girl." Her voice dropped and she spoke as if to herself. "In the meantime we must go about our business." She nodded in the direction of a bunch of goldenrod hanging from a rafter. "Yon goldenrod is ready to be ground."

Anna worked diligently all morning grinding the goldenrod into a powder from which a drink could be brewed to relieve a stomach upset. Afterward, Gudrun sent her to a place downstream where osiers, their long thin branches sweeping the surface of the water, were plentiful. The bark of the osier lowered fever and offered relief for pain. On her return, she caught sight of two horses outside the cottage.

She stopped short, nearly dropping the basket of bark she carried. As she watched from the shadows cast by the tall trees, Richard, Lord Emrys's chief steward, emerged from the cottage. Gudrun followed, carrying her healing satchel. Richard helped her onto the back of one of the horses, then swung himself up onto the other. Gudrun's horse was tethered to Richard's. Although Anna had made no sound, the older woman turned and gave a barely perceptible nod in Anna's direction.

The village gossips said that Richard held power over the staff at the castle, that they feared him, and that he had gained Lord Emrys's trust. Anna had no fondness for Richard. He leered at her whenever he saw her in the village, and she had seen Gudrun going out of her way to avoid him.

Once the horses were out of sight, she packed her own healing satchel with fresh moss, the osier bark she had gathered, and various ground herbs in small woven pouches. As well, she packed some strips of dried meat. Then she slipped her long, hooded black cloak over her shoulders, stuffing the pouch into one of the inside pockets Gudrun had sewn, and slid her feet into soft, tanned hide slippers.

She made her way to the edge of the forest, staying in the safety of the trees until the sun dipped below the distant hills and the orange glow around Lord Emrys's castle faded.

Only then, wrapping her cloak around her and concealing her face and heavy hair in the hood, did she approach the castle. She circled the building, keeping to the shadows, looking for a way in. Guards were posted at the main entrance and all the other gates were locked.

It was dusk when two servants climbed the path to the castle. Anna followed at a safe distance. The servants entered through the sally port near the base of the tower, and, engrossed in their conversation, left it unbarred.

She slipped into the castle and crept cautiously along a long hallway, dark except for occasional sconces holding rush lights. Firelight flickered some distance ahead and she heard the low murmur of voices. She stole forward, keeping to the wall until she could see and hear clearly. Richard, the steward who had come to fetch Gudrun, sat at table with two other men, both wearing Lord Emrys's black-and-gold livery. Richard signaled to a servant to fill his tankard from a nearby firkin of ale. He quaffed the ale thirstily. With a satisfied belch, he slammed the tankard onto the table, wiping the froth from his mouth with the back of his hand.

"Did you fetch the witch then?" one of his companions asked.

"I did. She attends His Lordship even now."

"And the comely maid that dwells in the cottage with her? The apprentice?"

With a start, Anna realized they were talking about her. She pulled her cloak more tightly about her and flattened herself against the wall.

With a lewd gesture toward his crotch, he added, "See where she has bewitched me already." The men laughed loudly.

Richard answered, "The maid was nowhere to be found. When I questioned the witch, she said only that the maid had gone into the forest and did not know when she would return."

"We shall go to the cottage under cover of darkness and fetch her."

"Wait until the moon is risen," Richard said. "You will catch her unawares."

Anna shrank back further against the rough wall. She had to find Gudrun. Talk of witches meant trouble. It was whispered among the village folk that the older woman was a witch, but still they sought her out for medicines and salves. As a child, Anna had often been taunted by the village children who called her "witch's spawn." Although Gudrun told her to pay them no heed, she became adept from an early age at using her fists and her cunning to silence her tormentors.

While she thought about what to do, a servant emerged from the room where the men drank and dined, carrying a tray with a covered platter. Hoping the servant might lead her to Gudrun, Anna followed at a safe distance. Once, she tripped over a loose stone in the floor. The servant turned, calling, "Who goes here?" Anna held her breath, her heart pounding. Her cloak and the shadows in the dark hallway concealed her from his eyes, and after a pause he turned and continued on his errand. Anna followed him.

At length, he came to a door made of richly carved oak, with tapers burning brightly on either side. With one hand on the wall, Anna crept as close as she could. The servant shifted the heavy tray to one hand and knocked with the other. A guard opened the door. Anna saw that it was a richly appointed bedchamber. Embroidered tapestries lined the walls, a small fire burned in a hearth, and Lord Emrys lay on a large bed, Gudrun sitting next to him. Two more armed men stood behind her. Near the head of the bed were Lord Emrys's lady and his young son. Seated across from Gudrun was Brother John. Anna shuddered.

The older woman raised her head and looked briefly past the guard, in Anna's direction, her dark eyes flashing a warning. Leaving the tray, the servant stepped out of the chamber, and the door closed. He hurried past Anna and was swallowed by the shadows. Off to one side was a small alcove with a chair and a window. Anna sat down, thinking over what she had seen. Gudrun had been brought to the side of the ailing Lord Emrys. But Richard's words and the presence of Brother John troubled her deeply.

The sound of voices floated through the window. Taking care not to show her face, Anna peered into the darkness. The moon was up and Richard's two drinking companions were waiting while a groom readied their horses. The men were unsteady on their feet. Their laughter was loud and their speech slurred.

In her mind's eye, she saw them clearly as they rode away. Their coarse laughter assaulted her ears. She slowed and deepened her breathing, as Gudrun had taught her, closing her eyes and willing herself to be an invisible companion to the men on their wild gallop through the woods to Gudrun's cottage. In the dark, they did not see the fallen tree that lay across the path. The lead horse shied suddenly, throwing his rider. The horse bolted into the forest, leaving his rider lying still on the ground. His companion pulled up short. He dismounted and examined the fallen man, rolling him over. There was no response from the fallen man. The servant climbed back on his horse and rode off.

Anna opened her eyes and blinked. She hurried along the passages until she found the door under the window where she had stood listening. She ran out of the castle and along the path the horsemen had followed until she came to the fallen rider. His breathing was shallow; by the light of the moon, she saw that his face was pale and beaded with perspiration. After taking his short sword, a baselard, from the scabbard at his waist, and a horn-handled hunting knife from his belt, she fetched some water from the nearby stream and forced it between his lips. He stirred, and his eyes flickered open.

She went back to the stream and mixed a potion. He watched, fear in his eyes. But the injuries from his fall were such that he was helpless. He thrashed to and fro, pressing his lips tightly together so as not to drink.

"If you answer my questions, I will give you this to drink. You need not fear. It will only make you sleep and when you wake, you will feel much better."

"And if I refuse?" he gasped.

She didn't answer, merely ran her finger along the sharp edge of the baselard. "Why has Lord Emrys sent for the healer?"

He tried to push away from her, but Anna grasped his hair firmly with one hand and held the point of the sword to his throat. "I can kill you now."

He closed his eyes. "It is Richard who has brought the witch to the bedside of my lord. He says she practices the black arts."

"Then why bring her to his lordship?"

"He is ill. If she cannot heal him, Brother John will say she caused his death and she will hang for a witch."

"Why is Richard sure she cannot heal him?"

He gasped, "I know not."

"Why are you here tonight?"

"We came to fetch you, but I had an accident with my horse."

"To fetch me? To violate me, you mean."

He shook his head. "I never wished you harm. My companion—" he gasped.

"You will not speak of our meeting tonight. Do you understand?"

He nodded and drank the draft, then fell back. His eyes closed.

The valerian would ensure he slept for many hours. Anna slipped through the trees until she came to the cottage. The horse, still lathered, was tethered outside, so its rider must have just arrived. Looking around her, she noted a familiar gleam, reflected in the moonlight, in the nearby oak tree. She smiled and stood in the doorway until her would-be captor turned. Seeing her, he smirked and advanced.

"So here you are, my pretty maid." He raised his arms and lunged at her. She turned as if to run from him. Something flew past her, hitting him on the head and knocking him to the ground.

A terrible cry rent the air. "My eyes, my eyes! I cannot see!" He fell to the ground, his face covered in blackness, shrieking all the while.

Reaching down, Anna gently lifted Ambrose, but not before the cat gave her attacker one last swipe with his sharp claws. The man's face and neck were a mess of bloody ribbons, his eyes swollen shut. He reached out, clutching at Anna's skirts. She took the baselard from under her cloak and slashed at him to loosen his grasp. He shrieked in anger and pain, letting go of her and rolling over. She stroked the cat's glossy coat and murmured her thanks.

Leaving the servant on the ground, she rode his horse to the woods. There, she dismounted and gave the beast a sharp slap on the rump, sending it galloping into the forest.

The bright moonlight helped her to find her way back to the sally port. She entered and, ensuring that she was alone, drew the baselard and held it before her. She found the room where Richard and his companions earlier had plotted against her, deserted except for two menservants. They talked as they cleaned and dipped the pith of reeds and rushes in grease to be lit as torches. Anna recognized the servant who had brought food to the bedchamber where Lord Emrys lay.

"How fares his lordship?" the second man asked.

The servant who had carried the tray shook his head. "He grows weaker daily, nay, hourly."

"They say Richard has brought the witch to work her powers."

"Ay. Richard brings medicines from the witch to put in his lordship's food, but even so he sickens."

Anna mulled over what she had heard. With Gudrun and her healing satchel by his side, why was Lord Emrys getting worse instead of better? What were they putting into his food? She waited until the servants had finished their work and departed. She wrapped herself in the long black cloak and found her way to the bedchamber, hoping to find Gudrun alone.

The door to the bedchamber was closed. Remembering the presence of the guards, Anna hesitated, wondering how to alert Gudrun to her presence. As she pondered, the door opened and Gudrun placed a tray on the floor.

"Anna! What are you doing here?" Gudrun whispered. "There is danger everywhere. Go now back to the cottage. I will come when I am able. Quickly! The guard sleeps, but he is sure to wake and must not find you here."

Anna shook her head. "The cottage is no longer safe. Listen to me. " Quickly she told Gudrun what she'd learned from the injured horseman and the servants.

Gudrun's face grew pale in the candlelight.

After a moment, the old woman spoke. "I have not given any medicines to be mixed into his lordship's food. You must find out what it is they are feeding him and tell me. Be very careful, Anna."

Anna laid her cheek against Gudrun's for a moment, then gathered her cloak around her and was gone. The old woman was the closest thing to a mother Anna had known. Since finding her as an infant abandoned on the doorstep of her cottage, Gudrun had raised Anna, caring for her and teaching her all she knew. The young maid proved herself a quick study, working hard so that she too could be a healer. Her skills were now almost equal to those of her mentor.

Anna could not imagine life without her. Although she said nothing, it troubled her to see Gudrun aging—her hair gray, her face lined, her step hesitant. She had vowed to care for Gudrun in her old age, as Gudrun had cared for her.

The first pale fingers of light probing the recesses and passages of the castle alerted her that dawn was at hand. She made her way back to the room from which the servant had brought the tray for Lord Emrys, and waited in a recess in the wall just outside the door. Before long, the servant arrived, stifled a yawn and threw peat on the fire. Richard swept into the room and handed him a small pouch. "The witch bids you mix this medicine into his lordship's ale." The servant placed the pouch on a table, then disappeared into the adjoining scullery.

Once Richard was out of sight, Anna crept into the room and seized the pouch. Quickly, she examined the powder as Gudrun had taught her, dipping her finger into the powder and placing a small amount on the end of her tongue. It was spicy and bitter. Foxglove. She put the pouch back on the table. Richard was poisoning Lord Emrys. If he continued to ingest the foxglove, he would die and Gudrun's life would be forfeit.

She looked around the room, then seized the firkin of ale and hid behind the scullery door. Soon after, the servant returned and set about preparing a meal of bread, cheese, and rashers of bacon. He was occupied with his task and did not notice Anna creeping up behind him. He turned at a slight sound, but too late. Anna brought the firkin down on his head and he slumped to the floor.

She tied the pouch to the girdle of her dress, and wrapped her cloak around her. Seizing the breakfast tray, she moved quickly through the passages until she came to the bedchamber. She set the tray down and knocked. The guard who opened the door barred the way. "Where is Francis? Why has he not brought his Lordship's breakfast?"

"Prithee, sir," Anna adopted a tremulous voice, "Francis has fallen and injured himself. I am bidden to bring the tray in his stead."

The guard nodded and stepped out of the way. The room was empty except for Lord Emrys, who slept fitfully, and Gudrun. Anna set the heavy tray down and caught Gudrun's eye. Her mouth formed the word *foxglove*. Gudrun gave a barely perceptible nod.

Anna was confident that Gudrun would prevent Lord Emrys ingesting any more of the poison, and would use her arts to restore his strength. Should she tell Brother John of the steward's plot? The Dominicans saw witchcraft everywhere, and Brother John had a particular hatred of women who practiced the healing arts. She sighed. There would be no help from that quarter.

Keeping her head bowed, she hurried back to the room and peered in past the open door. Richard breakfasted alone and was in a foul mood. The man Anna had hit with the firkin was nowhere to be seen.

Richard hurled his tankard across the room. It bounced against the wall and clattered to the floor, barely missing the servant bringing food to the table. "Two of my men missing. The young maid is nowhere to be found and the witch has not stirred from his Lordship's bedchamber. Yet I see her hand everywhere." He rose from the table and stormed out.

Anna drew back into the shadows, but not quickly enough. Richard saw the swirl of her cloak and stopped. "What have we here? The young sorceress herself." He grasped her firmly and drew her into the room, pulling her cloak from her in one fluid motion and hurling it onto the floor.

Anna stood silently, defying him.

His dark angry eyes roved over her. Spotting the pouch of foxglove at her belt, he seized it. "How came you by this? I gave it to my servant only this morning. A knife. And a baselard. What business has a maid with a sword?" He tossed the weapons to one side and circled Anna. "Now I know what happened to my men. Too bad such a fetching wench must hang with the hag." He drew a length of cord from a pocket and tied her hands.

He called for a servant and thrust Anna forward contemptuously, tossing her cloak after her. "Lock her up."

Grasping Anna's arms firmly, the servant marched her to a small room and shoved her inside, pulling the heavy door shut. She heard a key turn in the lock. From a slit in the stonework that served as a window, she could see daisies dotting an open field, their white heads dancing in the summer breeze. Anna wiped a tear from her eye, envying the flowers their freedom.

After a short while, she heard voices in the passageway.

"Where are you taking me?" It was Gudrun.

There was a creak as a door swung open and then slammed shut. Knowing that Gudrun must be imprisoned close by, Anna waited until she was sure the guards had gone, then put her mouth to the slit and called softly, "Gudrun, Gudrun."

She was rewarded by a harsh whisper. "Anna? Did I not bid you flee this place?"

"We have to get out. If Lord Emrys dies, they will hang us both for witches."

Their conversation was interrupted by the rattling of a key in the door of Anna's cell. The guard brought in a tray of bread, cheese and ale, set it on the floor, and turned to leave.

"Wait," Anna called, holding her bound hands in front of her. "I cannot eat or drink like this."

He hesitated, then removed his hunting knife from its sheath and cut her bonds. He locked the door again and left.

A moment later, she heard the door to Gudrun's cell open and close.

Anna pushed aside her cloak with her foot and as she did so, felt something firmer than the soft fabric. Her healing satchel. She quickly opened the bag and examined the contents until she found what she wanted. There was still enough valerian left. She mixed a strong measure into the ale, then sat down to wait for the guard to fetch the tray. When he entered the chamber, she smiled at him. "I cannot drink ale...I am too distressed. Can you bring me a little water please?" And dropped her eyes. The guard turned on his heel, leaving the tray and locking the door, but returned soon after with the water.

"Water for you, witch."

She held out the ale to him. "Please. Good ale should not go to waste." As she had hoped, he grasped the tankard and downed the ale thirstily, wiping his mouth on his sleeve. Bending down to pick up the tray with the untouched food on it, he passed his hand over his eyes and tottered to the wall, placing both hands against it for balance.

Anna watched silently. A moment later, he fell unconscious to the floor as the valerian did its work. With luck, she and Gudrun would be long gone by the time he awoke. She scrambled over to him, searching his clothing until she found the ring of keys.

Pushing open the door, she peered both ways down the hallway. Nobody in sight. She tried all the keys until she found the one that opened Gudrun's cell. "Quickly, Gudrun!"

The women crept down the passage, keeping to the shadows. At length they came to a narrow stairwell that led down to another hallway. Anna nodded to Gudrun, and began to descend. As Gudrun followed, she placed her foot on the first step, dislodging a bone lying there. It fell to the stone floor below, rousing one of the dogs that roamed the castle. Anna drew a strip of dried meat from her satchel and tossed it in the direction of the barking. The noise ceased, but not before Richard rushed into the passage carrying a lit torch.

He immediately spotted them on the stairs above him. A slow smile crept across his face as he withdrew his own baselard from its scabbard. "So. You found a way out.

No matter. I will kill you here." He began to mount the stairs.

Anna felt Gudrun tense behind her. She backed up against Gudrun, forcing the older woman to move onto the step behind her.

The steward sneered. He took his time advancing, knowing the women were trapped and at his mercy. He lifted his sword and ran his finger along its sharp edge. "This is what happens to witches, especially witches who meddle in what does not concern them."

"We are not witches," Gudrun spoke up. "We want only to heal the sick and relieve their misery."

"You are witches and will be blamed for his lordship's death." He climbed onto the next step.

There was nowhere for them to go. If they turned to climb the steps, hampered as they were by their long skirts, Richard would stab them in the back. Then a movement on the lower level caught Anna's attention. Intent on his prey, Richard did not notice that the dog had returned, looking for more dried meat. Cautiously, she moved her foot until she felt a loose stone. Giving it a nudge, she sent it hurtling over the edge. It hit the floor below with a sharp crack, causing the dog to erupt into loud barking and snarling.

The din caught Richard off guard. Startled, he turned his head in the direction of the sound. The distraction was all Anna needed. Pulling her skirt back, she raised her leg and lashed out with her foot, catching Richard on the chin. He lost his balance and tumbled backward off the stairs. He twisted as he fell shrieking, and landed upon his own sword.

Anna ran down the stairs and knelt beside him. "Steward, you have conspired against your master, and sought to kill my friend and teacher, and me. Say your prayers now, if you have any."

He worked his mouth, but no words, only angry red spittle, emerged. At last he gasped, "With his lordship dead and you blamed, I would have ruled the boy and found favor with the Dominicans. So close, so close…" His eyes rolled; his breathing grew shallower, and then stopped altogether.

She turned to Gudrun. "Let us go."

Some days later, the two women made their way through the forest. Gudrun's heart was heavy and her step slow. "We escaped from the death Richard planned for us and we saved the life of Lord Emrys. But it has been for naught. Brother John called us out for witches and his lordship has banished us."

Anna shifted the basket in which Ambrose slept, to her other hand. "We are banished instead of hanged. We live and for that we must rejoice. We will make a new home far from this place and continue our work." She turned one last time and beheld the flames leaping and dancing high in the air, consuming what was left of their little cottage.

About Joan O'Callaghan

Joan's short stories have been published in *EFD1; Starship Goodwords* (Carrick Publishing 2012) and the crime anthology, *Thirteen*, (Carrick Publishing 2013). Her story, "Runaway," took third prize in the national Bony Pete short story contest and has been published in *World Enough and Crime* (Carrick Publishing 2014). Her Flash Fiction story, "Torch Song for Two Voices" won first prize in a national competition, and was subsequently published in *That Golden Summer* (Polar Expressions Publishing 2014).

Joan has an active career in freelance writing, with over 30 educational publications to her credit. She is the author of three non-fiction books, two published by Scholastic Canada and one by Rubicon (Harcourt), as well as two e-shorts.

http://joanocallaghan.blogspot.ca
Facebook
Twitter
Mesdames of Mayhem

BEING LEDA FOX

By Lynne Murphy

Charlotte Manners had never stolen anything in her life. Not penny candy from the corner store when she was little. Not lipstick from Woolworth's as a teenager. If a salesclerk gave her too much change, she gave it back. Then, when she was in her 70s, she committed the worst theft of all—she stole another woman's identity.

It started with a small deceit. Charlotte and Leda Fox, her neighbor at Golden Elders Condo, both loved reading mysteries. They exchanged books by favorite authors, and were mutual fans of the well-known Regina writer Gail Bowen. They had both been born in Saskatchewan, although Charlotte's family had moved east when she was a child.

Leda was much more involved in the mystery scene than Charlotte. She went to conferences in distant cities and had met many of her favorite writers at autograph sessions. When one of the conferences was being held in Toronto, she signed up and told Charlotte about it. Charlotte didn't think she could spare a whole weekend, but when Leda made her offer, it felt like a gift.

"I can't go to the lunch on Sunday. I have an 80th birthday party I have to be at. How would you like to attend in my place? Gail Bowen is going to be the guest speaker. I'll give you my copy of her latest book so you can get it autographed for me."

"That's very nice of you, Leda. I'd love to hear Gail Bowen. I can miss church for one Sunday."

"Now, you'll have to wear my name badge to get in, but don't worry about it. My friend, Shirley, is the only person who really knows me at the conference, and she's coming to the birthday party, too."

Charlotte was a bit worried. In the end she decided to arrive at the end of the lunch and just hear the speech. That seemed more honest to her. She sat in the foyer outside the banquet room until the waiters started serving tea and coffee. Then she crept in and sat at an empty table.

Gail Bowen was very entertaining and Charlotte was glad she had been able to come. She joined the autograph line and spent the time watching a tall, handsome, silver-haired man, the type she had once called "a hunk". He seemed to be looking for someone.

She reached the signing table, complimented Gail on her speech and had her own book signed. Then she said, "And could you sign this one to Leda Fox, please? Spelled as on my name tag."

The hunk looked her way. "Leda Fox! I've been looking for you everywhere!" He rushed over and enfolded her in his arms.

Charlotte stood still for a moment, enjoying the hug. It had been a long time since she had been hugged by a good-looking man. Then she gently extricated herself, prepared to tell this stranger that she was not Leda Fox. She stepped back and looked way up into the bluest eyes she had ever seen. Peter O'Toole? Paul Newman? These eyes were bluer and they were set in a handsome, suntanned face. She hesitated and then she fell. She took a quick glance at his name tag.

"Gordon," she said. "Gordon Mitchell!"

"Leda. You haven't changed a bit."

It must have been a long time since he had seen Leda. She and Charlotte were about the same height, and they had both been blondes when they were younger. But Leda now outweighed her by at least 100 pounds. And she had stopped coloring her hair.

"How long has it been?" Charlotte asked, hoping to get some sort of handle on this.

"God, more than 50 years. You left Saskatoon after graduation to take journalism down east. Then we just lost touch."

He hugged her again in a more decorous way, but it was still pleasant. Gail Bowen had been watching the exchange with interest. She said, "Your book, Leda. Hi, Gordon. I enjoyed your panel." Charlotte managed a flustered thank-you and wondered if this would end up in one of Gail's books.

"You never answered any of my letters," Gordon said, taking her arm and moving her away from the table.

"I dropped journalism and went into nursing. Everything changed." There was no way she could pretend to have been a journalist although now she remembered Leda had worked in public relations. She might have been able to fake that.

"And you're still single? When I saw the name Leda Fox in the list of people attending the conference, I thought, 'How come she never got married? There must have been dozens of guys after her.'"

Charlotte might be prepared to lie, just to make this last a little longer, but she couldn't deny the existence of Jack and their children. And the grandchildren. That would be immoral.

"I'm a widow. My married name is Manners. I met Jack soon after I came east. He was studying medicine. That's the reason I switched to nursing."

Dear Lord, this is difficult. Quick, change the subject.

"What about you, Gordon? Are you married? Is your wife here?"

Let's hope his wife is here and comes along soon to end this. What had she been thinking?

"I'm divorced. I graduated in law after you left, married another lawyer. She was from B.C. I stayed in Saskatoon, my hometown, you know. Where were you from? Some little town down south?"

Charlotte froze. How could she explain being unable to remember the name of her hometown? Had Leda ever mentioned it in their conversations? She looked at Gordon and said, "You don't remember?"

"Kipling," he shouted suddenly. "I knew it was some old-fashioned author."

"That's amazing. You remember that. I have so many senior moments myself."

"Tell me about it. Listen, I have to leave for the airport at four, but could we have a drink or coffee and catch up? I'm sorry I had to check out of my room by noon or I could have asked you up there." He gave her arm a squeeze that bordered on being suggestive.

"Why Gordon Mitchell," she said, losing all restraint, "you haven't changed a bit."

They went to the bar where Gordon had a beer and Charlotte drank coffee. She had to keep her wits about her. Luckily, Gordon was happy to talk about himself. He had published a mystery novel after retiring as a criminal lawyer, which was why he was at the conference. She didn't have to contribute much, just details about her kids and grandkids. Gordon grew wistful when she talked about them.

"My wife and I didn't have kids. It's something I've always regretted. But you used to say you hated babies, Leda. You were going to be the great career woman."

"Nursing school changed me a lot. And when I met Jack, I knew I wanted children."

At quarter to four, Gordon took out his cell phone.

"I'm not going to lose track of you again. Give me your email address and we'll keep in touch."

"It's cmanners," Charlotte said, thinking fast. "My daughter, Charlotte, shares it with me. So don't you dare send me any explicit messages."

"I may have to come back to Toronto in the fall. I don't suppose you get to Saskatchewan much?"

"I'm afraid not. All my family there are gone." Which was true.

"Here, I've got a copy of my book in my carry-on. I'll sign it for you if you like."

And he did: "To Leda, with fond memories."

Dear Lord, just what is he remembering?

He threw his arms around her before he left and kissed her on the mouth. There was no doubt at all about what he was remembering.

***

On the subway going home, Charlotte sat in a daze. Lying was exhausting. And how could he have thought she was Leda? But she remembered people she had seen at her 50-year nursing reunion, changed beyond recognition. Time had altered them completely.

What was she going to do? To begin with, she would have to give Leda the book. It was meant for her and Charlotte had no right to it. She could buy her own copy. But she would have to explain to Leda about meeting

Gordon, without revealing anything about the mistaken identity. She would phone so Leda wouldn't see her blushing.

Luckily, Leda was still out and Charlotte connected with the answering machine. She explained about Gordon seeing the name tag and giving her the book, meant for Leda. She promised to leave it at Leda's door in a bag. If Leda wanted to get in touch with Gordon herself, she could search for him using Google or contact his publisher.

There was an email from Gordon the next morning. He didn't say anything too personal, just repeated how he had loved seeing her again and hoped that he'd have the pleasure again soon. Charlotte didn't reply even though it seemed cruel to ignore such a friendly message. Later that morning, Leda called to thank her for delivering the book.

"So you ran into Gordon Mitchell," she said. "I saw he was on a panel at the conference, but I didn't go to it. His writing isn't my kind of thing. All that courtroom detail. I suppose he's still full of himself?"

"He seemed very pleasant," Charlotte said. If Leda didn't remember Gordon as fondly as he remembered her, that was a good thing. She wouldn't mind Charlotte carrying on a long-distance relationship with him. Charlotte hung up her phone, went straight to her computer and replied to Gordon's message.

***

The email correspondence continued for the next month—regular messages, sometimes two or three a day. It was exciting, getting up in the morning, calling up her email, seeing what the night had brought. Then Gordon announced that he would be visiting Toronto in September. Was there a guest suite at her condo that he might use?

There was but Gordon couldn't come to the building. If he buzzed Leda's entry code, everything would be revealed. Charlotte needed someone to talk to. Her neighbor, Olive, came to mind.

Olive knew Leda better than Charlotte did because they were both Roman Catholics and often went to Mass together. And Olive had a lot of common sense though she could be judgmental. Charlotte spoke to her after their exercise group that morning.

"Could you come to my place for a few minutes, Olive? There's something I need to talk to you about."

"Of course. My son's picking me up for lunch, but I've got an hour before he gets here."

Olive followed her up to the suite. When they were seated in the living room Charlotte began her explanation. Olive listened, her eyes getting wider and wider.

"Gordon Mitchell," she said at the end of the story. "I wonder if he was the father."

Then she put her hand over her mouth, looking horrified.

"The father? Whose father?"

"Oh, no, Charlotte, I shouldn't have said anything. It was told to me in confidence."

"Of course, if it was a confidence you mustn't tell me." But her mind was working. She had read enough novels to help her along. "There was a child? Leda had a baby?"

Olive looked as though she might burst. Then unable to contain herself, she said, "You must swear never to reveal this to anyone."

"I swear."

"Leda and I got talking once after we had been to Mass. She told me that after she came east to take journalism, she discovered she was pregnant. She wasn't in love with the father, she didn't want to get married and she didn't want a baby. She wanted a career. Leda was very advanced in her thinking for those days."

"She was always a feminist."

"Of course, she wouldn't consider abortion. So she had the baby. He was adopted by a good Catholic family and she went on with her life. She never told anyone back home. She was feeling emotional that day because it was the child's birthday. Saint Patrick's Day, it was. She had named him Patrick."

"And you think Gordon was the father?"

"It all fits, doesn't it? Leda said she didn't regret the adoption, but she did get a bit teary-eyed talking about the baby. Which isn't like Leda."

The two women sat quietly for a while, thinking about a tragedy more than 50 years old. Finally Olive said, "It isn't true that time heals all wounds. Well, I have to get changed for lunch. If I were you, Charlotte, I'd ignore any more emails from him. This sounds like a can of worms to me. And remember your promise. I never told you anything."

"I'll remember," Charlotte said meekly, but her brain was whirling. Gordon had a son. In his 50s by now. There might even be grandchildren. She, Charlotte Manners, would become a detective and unite the family. Gordon would be so grateful that he would forgive her for her deceit. Or not. But at least she would have done a good deed.

People said you could find anything on the Internet. Now was the time to prove it.

***

It didn't take Charlotte long to discover that things weren't all that easy. There was a site for uniting adopted children with their parents, but you had to be a close relative and prove your connection. Luckily, she knew the day of birth and the approximate year—she and Leda were the same age. If only she had more computer skills.

Computer skills! Justin, her 18-year-old grandson had helped her whenever she had a computer problem. Could she enlist him now? She left a message on his phone. Better not to use email.

Justin called her back that evening.

"Hi, Nana. What's up?"

"Justin, I need you to do some hacking for me. On the computer. It's sort of illegal, so you mustn't tell your parents."

"Awesome. Who is it?"

Charlotte explained. Well, she didn't explain completely. Her story was that her friend, Leda, was looking for a son who had been adopted many years ago. Charlotte had decided to help find him as a surprise for her friend. Justin accepted the story and took down the details.

"We have to use the phone to communicate, Justin, not email. Legally, we're not supposed to be doing this. But I don't think Leda will ever do anything on her own even though I know she wants to."

"Awesome, Nana. I'll phone you when I know something."

They discussed Justin's summer job, coaching at soccer camp, which was "awesome," and ended their conversation with him saying, as usual, "Love you, Nana."

"And I love you too, Justin."

***

The next day, she emailed Gordon, telling him the condo guest suite was booked for the whole of September, but that she would love to spend time with him while he was in Toronto. If Justin was successful, she would have wonderful news for Gordon.

A few nights later, Justin phoned back.

"I found him, Nana. At least, my buddy found him. He's even better at computers than I am."

"Oh, Justin, I hope he's reliable."

"Nana, I've known him since kindergarten. The guy you're looking for is Michael Ryan. He's registered as looking for his biological parents. He's a bus driver in Ottawa, married, got three grown-up kids, and a grandson."

"A great-grandchild. My goodness."

Justin passed on the rest of the details. Michael Ryan sounded like a decent, ordinary person. Charlotte felt a glow of pride.

"Thank you for your help, dear," she said, when she had everything she needed. "Better tell your friend to delete all that information from his computer."

"He already has. Love you, Nana."

***

So there was nothing to do but wait for Gordon's visit. The rest of the summer seemed to pass very slowly. She and Gordon kept in touch by email, but there was always the deceit in the back of Charlotte's mind that kept her from enjoying the friendship. When she was able to be completely open, whether or not Gordon forgave her for lying, at least she would have given him his son.

Gordon phoned almost as soon as he arrived in Toronto in early September. He offered to come to her condo, but Charlotte suggested they meet at his hotel. "I have some errands to do downtown, so it will suit me better," she said.

That evening, he was waiting for her in the lobby.

"We can have a drink in the bar and then, I thought, dinner. You choose a place. You know Toronto restaurants."

"Let's go up to your room first, Gordon. I want to talk to you in private."

"Why sure," he said, his eyes lighting up. "Private is good."

Charlotte waited till they were both settled with drinks. Gordon had poured her rye and ginger ale without asking. Perhaps that had been Leda's drink of choice.

"Gordon," she said, coming straight to the point, "I am not Leda Fox."

Gordon looked at her as though she had suddenly lost her marbles. Finally, he found his voice.

"What do you mean? Of course you're Leda Fox. I met you again at the conference after all that time. You look just the same. You remember all about us."

"Gordon, Leda lent me her name tag. You called me by her name and you were so attractive that I couldn't help it. I pretended to be her. But when I tell you something, I hope you'll forgive me. If you can't, I'll understand."

Gordon stood up and bent over her chair to look at her more closely. "You're not Leda Fox?"

For a lawyer, he seemed to be slow on the uptake.

"I'm her neighbor. We live in the same building. But Gordon, this is important. After she came east, Leda discovered she was pregnant. With your child."

"She was pregnant? After just the one time?"

"Gordon, please listen to me. Leda didn't want to be a mother, so she gave the baby up for adoption. Well, I've found him. His name is Michael Ryan. He lives in Ottawa with his family."

Really, she couldn't blame Gordon for looking stunned.

"I have a son? With a family? In Ottawa?"

"Yes. I have his address. I can give it to you if you want. He registered his adoption information, so he must want to find his biological parents."

"What does he do?"

"He's a bus driver. With the Ottawa transit system."

A look of distaste came over Gordon's handsome face.

"A bus driver? My family have always been professional people. Lawyers and doctors and university professors. You must be mistaken. A bus driver?"

Charlotte looked at him in shock.

"How do I know he is my son? What proof does Leda have? I only slept with you—her—the one time." Gordon was shouting now. "You. What is your name anyway? Is this some sort of scam you've planned? You and Leda together? Well, I'm not going to be taken in by it. I advise other people about scams like this. You had better leave."

"But he has a grandchild, Gordon. You're a great-grandfather."

It wasn't just distaste on his face now. It was horror. He walked to the door and held it open.

"Get out of here, whatever your name is. And never contact me again."

***

Charlotte left the hotel with her tail between her legs, as her grandmother used to say. On the subway, she tried to think of some redeeming aspect of the episode. At least poor Michael Ryan had no inkling of what an awful man his father was.

By the time she reached home, Charlotte had thought things over. Leda was alone. She was in her 70s. Sometimes when the other women in the building talked about their grandchildren, there was a wistful look on her face. Charlotte made up her mind. She gathered the notes that Gordon had spurned and took the elevator to Leda's floor. Squaring her shoulders, she knocked on the door.

Mesdames of Mayhem

About Lynne Murphy

Lynne Murphy is a retired journalist who lives in Toronto. Her short stories have been published in a number of anthologies, including *Thirteen* by the Mesdames of Mayhem (Carrick Publishing, 2013).

She is a co-founder of the Toronto Chapter of Sisters' in Crime which is still going strong after twenty-three years. "Being Leda Fox" is for her daughter, Margo, and granddaughter, Asia, who suggested the plot, inspired by a borrowed name tag.

Facebook
Mesdames of Mayhem

LIFE LESSON

By Ed Piwowarczyk

Dana Evans held her head high as she approached the guillotine. Drums beat as the mob jeered.

"Your time's up!" someone in the crowd taunted.

"It's all over!" another yelled.

Dana shook her head. *Get a grip!* No mob, no drums, no guillotine—she was in a hallway at Wolfe College. No execution—just a meeting with the coordinator of continuing education, Lawrence Gardner.

But she still had a sense of foreboding.

She had been worried ever since she'd heard that Jack Pearce—a third-rate author, in her estimation—was joining the teaching staff. That news, coupled with rumors of cutbacks and this summons from Gardner, had her on edge.

Outside Gardner's office, she ran her fingers through her silver hair to give the pixie cut a stylish tousled look. She looked down at her calf-length black skirt and turquoise jacket. Fashionable yet business-like, she thought.

Let's get this over with. She knocked and opened the door.

***

"I'm afraid we're going to have to let you go at the end of this semester." Gardner looked down at his hands, folded on his desk, then looked up again at Dana. "I'm sorry."

Sitting across from him, she bit her lip to tamp down the rage and frustration building inside her. *Don't lose your temper!*

Lately she'd been lashing out at colleagues and friends over minor annoyances. Taken aback, they'd shaken their heads. "What's wrong with her?" she'd heard a colleague mutter.

Keep your cool!

"We'll do everything we can." Gardner leaned forward. "Within limits, of course. References—"

"What you can do is give me back my novel-writing course," she snapped.

"It's not possible, Mrs. Evans. There's only enough money in the budget for one course on the novel. Our continuing education enrollment needs a boost and, let's face it, classes with Jack Pearce will be an attraction."

"But he's a hack! He made his name with a piece of trash. That was five years ago. What has he done since?"

"Mrs. Evans—"

"What does he know about developing characters? About structure? About—"

"Now just a minute! *I'll Scream Again Tomorrow* may be trash to you, but it *was* on the best-seller list."

"But the critics said—"

"Who cares? He wrote a best seller. Can you say the same?"

"I got some very good notices for *The Bloom Is Off The Rose*," Dana replied. "Critics compared me to Carson McCullers."

"Those reviews were in literary journals that very few people outside academic circles read," Gardner countered. "And that was 30 years ago. What have you done lately?"

Dana said nothing. She'd had a few short stories published, but she couldn't get another novel on track. Her late husband Thomas had been a tenured university professor, so she'd assumed their financial future was secure. She'd taught novel writing as she waited for her muse to return.

Gardner peered over the top of his half-moon glasses. "I'm afraid time has passed you by."

Dana assessed Gardner's portly physique, graying hair and handlebar mustache. *You're the anachronism. A walrus in tweed, a pile of blubber.* She pictured herself on an ice floe, ready to sink a harpoon into a cowering Gardner.

"You're out of step with the times," he continued, interrupting her reverie. "Look at what sells. Kick-ass is in, sensitive is out. Students want to know how to create the next Lisbeth Salander, not the next Elizabeth Bennett."

"I *need* those classes," Dana protested. "Pearce doesn't."

Gardner shrugged. "I don't know why he wants to do it. Ego, maybe, or to get his creative juices flowing. But he was available, and we couldn't pass him up."

Dana closed her eyes. *It's so unfair!*

"Mr. Gardner, since my husband died, things have been…difficult." Thomas had been an expert in Elizabethan literature, not finance. His bad investments meant their nest egg was almost gone. "It's tough to make ends meet." She paused. "I'm pushing 60. At my age, what school will to take me on?"

"You have my sympathies, but…"

"After 25 years here, isn't there *something* you can do?"

Gardner shook his head. "I'm afraid not." Then he gave a small chuckle. "Unless, of course, Pearce were to drop dead."

"He's about 40, isn't he? So it's not bloody likely."

Dana glared at him, and Gardner busied himself with some papers on his desk. "Thanks for coming in, Mrs. Evans."

He looked up and began to rise, but Dana held up a hand as she stood. "Don't trouble yourself. I can see myself out."

She slammed the office door behind her.

***

I'm afraid time has passed you by. You're out of step with the times.

Dana shut her eyes and held her hands over her ears, trying to block out the words that had haunted her for the past six weeks. *Those are lies! I'm not!*

She opened her eyes, dropped her hands and glanced at her watch. With a good hour until evening classes began, the college's corridors were empty.

The start of a new term had made her nostalgic. *Can't hurt to have a look around.*

She had stopped outside a second-floor classroom. Room 227 had no windows, and students grumbled about how hot and stuffy it got, but it had been *hers*. She would miss it.

One little peek...

Dana rummaged in her purse for the key to the room—not the one she had turned in when the semester ended, but the duplicate she'd had made.

"Class doesn't start for another hour."

She turned with a start. Before her stood a fortyish version of a grunge rocker—lanky, a little over six feet tall, dirty blond hair parted in the middle and hanging down to his shoulders. He wore faded jeans and a blue plaid shirt. A Kurt Cobain wannabe.

"I'm Jack Pearce. Something I can help you with?" He held a fireplace poker in his right hand. A cardboard box was tucked under his left arm.

"I'm not a student." She unlocked the door.

"How come you have a key to this classroom?" he asked as he followed her in.

"This is *my* room. I'm Dana Evans."

"There's a mistake. This room's assigned to me." Pearce deposited the box and the poker on the teacher's desk at the front. "Evans...Evans..." He snapped his fingers. "The one I'm taking over from." He paused. "Sorry about how it worked out for you. Nothing personal."

"It's *very* personal, Mr. Pearce. It means the world to me. Can you understand that?"

"Take it up with Gardner." He began to unpack the box. "The way I look at it, it's a soft gig. And who knows? There might be some young thing who'd like private tutoring from the master." He winked.

Pearce refocused his attention on the box. "This is easy money while I finish my new book. It's the sequel to *I'll Scream Again Tomorrow.*" He paused. "I need another catchy title, though. Any ideas?"

She swallowed back her anger. *Say something clever to this arrogant fool.* "How about *I'll Scream Again The Day After Tomorrow?*"

Pearce laughed. "Good one, Dana."

"Mr. Pearce, I—" She stopped short when she saw what he had removed from the box. On the desk beside the poker lay a revolver, a butcher's knife, piano wire strung between two wooden dowels, a hatchet, an eyeless black hood, a hangman's noose, thin black leather gloves, disposable rubber gloves and a small dark-glass bottle with a skull-and-crossbones label. "What on earth...?"

"For tonight's class."

"What do any of these things have to do with your lesson?"

"You could call them teaching aids."

"You can't be serious. They're more like...like stage props."

"That's it exactly. It's show time. I don't want anyone saying my class is boring, so I'm going to make sure the students are entertained."

"Entertained? What about taught?"

"Oh, they'll learn all right. These are just to illustrate points." Pearce paused. "Tonight, it's an introduction to the murder mystery."

He picked up the noose and the hood. "We all know where murder ultimately led the killer in the old days, don't we? To the gallows."

Pearce returned the items to the desk and put on the leather gloves. "Of course, a killer wouldn't want to leave fingerprints, so he'd put these on." He tossed the disposable gloves at a startled Dana. "Or these."

Dana bobbled the gloves before catching them.

"Go ahead, try 'em on." Pearce grinned. Dana snapped on the gloves and clenched her fists.

"Looks like a good fit," he said. "So how would our killer go about his business?" he asked, picking up the bottle. "Aha! Agatha Christie and the Borgias might have suggested this—poison." He turned the bottle upside down. "Don't worry. It's empty."

He put the bottle back on the desk and picked up the revolver. "And this—" he pointed the gun at Dana "—isn't loaded." She heard a click when he pulled the trigger.

"That's not f-f-funny!" she sputtered as he returned the gun to the desk.

Pearce gave his head a mock shake. "Where's your sense of humor?"

He picked up the knife, raised it above his right shoulder and slashed downward through the air. "*Psycho*. Remember the shower scene?"

Dana winced.

Pearce dropped the knife and pointed to the piano wire and dowels. "Like my garrote?" He dropped his voice to a theatrical cross between Bela Lugosi and the Big Bad Wolf. "The better to strangle you with, my dear." He laughed.

"Then there's Lizzie Borden. How does the rhyme go? Lizzie Borden took an ax and gave her mother...I forget. How many whacks was it?"

He picked up the poker. "And we can't leave out the fireplace poker. A handy murder weapon on the old *Perry Mason* show."

"All this is a joke to you?"

"Hey, chill. It's not the way you'd do it, but I'm the teacher now. Haven't you learned any life lessons? It's every man for himself, survival of the fittest. Gardner thinks you don't have what it takes anymore."

Dana felt rage building inside her.

"If you want to get ahead—or hang on to what you've got—you've got to have a mean streak, be a little cold-blooded." He paused. "You don't have it in you. I'll prove it."

He turned his back to her. "We're all alone. You've got your choice of weapons. Go on. Hit me with your best shot. I bet you don't have the nerve." He picked up the hood. "I'll make it even easier for you." He slipped it over his head.

Dana stepped up to the desk, picked up the poker and held it in her gloved hands.

"C'mon, Dana," he taunted.

Her grip on the poker tightened.

"What are you waiting for?"

Dana raised the poker over her head, aimed for the back of Pearce's head and swung down as hard as she could. Pearce grunted and crumpled to the floor. She dropped the poker beside the unmoving body.

"Well, Mr. Pearce," she said, "here's a 'life lesson.' Never underestimate your enemy."

She picked up the hatchet. "Make sure you do a thorough job."

She swung it down at Pearce's motionless body.

"And watch out for the competition. It can kill you."

About Ed Piwowarczyk

Ed Piwowarczyk is a veteran journalist; he's worked as a copy editor for the *National Post* and *Toronto Sun*, and as an editor and reporter for *The Sault Star*. And on a freelance basis, he's edited Harlequin novels.

A lifelong fan of crime fiction, he is also a film buff and plays in the Canadian Inquisition, a Toronto pub trivia league.

He lives in Toronto with his wife Rosemary McCracken, author of the Pat Tierney mystery series.

Facebook
LinkedIn

GLOW GRASS

By M.H. Callway

Paula's fists clutched the steering wheel. The cottage, she had to reach the cottage.

Empty fields streamed past her car windows. She searched the deserted highway, desperate for familiar landmarks. Where was the drive-in theater? Grumpy's gas station?

So long since she last was here. Not since Dad died. The cottage had languished forgotten while she struggled with the wreckage of her life.

She almost missed the drive-in theater because its familiar sign had vanished. She slowed the Honda and pulled over to the gravel shoulder for a closer look. The drive-in's once-towering screen had collapsed into a chaos of spiky timbers. Half of its For Sale sign had blown away.

Told you. Brian's teasing voice jumped into her head. *Elton is such a loser town even its doughnut store closed down. It's the biggest dump on Lake Huron. No beach, no museums, no nothing. Time to kill it and put it out of its misery.*

It's quiet, she argued silently. Tourists stay away. That's why Dad liked it.

Sure. Always the contrarian, old Steve. And he threw away a fortune to prove it.

So what? It was Dad's money, not ours.

You know what I used to tell the traders at work? Take a look at Steve North's strategy. Then go be the contrarian of Bay Street's fabled contrarian. Old Steve, the shining icon of zero business sense. Runs in the family, doesn't it, Paula?

Shut up, Brian. I'm an artist, a painter. You know I can't do math.

Separated for nearly two years and Brian still lived in her head. Hour upon hour, his dark blue eyes taunted her, while his calm voice outlined her flaws. In detail.

Hey, Paulie, when were you last at the gym? And that stringy hair –time for an overhaul, bunnykins. But, hey, you need good bones, some basics to start with. Ah, forget it. Save your money.

Shut up! She stared through the windshield. When will I be free of him? When?

What if he never leaves my head?

She gunned the engine and bumped the car back onto the highway.

The road plunged on, woods alternating with barren fields. After a long stretch of pines, a weathered white building swung into view. Right at the crossroads, where it had always stood: Grumpy's gas station, her signpost to the cottage.

She flicked on her turn signal and drove over the familiar cracked concrete of Grumpy's parking lot. Too late, she spotted the rotten chipboard over the windows and the derelict, rusting gas pumps.

So the old fart finally retired. Brian again. *Or maybe he just died from being an asshole.*

Her fingers hurt from gripping the steering wheel. She'd counted on filling up at Grumpy's. Her car was riding on fumes. But the thought of driving 10 miles back to Elton for gas felt overwhelming.

I should drive back and gas up. But I have to see the cottage again. I have to make sure it's all right.

The shrill cry of her cell phone ripped through the silence, coupled with a vibration that bored into her side. She fumbled in her jacket and pulled it out. A name flashed on the call display.

Jay, checking up on her.

Again.

I should answer. We need to talk. But not now. I need to be alone.

She shoved the phone back into her thin windbreaker, stifling its nagging cries and gazed at the large muddy field that stretched along the road across from Grumpy's. A solitary man was driving a black tractor slowly and laboriously over the mangled earth. Old Sark. Still alive. Still farming 40 years on.

He's outlived everybody: Grumpy, Mum, Dad. Maybe he'll outlive me, too.

Hell, I'll risk it.

She tore out of Grumpy's ruined lot and turned down the dirt road that led to the cottage, Lake Huron a blue blur in the distance. Despite the cold spring, green buds studded the bare branches of the bushes lining the road. Soon the thick leaves and weeds would make the woods round the cottage impenetrable.

"And the green grass grew all around, all around. The green grass grew all around."

She chanted her favorite childhood tune as her car lurched down the road. Muddy water filled the potholes to the brim. When she reached the turn-in, her body seemed to sense it before her eyes did, as though it saw her instead of the other way round.

The cottage gate was a slender cedar log stretched over the drive, counterbalanced by a paint can filled with quick-dry cement. She remembered Dad fixing it, the last repair he did before he died.

And not fast enough, Brian loved to say. Then laugh so she wouldn't know if he meant Dad finally fixing the gate or Dad dying.

I remember how bright and clean the gate looked the day of Dad's funeral, she thought. I started crying again and couldn't stop. Only two years ago, and now the gate looks like it's been here forever. Things decay so quickly in the country.

She climbed out to deal with the gate, leaving the driver's door open with the engine running. For a quick getaway, Dad liked to joke.

The air felt chill on her skin. Tall pines shut out the sun, everything lay in shade. She longed for the homey scent of wood smoke, a hint to show that other people lived nearby, but all she could smell was mud, wet grass and leaves.

A lilac bush sagged low over the gate. She forced up its heavy branches and peered down the long, narrow drive. At the far end, all she could make out was a patch of silvery green.

Where's the cottage? Why can't I see it?

She heaved the lilac branches aside, hauled up the gate and secured it, the cedar pole slimy under her shaking hands.

The cottage is fine, she told herself. Nothing's happened. If it caught fire and burned down, they'd have called me.

Or would they? And who were "they" anyway?

She shivered and climbed back into the warmth of the car.

No one lives out here except Sark now that Grumpy's gone. And Sark refuses to own a phone. Even if he drove in to Elton to use the gas station's payphone, he'd use Dad's old number. And who would he reach? Brian, not me.

Brian even stole my family's old phone number, she thought. Keeps it for business reasons, he says. And he always "forgets" to pass on my messages. Every time I confront him about it, he just laughs and says he already gave them to me. Ages ago.

Please, please, please let the cottage be all right.

The lilac branches rasped over the roof of the car as she eased it through the gateway. She steered down the overgrown drive, ignoring the scrape of muddy ruts on the undercarriage, her eyes fixed on the green glow of the clearing.

At last, she broke free of the trees.

She let go her breath and turned off the engine.

***

The cottage seemed to shift and shimmer under the trees, its dark brown logs merging with the shadows. The late afternoon sun glinted off an upstairs window.

Silence flowed in through the open driver's window. No birds, no rustle of leaves, no distant murmur of highway traffic.

The cottage watched her, dark, still and vacant.

Her eyes strayed down its east side. The horrible shed was gone. Sark had hauled it away, thank God. Just as he'd promised her the day of Dad's funeral.

Oh, why am I here? I imagined...I thought maybe I'd feel Dad somehow. Now even the air feels empty.

That strange grass, the kind that only grew under the pine trees by the cottage, now filled the spot of ground where the shed once stood. From there, it flowed out to embrace the cottage, indeed to carpet the entire clearing.

Spidery and thin-leafed, an unusually pale green, in the dim afternoon light it almost seemed to phosphoresce.

My special grass. My glow grass. That's the green I saw at the end of the drive.

Glow grass? Are you kidding me? The cottage isn't fairyland and you aren't 12. Why don't you do something useful on the Internet for once and look up its real name? Get suckers to pay for weeds that only grow under pine trees. Go on, move that fat butt of yours.

I am not fat, she shot back silently. I'm borderline anorexic. The doctor said so.

Her phone rang. She hesitated for a heartbeat, then answered it.

"Paulie, thank God!" Jay shouted over the blare of traffic noise. "I'm standing outside your apartment building. Buzz me in, will you? We need to talk. It's crucial."

Always the drama, Paula thought. Probably why Jay loved being a lawyer.

She roused herself. "Sorry, Jay, I…I had to run an errand."

"You promised you'd stay at home today. You promised you'd call me if you went out, remember?" A rustle as Jay shifted hands. "When will you be back?"

"I don't know."

"What do you mean you don't know?"

"I need some time alone. To think." She listened to Jay gathering breath. "Please don't badger me, Janet."

"Don't call me that."

Janet, Jay's childhood name, simply slipped out from time to time. Paula couldn't help it. "Sorry, *Jay*. What happened with Brian this morning?"

Jay stayed quiet for a long moment. "Look, do you really want to discuss your private affairs while I'm standing out here in the open? Anybody could walk by and overhear us."

"I'm fine with it." Paula worried her bitten thumb nail. "Tell me, how was His Majesty?"

Jay sighed. "Gorgeous as ever. Fit, training for a marathon. But the minute he walked into my office I sensed a change in him, an undercurrent of…something. Well, you know how hard he is to read, but my intuition says he's weakening."

"Really?"

"Yes, really. He muttered something about feeling worn out by this long, drawn-out negotiation. Then the mask slips back on and he's Mr. Hard-ass. But he's a mere male, Paulie, not tough like us babes. Bottom line: He's handed over a written offer. One we can work with. Finally. But we are still dealing with Brian, right?"

"He wants something."

Jay's hesitation confirmed it. "That's how negotiation works—or doesn't. I admit that my gut reaction was negative, but then I sat down and did the numbers. And much as I hate to say it, his offer does make sense."

"Okay, I'm listening."

"It's complicated. We can't do this over the phone. Where are you?"

Paula didn't reply. She could almost hear Jay bristling.

"Look, I don't blame you for feeling skeptical. We both know how Brian loves to play games, but this time, I believe he's ready to settle."

"He's met someone."

Jay sighed. "Okay, yes, but so what? Press your advantage while he's starry-eyed."

"Well, that depends on what he wants."

"Okay, fair enough, but tomorrow he could get a wasp up his ass and drag things out another two years."

"Is his new girlfriend rich?"

"Look, forget about her. Sign his damn offer and get on with your life."

"What life? My life's been hell ever since Dad died. My money, my home—everything's gone. Brian made sure of that."

"Let it go, Paulie. Brian doesn't have any money either."

"He's lying! What about that line of credit he ran up against our house —*my* family home—after we split up? The loan that bank manager gave him without my signature, even though she knew the house was in both our names. The bank's never been clear on that." For a moment she thought she'd lost the connection. "Jay, are you still there?"

"Yes, I'm still here trying to get a word in. We've been through this a thousand times. You don't have the money to take the bank to court. Your money's gone. That's why we decided to negotiate with Brian. Formal mediation costs too much, remember? Look, everyone loses in a divorce. That's the way it works."

"Then why am I the one who always loses? Brian always wins. Even when he and the damn bank break the law, he wins."

"Okay, I'm the first person to admit that our legal system isn't perfect. You're in a dark place. I understand, believe me. Disentangling a marriage can be tough."

"Disentangling?" A worn-out weasel word to obscure the pain and humiliation of divorce, Paula thought. And how would Jay know? She'd never been married.

"Look, try to view your divorce as a life process. You die a little now in order to grow, to become the person you were meant to be."

Process—Jay viewed every human trauma as a "process."

"Forget it! You tell Brian, no! Absolutely no way! Whatever he wants, it's NO!"

She pressed End Call and flung her phone down on the passenger seat. Roaring the engine back to life, she gunned the car across the clearing.

And immediately lost control. The Honda fishtailed over the wet grass. She slammed on the brakes, slewing and sliding—and slammed head-on into the porch.

Oh, God! Waves of heat roared through her.

She shoved the gears into reverse, but her back wheels spun, whined and failed to get a grip. Jammed up against the porch, she couldn't go forward. She tried reversing again, several times, but the wet grass grabbed her tires like thick mud. The Honda was well and truly stuck; she'd only burn off the last traces of gas trying to get free.

Never pull up to the porch in spring, the ground's too wet. Always park at the end of the drive. For a quick getaway. I should have remembered, Dad.

She turned off the engine and climbed out, sinking ankle-deep into the soggy grass.

Now what? She'd cancelled her CAA membership to save money. What about the gas station in Elton? She could call there for help. And pray the staff didn't check her maxed-out credit card first.

Or…she could trek over to Sark's farm. Ask him to pull her out. He was always driving around on his tractor doing some mysterious farm thing or other. She shuddered. Sark's stoop-shouldered, hulking presence had unsettled her since childhood.

Dad never minded going over to visit Sark or even sharing a shot of rye with him, but she hated Sark's place. It was filled with junk—empty freezers, chains and rags everywhere, cans of oil and jars filled with murky fluids. Everything overlaid with the smell of decay and soiled laundry.

Don't judge him too harshly, Dad would say. He's been that way since his wife died.

But Mum died and you aren't that way, she'd argue. You aren't like Sark at all.

I have you, kid. Sark has nobody. He's alone, buried in his memories. That does strange things to people.

Memories...the cottage lay wreathed in them.

I need to look inside. Then I'll figure out what to do.

She fished the round-headed cottage key from her jeans, went up the porch steps and unlocked the front door. The wrought-iron latch lifted with a loud click.

She swung open the door.

And thought: I'm home now. Back with Dad.

***

Dank, moist air rushed over her. I must be the only person in the world who loves the smell of mildew, she thought.

The setting sun streamed in through the open doorway. Slowly, the long, plastic-shrouded kitchen table emerged from the dark, and beyond it, the shadowy, coffin shape of the refrigerator, its door propped open.

Step one, turn on the power.

The main floor of the cottage was divided by a fieldstone fireplace—a sitting area to her left, a country kitchen to the right. The power switch, a heavy black lever on a rusty metal box, rested on the side wall above the stove.

She stepped inside, the dusty plank floor crunching beneath her feet. Almost immediately, the outside light deserted her. She groped her way along the edge of the pine table, the plastic sheet rustling against her thighs. At the far end, she threw out her arms and felt the smooth surface of the electric stove. With one hand pressing down on a dead burner, she stretched up and found the switch.

She took a breath and pushed. It refused to budge.

That's my Paulie, skinny little arms but plenty of fat in the can.

She braced both hands on the stove and jumped. Shoes sliding on the slippery enamel, she scrambled up. A burner cracked loudly under her knee. Using both hands, she threw her weight and rage against the switch. And felt it clunk into position.

Nothing. No power.

Now what? No power meant no heat, no light, no hot water, no stove. Had she forgotten to pay the cottage hydro? No, the bank paid the bill directly out of her account. But what if the bill had arrived during one of the many times her funds had run dry?

I've got to get some light in here.

She grabbed the roller blind over the window beside the stove and pulled. With a huge clatter, the blind flew out of her hand, ripped free of its mountings and crashed down onto the floor.

Gray light filtered in through the dusty windowpane. She slid down off the stove and picked up the fallen blind. Dead insects littered the floor, the plastic sheeting, everywhere she looked.

God, that's disgusting. Never mind, step two, turn on the water. Don't need electricity for that.

She dumped the blind on the table and went over to the sink by the far wall. The inlet tap connecting the cottage's water system to Sark's well rested in the cupboard beneath it. She crouched down, opened the cupboard door, grabbed the inlet tap, and tried to turn it. The bloody thing wouldn't budge.

She leaned her head against the open cupboard door, sweat beading on her forehead. I have got to do this, she thought.

She groped through the darkness of the cupboard for Dad's wrench. Mum always needed it to turn the water back on.

Found it! The jaws of the wrench slid perfectly over the nut at the base of the tap. She breathed in, pushed down on the wrench and felt something give.

A familiar hiss and clanking in the intake pipe. Air rushed out of the kitchen tap in the sink above her head, followed by a belch of foul-smelling water. She stood up, feeling light-headed. Rusty water gushed out of the tap, but as she watched, it began to run clear, flushing two years of dirt and debris down the drain.

I did it!

She left the water running and dropped the wrench on the counter by the sink. Now to get some light and fresh air in here. I feel like Pip in *Great Expectations* tearing open Miss Havisham's apartments. I've come, come to let the light in!

She moved swiftly from the sitting room to the back bedroom to the cramped bathroom tucked behind the kitchen, raising blinds, fumbling with the rusty catches on the windows, hauling up their heavy frames and propping them open with the wooden sticks Dad had cut so long ago. They still bore his handwriting in black crayon: Back bedroom left, back bedroom right.

Dad's cottage exactly as he left it. How easy to pretend he was out by the beaver pond cutting trails. Or off to Elton for groceries.

Yeah, Elton's King Tut and his dump of a tomb.

That's enough, Brian. You've always hated the cottage.

She rubbed her arms and retrieved the wrench to get water flowing in the toilet. Retracing her steps back to the kitchen, she glanced up the narrow stairs that rose behind the stone fireplace. Her old bedroom lay up there in the loft with her favorite toys. But with the power out, all she could see was darkness.

Funny how Dad always slept in her bed upstairs whenever she and Brian visited. Switching places, kid, now that you're married, he'd say. You two take the master bedroom out back.

Hoping for the grandchildren that never came, she thought. I'll look upstairs later once I get the power back on.

She dropped the wrench beside the blind on the table and turned off the taps. How much better to *act* instead of sitting around. She'd been drowning in thoughts since Dad died.

Out in the car she could hear her phone ringing. She ignored it.

I'll get a fire going in the fireplace, she thought. Boil some water and make a cup of tea. Dad always left tea bags in the cupboard. I'll eat that chicken sandwich I couldn't finish at lunch. Tonight I'll sleep on the sofa in front of the fireplace and pretend that I'm camping. Come morning, I'll walk the 10 miles to Elton's gas station. I can do it. That's all I've been doing lately, walking and thinking. Endlessly.

She ran her hand over the rough fieldstones of the fireplace, remembering when Dad and Sark built it, their grunts of effort as they lifted the stones and mortared them into place. The cement for its base spread out like a strange moist cloth. And the repellent yet magnetic scent of their sweat.

Charred pieces of wood rested in the grate, remnants of the fire Brian built during their last, dreadful visit.

I'm throwing those ashes into the woods as far as they will go.

She jerked open the mesh curtains of the fire screen. A loud snap. A piece of wood struck her shoulder. She jumped, stifling a cry.

A mousetrap!

She glanced at the copper box holding the firewood. Another trap lay half-buried in the logs, a small mummified form caught under the rusty metal spring.

I hate those traps. They're so cruel.

Mice are vermin. They bring death on themselves.

She unhooked the little brass shovel from the stand holding the fire irons and slid it under the trap. Trying not to look at the dead mouse, she carried the trap outside. At the edge of the woods, she swung the shovel in a wide arc and heaved everything into the bush.

Done.

She breathed in the chill evening air. When had Brian put out those mousetraps? The day of the funeral or the day of the accident? She remembered nothing but chaos from that day: ambulance, police…and in the laneway, Sark sitting silently astride his brush cutter. She rubbed her cold hands.

Dad dies and you find time to set out mousetraps? You're sick, Brian.

Hey, you and Steve always complain that I never do anything at the cottage. Can't have it both ways.

Where else did you hide traps, you jerk?

She heard the growl of a faraway engine on the road down to the lake. She tensed. A car? No, too rough. It sounded like heavy machinery. Farm machinery.

Sark!

He had an uncanny way of knowing everything that happened at the cottage. And she sensed that he liked her knowing that he knew. Sometimes a faint smile would steal across his face—she'd notice it though Dad never did.

Dad always maintained that Sark didn't have a bad bone in his body, but she dreaded his sealed silence—and the oppressive obligation she felt, whenever she ran into him, to make one-sided inane conversation until she devised a lame excuse to escape. His sly smile would creep back then, too.

The motor sounded much closer. Definitely a tractor.

Turning into the cottage drive.

***

He'll realize I'm here alone.

She ran down the eastern side of the cottage away from the drive, her mind working. *I'll head up to the beaver pond while it's still light,* she thought. *Wait him out.*

The trail to the beaver pond started behind Dad's shed. She had no choice now; she had to cross over the horrible spot. A shimmering tongue of glow grass leaked out into the trail as though pointing the way to the pond.

Fire shovel in hand, she dashed over the sinister spot and plunged down the narrow track into the safety of the trees. The path snaked deeper into the forest, the glow grass dwindling out behind her.

The beaver pond lay buried in the woods half a kilometer north of the cottage. At one time, homesteaders owned a farm there with an apple orchard—or so Sark had told Dad. But the settlers had departed long ago and over time their log house had crumbled into the forest soil. The orchard had grown wild until beavers dammed the creek that cut through the forest, drowning the apple trees, turning their dead trunks silver.

The lost farm made Dad melancholy. It reminded him of time's passing, he said. But in the beaver pond all she saw was life—frogs, dragon flies, turtles, snails, and minnows. Once a pair of Canada geese nested there. Another time, she caught a perch, which Dad cooked for dinner. She'd always meant to find out who owned the land around the beaver pond. All Dad could tell her was that it lay well beyond their property line.

The trail suddenly veered right not left. She stopped, bewildered, faced with a tangle of brambles and reeds.

The path turns left here, she thought. Dad cut the trail along the *left* side of the pond so we could walk along its edge to the far end. Too many cedar trees on the right side: Dad never owned the heavy tools he needed to cut through them. I've used this trail since I was a kid. It turns left here, not right.

She clutched the fire shovel as though she could beat her memory into submission.

Oh, God, this divorce is driving me crazy.

Crazier, wouldn't you say?

Go away, Brian.

She took the path to the right.

It led into the shadows of the now-towering cedar trees. A short distance along, she spotted a soft green light—glow grass growing into the trail.

It spilled out from a tiny track that branched away through a clump of alders. Dodging the leafless bushes, she followed it into a small clearing.

A stone garden bench rested in a soft carpet of glow grass. Several small stones bordered its circular edge. On closer inspection, the stones proved to be store-bought garden ornaments, inscribed with a single word like *Forever* or *Remember*. Between the stones stood small plaster statues of angels holding soiled plastic flowers or soggy, bedraggled ribbons. One angel held a glass engraving of the poem "Desiderata," the relic cracked and damaged by the weather. Votive candles in red glass holders lay scattered among the stones, most burned down to the end.

This was a memorial garden. But for whom?

She sank down on the bench. The tiny monuments were cheap; she'd seen them for sale in dollar stores. None bore a date or name. Perhaps the strange garden was an amateurish, heartfelt tribute to a family pet.

But what if it wasn't?

She shivered. Who built the garden? Why hide it in the woods away from prying eyes? Was it the unknown owner of the beaver pond?

Over the years, she and Dad had found evidence of strangers round the pond—cigarette butts, fish line and hooks, empty beer cans. Anyone could pass through their property when she and Dad weren't there.

The mysterious gardener had taken glow grass from the cottage and replanted it here. That felt like a warning, a challenge even. As if the unknown gardener was telling her: *You abandoned the cottage. Now it's mine to do with as I like.*

The woods were deathly silent. Yet she had an uneasy sense that someone lurked in the shadows. Watching, waiting, matching her breath for breath. She felt in her jacket for her phone and remembered she'd left it in the car.

She stood up slowly, wielding the puny fire shovel. Saw nothing but lifeless bushes and dark cedar trees.

Heart pounding, she stumbled back to the main trail. She walked briskly, faster and faster through the waning light until she was running flat-out. She didn't stop until she burst clear of the trees.

The porch light was on. Under its harsh light, the glow grass had turned a chalky, sepulchral white.

Sark stood on the front porch, his bulky form blending into the dusk.

***

He sensed her presence, turned and stared in her direction. She shrank back against the cottage wall.

Slowly, laboriously, he lumbered off the porch. Stood there without speaking, the hard bones of his face sculpted by the evening shadows.

She had no choice; he'd seen her plain enough. She stepped forward.

"Hello, Mr. Sark." She gripped the fire shovel, held it close to her side. "Thank you, um, thank you for clearing away the shed." She gestured feebly at the spot behind her.

He grunted.

"I see…I see the power's back on."

"Weren't out. It's yer switch."

"My switch…Oh, but I turned it on." She cursed the defensive tremor that crept into her voice.

"Gone rusty. From sitting around. It's the damp what does it. Had to work it but good." With a gnarled fist, he motioned turning the black breaker switch off and on.

"You were inside? You went inside my cottage?"

"Wet kills a place." He took off his flat gray cap and ran a huge hand over his bald scalp. "You selling?"

"What?" Had he really said that? "Um, no, I-I'm not selling. Not now. I'm…I should say *we*, dropped by. To make sure, you know, everything's still all right."

"Long time."

"Yes, it's been very emotional." Under his stare, she struggled to find a simpler word. "Hard."

He nodded. Settled the cap back on his head.

"I see that Grumpy's gas station is gone."

Something stirred in the deep-set dark eyes. A slight shift in the heavy shoulders. She'd forgotten how large he was, how he towered over her even now as an elderly man. He gazed at a point past her shoulder, waiting, listening. She felt helpless. Maybe mentioning his old enemy, Grumpy, had been a mistake.

"I'll be going now." He nodded and trudged toward the mouth of the drive, cutting a dark line through the glow grass. She watched his hunched form turn down the road and vanish into the twilight.

Where was his tractor? She could have sworn she'd heard it turn into the drive.

She rushed over to her car and retrieved her phone. Her hands shook so badly, her fingers slipped on the touch screen.

He was here. Inside. My. Cottage. He knows I'm alone.

She punched out Jay's number.

No ring. Nothing.

Instead the phone uttered its inanely happy call tone and turned itself off. The outline of an empty battery flashed on the screen.

Out of power.

The sound of a vehicle on the drive. The phone slipped from her hands, bounced back onto the passenger seat.

He's coming back. He's coming back!

She stared, blinded by the oncoming headlights.

***

A car door opened. Someone called her name.

"Jay?" Had she heard right? "Oh, thank God, it's you!" Paula didn't know whether to laugh or cry.

Jay appeared from behind the open driver's door, her red cashmere coat swinging, her arms full of groceries. Paula rushed over to hug her.

Jay laughed, extricated herself. "What's going on? You look like a scared rabbit!"

"Sark was here. He knows I'm alone." Paula felt abruptly, chillingly sick. "You must have driven right past him on the way in."

"No, I did not see Old Psycho McDonald."

"He was here just a minute ago. How could you miss him?"

"I don't know. Hey, relax, will you. What were you planning to do? Beat him to death with that silly little shovel?"

The shovel felt slippery in Paula's sweaty grip. Sark wasn't the only one who could make her feel like an idiot. "How…how did you find me?"

"How long have we known each other? Twenty years! Think about it. We met in Grade 6 when we were 11. Here, take these groceries, will you? My arms are falling off. " She pushed the heavy bags into Paula's arms. Tossing her oversized Prada handbag over one shoulder, she headed back to where her Mercedes stood idling.

"Jay, wait! Leave your car on the drive." The driver's door slammed shut. "Don't! Wait!"

The noise of the V6 engine drowned out Paula's words. The Mercedes churned through the wet grass, heading directly toward her. Paula staggered under the burden of the groceries, barely sidestepping out of the way. With a spray of mud and grass, Jay skidded to a stop inches from the Honda's back fender.

"Why don't you listen?" Paula shouted as Jay reappeared. "You nearly ran me over!"

"What *are* you talking about?" Jay locked her car with a beep of her electronic key.

"The grass is too wet. My car got stuck. Now we're both trapped!" Paula stumbled over to the porch and dumped the groceries on it with a loud clank of bottles.

"Hey, take it easy! I bought us some decent merlot for once." Jay bounded up the porch steps and flung open the front door. "Phew, I'd forgotten the awful mildew smell in this place. I never could understand why your dad loved this old dump so much. With his money, why didn't he invest in Muskoka?"

They both knew the answer: Dad avoided the rich outside of work. Farmers and working men were the folks he admired. Why he loved that Jay, the scholarship student, became Paula's best friend at school. She remembered Dad telling her: "Jay's father is nothing but an old drunk. Let's give that girl a real family."

"Earth to Paulie: bring in the groceries, will you? Before the damn raccoons eat them."

"Hold on a minute. We need to talk."

"That's why I drove out here." Jay charged ahead of her into the dimly lit cottage.

It occurred to Paula that Jay didn't merely move through the world, she bored through it, light and air fracturing around her. Or so it seemed. In fact, ever since their childhood, it had always seemed so.

Paula trailed after her, lugging in the groceries. Nowhere clean to set them down. Even in the faint light shed by the wagon wheel chandelier, the insect bodies littering the plastic sheeting looked disgustingly obvious. Jay hadn't noticed the bugs yet, intent as she was on her cell phone. She'd dumped her precious Prada bag on the encrusted table. And her red Armani coat.

She'll freak, Paula thought. She hates bugs. I should dig out the vacuum cleaner and disappear every last one of those little buggers. But Sark...I want to get out of here.

Her legs were trembling. "Can you forget about your job for one minute? Please call the CAA."

"What did you think I was doing?" Jay frowned, staring at her phone. "There's no signal in here."

"But you got through to me earlier. Maybe it's your phone service. Try my phone instead." But her phone was out of juice, lying outside in her car, Paula remembered.

Jay made a gesture of frustration. "Never mind. I'll walk out to the road and try there."

"No, don't! Not with Sark around."

"Hello, he lives here. On the farm next field over."

"Will you listen for once? Sark was here. He was here *inside* the cottage."

Jay stared at her. "Why did you let him in if he scares you so much?"

"I didn't let him in! He walked in like he owned the place when I was out in the woods. He told me so to my face!"

"What were you doing in the woods? I'm confused."

Paula took a deep breath and blurted out her story, her words tumbling over and over each other like a rock fall: the stuck switch, the overgrown trail, the strange garden.

Jay frowned. "Okay, that's creepy. Maybe Old Psycho McDonald thought he was being neighborly. Out here in Braindead, Ontario, nobody locks their doors. People walk in and out of each other's houses all the time. Country crap."

"No, when Dad was alive, Sark always knocked first. Don't you see? He walked in here because he *knew* I was alone!" Paula realized she was shouting.

"Oh, for God's sake! If Sark was going to rape and murder you, he would have done it already."

"Thanks a lot."

Jay held up a hand. "Okay, okay. If you insist on talking about psycho farmers and weird graveyards in the woods, I need wine. Where did you put the groceries?"

Paula pointed to the spot by the table.

Jay reached down and gasped. "Oh, my God!" She snatched up her coat, brushing it off frantically. "Nice of you to tell me about the dead bugs before I dumped my new Armani on them."

"Sorry." Paula tossed the wrench and the broken blind under the table and peeled off the plastic sheeting over it. She took great care to wrap up the dead insects inside the plastic. At a loss when she was done, she shoved the rolled-up bundle under the table as well.

Jay banged an oversize bottle of red wine down on the counter. "I can't remember where your dad hid the wineglasses."

Paula pointed to the cupboard above the sink. She watched Jay extract two wineglasses and grimace at their dusty interiors. She took a breath. "You don't believe me about that strange garden, do you?"

Jay frowned while she rinsed the glasses under the kitchen tap. "Well, you do tend to exaggerate just a little. Goes with being an artsy, I guess."

"My being an artist has nothing to do with it! I know what I saw."

"Relax, I'm just teasing you." Jay shook the excess water out of the glasses. "Look, your mystery garden is a leftover from Halloween. Teenagers having a party. More country crap." She unscrewed the metal cap on the bottle. "Come on, don't stand there freaking out. Go build us a fire. It feels like the inside of an aquarium in here."

Wordlessly, Paula picked up the shovel from where she'd dropped it next to the groceries and made her way over to the fireplace. Light beamed down from the brass floor lamp over the worn brown sofa. She sank down into its chilly cushions, twisting the fire shovel handle in her fists. Time to come clean with Jay. She should have done it right after her meeting on Monday.

I hope we're still friends afterward, she thought. But if we aren't, well, maybe it's time to move on. For both of us. When we were kids, we were the school rejects, so we had to stick together. But we're so mismatched, we always have been. Jay's always been the pretty one, tall and athletic, while I'm the short, dumpy one who failed gym. She's the super bright math whiz, but I only had A's in art. So much has happened since school: Jay's a lawyer with a big Toronto firm. I got married and divorced. Well, I'm trying to get divorced.

"How's that fire coming along?" Jay shouted from the kitchen.

"I'm working on it." Paula bounced off the sofa and kneeled down next to the wood basket.

I'll burn you to nothing, she thought, glaring at the charred wood in the grate. Cleanse the cottage of you. And you with it, Brian.

Hey, our marriage is over. No need to get violent.

I wish you were dead. I wish you were dead instead of Dad.

Ooh, I am so scared. What are you going to do, bite me?

She reached for the kindling in the wood basket and hesitated.

You scared of another dead mousie? Go on, dig deeper. See if I left another surprise, you scared little bunny.

I'm sick to death of you and your traps. Go away!

She yanked kindling and logs free of the basket and threw them on top of the ashes. Standing up, she reached for the green biscuit tin where Dad stored the matches. But when she tried to pry the lid off, it wouldn't budge.

"Jay, I need your strong fingers."

Jay appeared, a full wineglass in each hand, her Prada bag slung over her shoulder. She set the glasses down on the mantelpiece and dumped her bag on the floor.

"Cheers!" She grabbed the nearest glass and flashed Paula a broad smile, showing off her brilliantly bleached teeth.

Sensing Jay's eyes on her, Paula picked up the other wineglass and took a sip of Jay's "decent merlot." The dark red wine tasted strangely sweet, but with a faint under taste.

"What's the matter? Don't you like it?"

"It's okay." Paula took a second sip to keep things pleasant. There it was again, that off-putting, almost metallic flavor.

"Let's get down to business." Jay dropped down on the sofa and patted the sofa cushions. "Come, sit down."

"First tell me what Brian wants. And be up front with me this time."

"I'm always up front with you."

"Answer my question!" Paula banged her glass down on the mantelpiece. Wine slopped over the brim.

Jay shrugged and sighed. "He wants the cottage."

Gotcha, Paulie.

***

Paula's throat constricted. Surprise had rendered her speechless.

"I know, I felt the same. Outrage, disbelief." Jay waved her wineglass. "But look at what this place costs you: there's property tax, insurance, water and power, plus your car and the gas to drive up here. And that's not counting repairs. You can't even begin to cover the costs on the pittance they pay you at the art gallery."

Paula stared into the dead fireplace. Jay was right: The cottage bills had eaten through her slender savings. And the nasty letters from the county tax office were getting nastier.

"Would giving up this place be so bad?" Jay went on. "It's falling apart. You haven't been up here since …well… since your dad's accident. To be honest, I thought you'd *want* to be rid of it."

Paula wiped her eyes. "You don't understand. It's all I have left of Dad. And he didn't die in the cottage. He died out in the shed."

So much blood. It had looked black not red. Splattered over the garden tools, leaking through the wooden floor, soaking into the grass beneath it…the glow grass. She hadn't understood what she was seeing when she opened the shed door to look for Dad. Her mind couldn't process the horror.

A severed femoral artery, the medical examiner said. Your father tripped over the garden scythe.

She remembered crying: But Dad was always so careful with his tools.

Jay looked subdued. "I'm sorry, Paulie. I shouldn't have stirred up those bad memories."

Paula found her voice. "You know, I never thought I could hate anyone. I mean, truly hate someone. Brian's always despised the cottage. He only wants it now because he's figured out a way to get money for it."

Jay shrugged. "Makes sense."

A cold gust of wind blew in through the open back window. Paula rubbed her arms. "That's why Sark asked me if I was selling when he was here. Brian cut a deal with him. Probably told him it was a sure thing."

"Maybe you're right. So what if Brian cut a deal with Sark? Who else would buy this swamp pit? After all, Sark's the one who sold it to your mum and dad in the first place."

"Dad said Sark needed the money." Paula rubbed her forehead. "Sark's poor. He's always been poor. He could only pay Brian a fraction of what the cottage is worth."

Hey, money's money. The cottage isn't an asset, it's a liability. Time to trim the fat.

Go to hell, Brian. The cottage isn't yours to sell.

Yet. You'll cave, bunnykins. You always do.

"Sark's got a thing about land." Jay drained the rest of her wine. "Remember how he moaned to your dad that Grumpy stole the gas station land from him? And how Grumpy called Sark dumb as a pail of hammers. Well, guess who owns the gas station now? Sark!"

"How do you know that?"

"I got curious when I saw Grumpy's was gone. So I stopped and called my assistant. Got him to check the land registry."

"What happened to Grumpy?"

Jay shrugged. "Maybe Old Psycho McDonald ploughed him into the back field."

"That's not funny. When Sark was here, I told him I'd never sell. I thought I was reassuring him. Instead he's going to be furious."

Jay slammed down her empty glass. "So what do I tell Brian?"

"Tell Brian…" Paula clenched her fists. "You tell Brian I'll burn the cottage to the ground before he takes it away from me."

"Now you're being unreasonable."

"No, I'm not." Paula picked up the matchbox tin again and forced her nails under its lid.

"Look, I can't spend any more time on you and Brian. I'm in big trouble with the firm. If I don't bill a ton more hours, they'll fire me. Just sign Brian's damn offer and move on."

"No, I said no and I meant no." She wrenched on the lid. "You never listen, Jay, that's why I have to tell you…"

The tin exploded in her grip.

Clumps of black matter showered down over the hearth. A strange powdery dust drifted through the air, settling over the scattered match sticks.

Paula looked down and screamed.

***

"There—there was something in the tin." She forced herself to look. Saw feathers, claws. "Oh, God. I think…I think it's a burned bird."

Jay bent over the fallen matchsticks. "You're right, it is a bird. Well, that's gross." She grabbed the brush hanging with the fire irons and began sweeping up the fragments.

"A pair of swallows used to nest in the eaves outside the back bedroom. They came back year after year. I loved them." Paula leaned her forehead against the cold, rough stones of the fireplace. "I know who killed the bird and put it there."

"Your Brian obsession is getting tired." Jay pushed the black remnants into a little pile.

"He built the fire last time."

"Enough about Brian!" Jay picked up the fire shovel from the floor by the sofa. "Look, a bird got caught in the chimney when you had a fire. It could have happened any time. Maybe your dad put it in the match box to bury it."

"Are you crazy? Dad believed what the Navajos believe, that death poisons everything it touches. He and Mum bought that tin on their honeymoon. It was special to him. Now it's spoiled forever."

"Oh, come on! Going mental over a cheap old tin." She made to toss the bird fragments into the fireplace.

"Wait, stop!" Paula grabbed her arm. "Throw it in the woods. The tin, too."

"Okay, fine. But after this, I want more wine. And since you don't like the stuff I opened, let's try the other bottle I brought. It's got a cork, so we'll need your corkscrew."

"Okay," Paula murmured.

She watched Jay brush the bird's ashes into the fire shovel, grab the matchbox and carry everything outside into the night.

Cold sweat prickled down her back. Her stomach burned. She thought back to the watery chicken sandwich she'd bought at the gas station on her way out of Toronto. And Jay's sickly sweet wine.

I think I'm going to be sick.

A faint noise, a creaking overhead. She looked up. A soft thud, as though someone had dropped a book. Directly above her head.

Someone's upstairs!

Sark!

Hey, I always thought Old Psycho McDonald liked you, Paulie. I mean, really liked you.

Helpless, she gazed up to the steps to the loft. Shadows smudged the stairs. Darkness hovered at the top of the landing.

Sark crept back through the woods. That's why Jay didn't see him. He climbed in through the open back window while we were outside.

She couldn't breathe. Couldn't move.

A car door slammed. The sharp crack of sound unfroze her legs. She stumbled, tripped and blundered her way outside.

A faint mist hovered over the glow grass. The fluorescent blue of Jay's cell phone screen floated in the dark beyond the cars.

"Jay," she managed. And then louder: "Jay!"

Jay materialized from the darkness, swishing through the mist like a ghostly surf, the fire shovel swinging in her free hand. She shoved her phone into the back pocket of her tight-fitting designer jeans.

Paula staggered down the porch steps. "There's someone in the cottage." She tried to keep her voice low, looked back over her shoulder.

"No way!" Jay's dark brows, such a contrast to her shining blond hair, pulled down in a deep frown.

"It's—it's Sark!"

"No, it can't be. Listen!" Jay pointed down the drive.

Faintly, in the distance, the unmistakable growl of a tractor. Revving back and forth. Driving over the black muddy field the way she'd seen him when she first arrived.

"Jay, we need to leave. Right now."

"Make up your mind. Is Old Psycho McDonald inside or outside?" Jay brushed past her, bounded onto the porch and disappeared back inside.

I am not imagining it, Paula told herself. She needed her phone. With the cottage power back on, she'd recharge it.

She rushed over to passenger side of her car. And felt a crunch underfoot.

***

No! It can't be!

She dropped to her hands and knees, groping through the wet grass. Impossible to see in the dark. Her fingers struck something hard. She felt a sharp jab of pain.

Glass! Even in the dim porch light, she could make out the bloodied fragment in the grass.

Biting back the pain, she combed through the grass. In a few moments, she'd retrieved the shattered pieces of her cell phone. She'd stepped on it, crushed it beyond repair.

But I left it on the passenger seat. How could it have slipped out of my car?

"Are you going to sit out there all night?" Jay called from the cottage.

Paula forced herself to stand up. She opened the passenger door and tossed the remains of her ruined phone inside.

"Have you calmed down now?" Jay was standing in the doorway of the cottage.

"I'm fine." Paula clutched her bleeding hand. "I really did hear a noise upstairs."

"Fine, you heard something," Jay snapped. "Probably a mouse. This swamp pit is a rodent highway. Are you coming back in or not? I'm starving."

Paula made herself climb up the porch steps. "It's only a mouse, it's only a mouse," she chanted under her breath. She eased in through the front door.

"Will you stop muttering to yourself!"

'I'm fine, Jay. Let's eat. I'll open the wine." Action was better than thinking. Action would calm her nerves.

She walked over to counter and pulled open the cutlery drawer where Dad kept the corkscrew. She reached in blindly.

And heard the snap of a mousetrap.

***

Hot tears ran down her cheeks. She tried to free her hand from the drawer. It was caught.

"Jay…" she gasped against the fierce pain. "Help me."

Jay rushed over. "What's wrong with you?"

"A mousetrap. Pull the drawer out."

Jay seized both sides of the drawer and heaved. Nothing happened.

"Yank it out all the way." Paula's breath was coming in gasps.

Jay hauled on the drawer again. It wrenched free of its slide and crashed to the ground, sending a glittering cascade of knives, forks and spoons skittering across the floor.

"Holy hell!" Jay grabbed Paula's arm, making her wheeze in pain.

Paula stared at her injured hand in the trap. My finger doesn't bend that way.

"Hold still." Jay's strong fingers bent back the shiny copper hinge of the trap. "Now! Hurry! Pull it out!"

"I…I can't."

"Do it! I can't hold it open."

With a savage tug, Paula twisted her finger free. A vicious snap shot the trap from Jay's grip.

Paula clutched her left wrist. Her finger refused to move. It was already darkening and swelling. "I…I think it's broken."

Jay looked pale. "I'll get the first aid kit. You still have it, right?"

Paula nodded. "Please hurry."

Jay disappeared into the bathroom.

I call that sweet irony, don't you? Broken marriage, broken ring finger.

I hate you, Brian! A shining bolt of pain shot down her left arm.

Jay returned, carrying a battered metal box with a red cross on it. The old first aid kit Dad had used to patch up their childhood scrapes.

Must think… Paula's finger throbbed in agony. Jay made a splint for it with an emery board and some ancient gauze. But there was no aspirin inside the first aid kit.

Paula stumbled over to the side fireplace and leaned against the stones. She might as well tell Jay now. Anything to take her mind off the pain.

"Jay, I…please sit down. We need to talk."

Jay slouched down on the brown sofa. "Okay, I'm listening."

"I owe you so much. You were the friend I turned to when Dad died and Brian took off." Paula gathered her breath. "I couldn't think straight after finding Dad like that. And losing the house, Dad's money gone. Brian turning ugly…the stress was crushing me."

Jay frowned. "So what's the problem?"

"Trying to negotiate with Brian has been a disaster!"

"What are you talking about? We're done! I have the papers with me. Sign and Brian's out of your life forever."

"No." Paula shook her head. "He's relentless. He'll never stop."

"It's because he wants the cottage, isn't it?"

Paula straightened up. "Well, that certainly made up my mind." There was no easy way to tell Jay other than to say it. "I've been doing a lot of thinking lately. I…I went to see Michael Rothstein on Monday."

"What!"

"He's the family lawyer who's always in the news."

"I know who Michael 'Barracuda' Rothstein is." Jay picked up the fire shovel, twisting its handle between her hands. "You're unbelievable! Wasting everyone's time lawyer shopping. Thanks a lot, 'best friend'!"

"It's my life, Jay."

Jay threw her a hard look. "The Barracuda will tell you exactly what I've told you a thousand times already: You don't have the money to take the bank to court."

"Mike thinks I have an excellent case."

"Mike?" Jay pulled a face. "Of course, he'd say that. Do you have any idea how much The Barracuda charges per hour? You'll spend the rest of your life paying off his legal fees."

"He's offered to do it *pro bono*."

"You heard what you wanted to hear. The Barracuda never does *pro bono* work."

Paula cleared her throat. "You wouldn't necessarily know this, but Dad and Mike's father were in school together. Mike's father was the poor Jewish kid there on scholarship, so the other boys gave him a rough time. Dad stuck by him. Mike says his dad never forgot that. He wants to help. He's offered to handle my case personally...and now I've decided to say yes."

"You...you're *firing* me?"

"Yes, I'm really sorry, Jay. I should have gone to see Mike in the first place." Paula tried to ignore the throbbing pain in her hand. "Negotiating with Brian seemed like the best way when you suggested it, but he's fooled both of us."

Jay stared into the cold fireplace in stony silence.

"Don't you see? You, Brian and I...we know each other too well. You knew him before I did. Remember how you introduced us at the golf club? That's the problem. He's manipulated both of us."

"You're crazy!" Jay squeezed the handle of the fire shovel so hard that Paula thought she could see it bend. "You want to blame Brian for everything that's wrong with your life. None of those therapists helped you. No one can."

"I'm sorry I dragged you into my mess. I asked too much of our friendship, Janet."

"Don't you call me that!"

The shovel clanged against the stones of the fireplace, inches from Paula's head.

"Did you just throw that at me?"

Jay stalked off into the kitchen.

Well, that went horribly, Paula thought, heart churning.

"I need a drink," she heard Jay mutter. Then louder: "Where the hell did you throw the corkscrew?"

A loud clatter as Jay scooped up the fallen cutlery from the floor and dumped it back into the kitchen drawer. The white-hot pain from Paula's broken finger was blurring out the world. "Jay?" she ventured.

"What do you want?"

"Do you have an Advil in that big Prada bag of yours?"

Jay sighed with drama. "Fine, you're in luck. Go sit down. I'll bring it."

Relieved to restore the peace, even for a moment, Paula turned to sit down on the sofa. That's when she saw it: a tiny pinpoint of blue light winking at her from between the sofa cushions like a snake's eye.

With her uninjured hand, she reached down and found Jay's cell phone. It had slipped out of the shallow back pocket of Jay's tight-fitting jeans.

She swept her finger across the phone's screen to unlock it.

A message appeared: Keep her busy.

The message was from Brian.

The world stopped.

***

The pop of a cork broke the spell.

The shattered pieces of Paula's world kaleidoscoped back into a new, chilling reality. Jay and Brian. Working together.

The proof rested in her hand.

Her throat had dried up. Her heart was beating so wildly she could barely breathe. She slipped Jay's phone into her jacket.

She edged round the end of the stone fireplace and peered into the kitchen. Jay stood by the pine table, turned away from her. Though slender, she possessed athletic strength.

Brian's equal in every way. Especially in deceit.

Think. I must think.

Paula watched Jay fill their glasses with a murky red wine.

How could you do this to me, Janet? she thought. Dad called us spirit twins. He paid your way through law school, so you'd never be poor again. It can't just be because of the money. It can't just be because you and Brian wanted all Dad's money.

But of course, it could. Dad had always told her that money made people crazy. He'd seen too much in the brokerage business. People did unspeakable things for money. To strangers, friends and family. Especially to friends and family.

She'd asked Brian again and again for the financial documents, the hard copy proof that Dad's money had vanished in the recession, only to be told by Jay that she'd never be able to decipher them. Because she couldn't do math.

But Jay could. And she had the legal knowledge to funnel Dad's stolen money to an off-shore account.

"You're muttering to yourself again." Jay turned to face her, a glass of wine in her hand.

Paula met her gaze, but kept still.

"Here, drink this." Jay shoved the glass into Paula's uninjured hand.

"Alcohol won't help the pain." Paula's mind was whirling.

"Best cure there is." Jay dug through the front pocket of her jeans. "And take these."

Paula stared at the two elongated green capsules in Jay's hand. "Those aren't Advil."

"Advil won't help a broken finger. My sports doctor prescribed them when I tore my hamstring. Go on, take them and drink up."

"You're not supposed to mix alcohol and painkillers."

"I am beyond tired listening to you whine. Take them or I'll shove them down your throat!"

"What's wrong with you?"

"What's wrong with me? You went to The Barracuda behind my back, wasted two years of my professional time, got me in big trouble with my law firm for not billing enough—and you're asking me what's wrong?"

Paula's eyes strayed to the front door. She had to get outside. But Jay was standing between her and the door.

"You're not drinking." Jay held out the pills, her eyes never leaving Paula's face.

Paula motioned with her bandaged left hand. "I only have one hand." She squeezed past Jay to the opposite side of the table.

Nothing now between her and the front door.

She took the pills from Jay. She made a display of shoving them in her mouth. Praying they wouldn't dissolve, she picked up her wineglass.

Heart beating, conscious of Jay's ever-watchful eye, she drew in a mouthful of wine. She pressed the pills hard against her bottom teeth with her tongue, a trick she'd mastered in childhood to avoid swallowing medicine.

"You're not drinking."

She had to swallow now. She downed as little as possible and choked. Coughing and spluttering, she doubled over. And spat the pills into the wine.

"What the hell are you doing?"

To cover, she drew in a rasping breath. "Took too big a drink."

Jay wasn't convinced.

Paula straightened up, pasted on a smile and took another sip, curling her fingers tightly around her glass to hide the pills in the depths of the blood-red wine. "There, that's better." She smiled again. "Much better."

Jay picked up the other glass and took a swallow of wine. Said nothing.

She had to distract Jay. Her mind ricocheted from one idea to another. She cleared her throat. "That illegal line of credit on our house that forced me to sell…"

Jay made an impatient gesture. "Will you stop! Brian got caught in the recession, okay? He made some bad choices. Give it up. That money's gone, it's never coming back."

Paula closed her eyes, persevering. "You and I know what the bank did. But we should have been asking *why*."

"This is pointless. I'm not your lawyer anymore."

"Mike knew why right away."

"Oh, really?"

Paula licked her lips. "I felt so stupid when he pointed it out. The answer's obvious: Brian had sex with the bank manager."

Jay clutched her wine glass. "That's not possible."

"Why? Because she's married and 20 years older than we are? Brian held his nose and did the necessary, as he puts it. He's always used sex to get whatever he wants. I should know! He couldn't get Dad's money with just a little sex. But if he married me, he'd get it *all*."

"Believe that if you want. And if you keep repeating that idiotic lie about the bank manager, she'll sue you. And *she'll* have 'an excellent case.'" Jay mimed the quotation marks with her free hand.

Paula felt a prickle of heat in her throat. She had to convince Jay, she had to. "Oh, Brian did her all right. Big-time. Mike's junior did some digging. Finding the proof turned out to be easy. Mike told me this morning. I felt so upset, I had to get away. That's why I drove up here to the cottage."

"I don't believe you!"

"Why? Every woman we know wants Brian. *I* fell in love the minute I saw him. I'd never met anyone that good-looking. I thought he was a movie star when you introduced us." Her limbs shook with a chill foreign to the damp in the cottage. "He had at least three affairs while we were still together. And they weren't just one-night stands."

"You're making this up!"

"Brian told me himself. Rubbed my face in it. And those are only three affairs I know about."

Jay said nothing, her expression unreadable.

"Don't you remember? I asked you about infidelity when Brian took off. In a general sort of way. You said adultery doesn't count for much nowadays, even in divorce court." She took a step back from the table, feeling dizzy. "I never told anyone, not even you, because I felt so humiliated."

"You're lying."

Paula shook her head. "I wish I were." She set glass down on the table. "Do you really think Brian will stay with you once he has all my money?"

"SHUT UP!"

Jay's glass shattered on the log wall behind Paula. The acrid scent of spilled wine filled the room.

A loud crash from upstairs stunned both of them.

No mistaking that for a mouse.

***

Paula ran for the front door. It wouldn't open. She wrestled madly with the latch. Heaved her weight against the wood, her terror obliterating all sense of pain.

"It's locked," Jay said behind her.

Paula turned to face her.

"Let me show you the key." Victorious, Jay dug through the back pocket of her jeans. Her smile died. "Where is it? Where's my phone?"

Paula shook her head, refused to speak.

Jay stared at her. "*You* took it." She grabbed the wine bottle from the table. "Give it to me!"

"NO!"

"Give it to me or I'll smash your finger to a pulp!"

The open back window! Paula plunged past her, but Jay latched onto her like a wild animal. She caught hold of her hair, yanking, twisting and pulling.

Paula screamed, desperate to free herself. She flailed out with her good arm. Jay hooked her ankle, threw her off balance. A horrible sensation of falling. An agonizing thud down onto the dusty floor.

Then Jay was straddling her, weighing her down, pummeling her unmercifully. She screamed again, frantically fending Jay off with her good hand, but all she struck was air.

A glint of light. A flash image of Jay raising the wine bottle.

White-hot agony burst through her broken hand.

She couldn't cry out, the pain was so great. She retched.

"You little bitch!" Jay scrambled off her.

Paula rolled over. Foaming acid liquid roared up her throat and splattered over the floor. Splashed onto Jay's jeans.

Jay raised the wine bottle: A glass baseball bat, aimed at her temple. Paula lifted her limp arm—a ridiculously puny shield.

"Stop playing around, you two!" someone shouted.

Jay froze in mid-swing. Paula coughed through a haze of anguish.

Brian had left her head and re-entered the real world.

He was upstairs in the cottage.

***

Jay leaped up. "*You* stop playing around! Get your ass down here and help me with her!"

Brian laughed. "Listening's more fun."

Jay swore and stomped over to the stairs, wine bottle in hand. "I'm tired of doing all the work."

"But you do it so well. And hey, Jay-bird, you told me you could handle this. Sounds like you lost it."

"Get down here!" When Brian didn't reply, Jay reached over and flicked the light switch by the back bedroom door. It controlled the light up in the loft.

Nothing happened.

"What did you do to the light?" she shouted.

Brian chuckled. "Come up and find out."

"Is she lying about the bank manager? Those other women? Tell me she's lying."

"Hey, Paulie doesn't have the brains to lie. Like her old man that way.'

"You bastard!"

"Aw, you're so cute when you're mad."

Jay charged up the stairs, clenching the wine bottle.

Now was her chance. Paula tried to stand up, but her legs buckled. A deadly lethargy had invaded her body. She dragged herself onto her hands and knees. The window... she had to get to the back window.

She retched again, bringing up the dregs of Jay's drug-laden merlot.

Upstairs Brian and Jay were arguing in urgent, intense bursts. The world was fading. She shook her head violently. *If I pass out, I'll die.*

"Hey, Paulie," Brian called down. "Come up here and play. We're waiting."

"Who were those women? Tell me!"

A thud and a crash. "Cut it out, Jay." Another crash. "I said cut it out!"

"Tell me!"

Brian swore. "I just tripped over your damn toy box, bunnykins."

A blue iridescent light cut through the upstairs darkness, strobed back and forth across the landing at the head of the stairs. So Brian had a phone, too.

Paula fought to hang on to consciousness. Jay had been texting Brian all along. They must have driven up together. Jay probably dropped him off at the end of the cottage drive. He could have slipped in unseen any number of times.

Suddenly Jay let out a cry of rage. Brian shouted back. They were getting physical. Splintering the upstairs furniture.

The world was growing dark. Paula dragged herself over to the kitchen table—the only hiding place she could reach. She crawled underneath it, grappling with the bug-infested plastic sheeting. The noise of the fight upstairs drowned out the ghastly rustling sound it made as she burrowed in next to it.

With her undamaged right hand, she extracted Jay's phone from her pocket. Punched in 911 with her thumb. It rang and rang.

Please pick up, please pick up!

"Emergency services. Fire, ambulance or police?" a faint voice said in her ear.

"Police! *Police!*" Paula shouted against the din of the rampage upstairs.

"Stand by." The dispatcher's voice died out. He must have put her on hold.

Answer, please answer.

Shrieks and blows overhead.

Why didn't the police answer? She stared at the phone screen. Only half a reception bar. So Jay hadn't lied about the poor service after all.

A thunderous thump from upstairs. Glass shattered.

Silence. They'd stopped fighting.

The bing of Jay's phone sounded unnaturally loud.

A message appeared: Call lost.

***

"Hey, bunnykins," Brian called down.

Her heart beat like a trapped bird. The police tracked emergency calls, didn't they? They'd track her call to the cottage, wouldn't they?

But even if they did, it would take too long. They'd arrive too late.

"I'm losing patience, sweetie."

She pulled herself onto her knees. Her legs trembled. She had to get out. She had to get outside or she would die.

"Who the hell keeps Ninja Turtles when they're over 30?" Brian said. A horrible crunch followed. "Hey, that was fun."

He's trying to lure me out. He's counting on me to be weak. But I will not let him kill me!

"Got a whole toy chest to play with up here. Better come up and stop me."

She refused to utter a sound. She would not be drawn out.

"Bye-bye, Snow White," Brian said. Glass and china smashed.

She wouldn't think about her beloved toys, she wouldn't.

"Bye-bye, Mickey Mouse."

Blue light flashed through the gaps in the planks of the ceiling as Brian worked his way through the loft. Destroying her precious memories one by one.

Paula wiped away her tears with her good hand.

The stairs creaked. Someone was coming downstairs.

Through the maze of table and chair legs, she spied Brian's trim, muscular form on the steps. He was dressed in his running gear: black tank top, black shorts, black and gold-trimmed running shoes. No sign of Jay.

"I know where you're hiding, Paulie. Bad things happen in showers."

He vanished into the bathroom. She heard the plastic shower curtain rip. And the clang of the shower hooks as they hit the tub.

The bathroom window banged shut. She jumped, smacking her head on the underside of the table.

"I heard that." He was standing outside the bathroom door. "Come on out. Make it easy on yourself."

She dared not breathe. He dove into the back bedroom. A huge clatter as he heaved aside the wooden sticks propping open its only window. He crashed it down. Glass splintered.

Oh, Dad, help me.

Her knee knocked against the fallen kitchen blind. She reached for it with her good hand.

And found the wrench.

She watched him leave the back bedroom. He headed for the open back window next to the fireplace. Her last chance of escape.

She wrestled free of the plastic and hauled herself out from under. She tossed the blind onto the table. Clinging to its edge for support, she pulled herself up onto her shaking feet. Only the kitchen table stood between them.

"There you are, little mousie." He turned and flashed her an engaging smile. Who would believe he was about to kill her?

She kept her uninjured right arm close to her side. "Stay where you are. Don't come near me."

He sauntered over. "How'd you like my traps?"

"I thought Jay set the traps."

"Not her style. No sense of humor. Had to work fast while you and Jay-bird were outside. Except for the swallow in the tin. Did that the day of old Steve's funeral."

He stepped closer. "Clever girl, Jay-bird. Learned lots of tricks in law school. Except the whole 'drain the assets, hide the money offshore' thing took so damn long."

"Where is she?"

He shrugged. "Taking a break. She's played her part."

"She drugged me."

He threw out his hands. "Hey, makes sense you'd off yourself in your crappy childhood dump, crying for dear old Dad. After all, you're not the most stable person, are you, bunny brain?"

"Fuck you, Brian."

He'd reached the other side of the table. Behind him, the blackness beyond the back window beckoned. "You know, you could have sucked downed that nice merlot and gone to sleep like an old cat at the vet's. A sofa cushion to the face to make sure and a soft exit from your pathetic life. Now you force me to improvise. I'll have to burn down this swamp pit." His face brightened. "But hey, there's an upside to everything. You kept up the insurance. Jay-bird checked."

He lunged for her. Batted the blind off the table like a scrap of paper. It clattered to the floor.

She wheezed in fear. No need to act.

"God, you're a pain. Tell you what." He clapped his hands in a theatrical gesture. "I'm going to string you up on this chandelier thing." He gestured at the wagon wheel above the table. "I'm going to make it nice, slow and painful. Let you catch your breath, pull you back up." He flashed a boyish grin. "Make you last all night."

"Why…" Her voice died, refused to come out.

He crashed his fists on the table, making her leap in shock. "Because you won't cooperate!"

She found her voice. "Jay, don't do this. We were friends once, best friends. Answer me, Jay. Where are you? Where…?"

Water hit her forehead. She swiped at it with her injured hand. The gauze on her broken finger turned scarlet.

She felt a drop on her cheek. And another.

A red rain was leaking through the gaps in the ceiling planks. Skittering over the tabletop, dropping down on her.

And hitting Brian, too.

A strange, humid smell. Not rain. Blood!

He killed her. He killed Janet!

She screamed in horror—and that saved her. Distracted him for a heartbeat as he jumped the table.

She swung the wrench. Crunched it against his cheekbone.

He roared in pain and outrage.

She ran for the window. He scrabbled after her.

She was halfway through the window when his fists seized her. She struck out again with the wrench, fighting and screaming. He got it away from her.

A gleam of metal in the tumult of their fists. Brian yelled and grabbed his head. The fire shovel bounced onto the floor.

A voice shrilled at her to run. A nightmare vision stood on the stairs. Sodden with black and red blood. Holding a broken wine bottle.

Brian threw himself at the phantom. They grappled for the bottle in a deadly tug-of-war.

Paula rolled over the window sill. Tumbled into the wet grass.

And charged blindly into the woods.

***

The moon was up. The glow grass shimmered all around her with a chill white phosphorescence. Mist rose from it like smoke.

She ran mindlessly. Her shaking legs moved with a will of their own. The pain in her hand dwindled to a distant thing.

I must not fall. If I fall, he'll kill me. Must get into the trees. Hide in the dark.

The turn-off to the beaver pond loomed before her. She could hear his footsteps on the path like a cold wind behind her.

She dove into the darkness under the cedar trees. The track to the hidden garden shone like a silver thread.

Must hide. *Must hide.*

The moon shone down on the empty garden bench, bathing the tiny angels and stones in an eerie pattern of light and shadow.

He'll find me.

She fought her way into the woods, struggling through a ferocious tangle of bushes. Branches and thorns scratched her face. She could penetrate no further. Already she could hear the huff of his breath on the trail.

She dropped to the ground. Huddled to make herself small.

A mad thrashing of bushes. He's coming down the track.

"What the hell!" He'd found the garden. "You build this for dear old dad, bunnykins? It's tacky enough."

She peered through the web of undergrowth. Moonlight outlined his head and bare torso. It glinted off the broken wine bottle in his fist. Black matter stained its gleaming edges. He'd made short work of Jay.

"I know you're in here."

She held her breath. She dared not move.

No one out here in the depths of the woods. Her cries for help would die out as they did for all prey.

He was circling the garden now, peering into the shadows. Suddenly, an intense brightness flooded the woods. His cell phone!

He stood by the stone bench, beaming its light over the undergrowth. A fiendish beacon, searching, probing.

She pressed her pale face hard against her knees, squeezing down even smaller. To be one with the dark.

"You're making me very angry." His voice sounded too close. "You really don't want to do that."

She sensed the light moving away. A quick glance showed him sitting on the bench, phone in one hand, broken bottle in the other. His foot bounced in annoyance, as though she was late with dinner. Or boring him.

"I'll find you when the sun comes up. Getting cold here, waiting around. Tell you what. Come out now, and I'll make it quick."

He paused, thinking. What was he doing now?

She sensed a vibration. A light shone through her pocket. The phone. He was calling Jay's phone!

She yanked it out and heaved it into the trees. Its throbbing techno beat ring sounded as loud as a jet plane. It landed too close to her, its blue light pulsing through the brush.

He was on it in an instant. Foraging through the weeds and bushes like a wild dog. He was so close she could smell his acrid sweat. One more step and he'd land on top of her.

She broke free of the bushes. Landed in the garden.

The glowing track had vanished. She ran for it anyway. And smashed into a wall.

A terrible force caught hold of her. She struggled madly. Felt her jacket rip away. She tried to run. The stone bench struck her knees. She fell heavily.

Brian loomed over her. She screamed in icy terror.

He slashed down with the wine bottle. It shattered on the bench in a glittering mass of shards.

She couldn't escape the glass, the darkness, his rage.

He uttered a wet cough. Strangely he'd grown a second smile. His hands clutched his throat. A black fountain gushed over his naked chest.

He toppled onto his knees beside her.

She struggled away from him. He threw her a beseeching look. Reached out his hand.

And fell to the ground, shaking in a lethal seizure, twitching and shuddering, as his life's blood emptied into the glow grass.

Her breath had left her. She could only watch, paralyzed.

A piece of the darkness detached from the woods. A shape as big as a mountain. The moonlight shone down on a pale and pitted face. Gleamed on the scythe in a huge fist.

Sark!

His free hand reached for her. Gathered her up. Pressed her against his stony chest. She smelled wet wool and earth.

"You all right?" his hoarse voice asked.

She burst into desperate, gulping sobs. They tore out of her, the way the blood had gushed out of Brian. "You...you killed him!"

"Like a hog. Done lots in my time."

"You ...saved me."

"Swore to Steve I'd look out for you." He kicked Brian's now flaccid leg. "This one needed killing."

She tried to contain her crying. "He-he killed my friend Jay."

"She weren't your friend. She was with him."

So he'd heard everything through the open windows! She'd sensed him out there, lurking, listening.

"Brian killed Dad. He set a trap for him in the shed. I know he did it, but I'll never be able to prove it."

"Your dad's blood made the grass glow."

"Wh-what?"

"His spirit makes the grass shine."

She backed away from him, wiping her cheeks with her good hand. "You built the garden. You made it for Dad."

Sark nodded his massive head. "Steve was a good man." He wiped the scythe on the leg of his overalls. "I'll clean up the mess. They won't bother you again."

"What-what will you do?"

"Back field needs ploughing."

She wanted to tell him to stop. That they must call the police. But the strength that had saved her was ebbing.

"You selling?" His hard dark eyes met hers.

"No, never." The glow grass in the track shone like the sun. She edged down it. "The cottage is yours if you want it. Take it! Take it back!"

She fled down the trail. All around her, the glow grass shimmered with an unearthly light.

She ran down the trail, skirting the spot where the shed once stood, passing the dark hulk of the cottage and the two cold, useless cars parked end to end. She ran and ran. Down to the end of the drive and up the road to the highway.

Her lungs burned. Somewhere during her wild flight, she lost her shoes. She hobbled over the dirt road in her bare feet, fear and pain beyond her.

A faint greenish light rimmed the eastern horizon. Dawn was breaking.

Grumpy's abandoned gas station was flooded with a red light. A police car stood idling on the cracked concrete.

With a cry, she staggered toward it and collapsed. Car doors opened, footsteps ran toward her. Two police officers bent over her.

"You...you found me," she stammered.

Their kind hands lifted her up.

And she felt the new day's light embrace her like her beloved glow grass.

About M.H. Callway

M. H. Callway is the founder of the Mesdames of Mayhem. Her critically acclaimed debut novel, *Windigo Fire* (Seraphim Editions) was short-listed for the 2015 Arthur Ellis Award for Best First Novel. Previously it was nominated for both the Unhanged Arthur and the Debut Dagger Awards. Margaret Cannon of *The Globe and Mail* called her "a writer to watch".

Madeleine's award-winning crime fiction stories have been published in several anthologies and magazines. Her speculative fiction story, "The Ultimate Mystery" in *World Enough and Crime* (Carrick Publishing 2014), was a 2015 Derringer finalist.

She is a longstanding member of Crime Writers of Canada and Sisters in Crime. An avid cyclist, runner and downhill skier, she has participated in the Toronto Ride to Conquer Cancer every year since 2008. She and her husband share their Victorian home with a very spoiled cat.

http://mhcallway.com/
Amazon Author Page
Facebook
Twitter
Mesdames of Mayhem

Mesdames of Mayhem

THE TEST OF TIME

By Melodie Campbell

"Another missing female—you better see this, Jack."

Jack Connelly looked up from his cluttered desk and scowled. The third one in two months, and each case a dead end. No body, no witnesses, no traces of violence, not even any close relatives to grieve over them. It was as if they had disappeared into thin air.

He scanned the details and saw they checked out, same as before. This one was 28 years old, a PhD student in engineering physics, whatever that was. Bright girl, obviously. That fit, too.

He looked at the photo. Good-looking kid with shoulder-length auburn hair and big, brown eyes. Nice smile.

He continued reading. Used to be engaged, but broke it off last year. No history of violence on the part of the ex. No known current boyfriend.

"Girlfriend reported her missing when she failed to show up for lunch and shopping." Marco said. "Not like her. When she didn't answer her cell or home phone, the friend started to worry about meningitis."

There was some of that going around, for sure. But both of them knew this wasn't a medical case.

"Any signs?" Jack stuck a pencil in his mouth in lieu of a cigarette. Quitting smoking was hell, and he had to stop eating; the pounds were piling on.

"Not a thing. Same as before."

"Work? Hobbies?"

"Not teaching this term. Off for a few months, doing her thesis. Took dance lessons—ballet—and likes classical music, books. All highfalutin stuff." Marco was a beer-and-hockey kind of guy.

"Not exactly a hotbed of criminal activity in symphony and ballet." Jack sucked on the eraser end. Who was taking them? And why these ones? All bright, all well-educated... not a single barfly in the bunch. Toss in the lack of close relatives or boyfriends, and it smacked of premeditation.

"White slave trade?" his young detective constable asked.

Jack shook his head. "Too old. They target teens and runaways." He bit down hard on the pencil. "Someone with an agenda, I'll lay money on it. One perp, working alone. Done his research, and knows what he wants." And good. Careful. *God, I hate cases like this.*

"Any leads at all?" he asked.

Marco shrugged. "Her computer was wiped clean. That's a little strange."

Jack's cop radar switched to full alert. He shifted out of the leather chair. "Let's go there. I want to see for myself."

***

Jack Connelly traipsed through Valerie Revel's modest apartment with a sinking heart. There was nothing—nothing to lay a trail to where she had gone. Lots of clothes still there in drawers; a few underthings in the dirty clothes hamper. The small closet was stuffed with loaded hangers. A suitcase lay on the floor of the closet, empty. Of course, that didn't prove anything. She might have had a second suitcase.

No messages on the answering machine, except for the girlfriend trying several times to reach her.

Jack walked back to the kitchen.

"Anything in the fridge?" he asked the detective constable.

"Basics," Marco said. "Milk, orange juice, eggs. Not a lot of cooking ingredients."

Breakfast dishes were stacked neatly in the drying tray. The garbage contained a coffee filter, recently used.

And yet her computer had been wiped completely.

It was peculiar and inconclusive. Jack's heart sank.

"Here's something. On the calendar, here on the wall. 'E-Galaxy' marked on the day she went missing."

"E-Galaxy? Isn't that the online dating site that's been advertising on late-night television?"

"That's the one. You think some pervert was stalking her online?"

He gazed out the window at the growing twilight.

"What's her name again? Valerie Revel...pretty. Well, Valerie darlin', where the hell are you?" he muttered.

***

Valerie felt sick. Lights were flickering, and her head hurt. Somewhere, a machine hummed a pleasant drone.

"Vital signs look okay. I think she's coming out of it."

Her eyes blinked open. Valerie looked around and immediately began an environmental assessment, second nature from years of engineering training. She appeared to be lying on a soft white leatherette bench against one wall of a scientific lab. The far wall housed a floor-to-ceiling unit of electronic equipment that spanned a good 10 feet; the equipment was obviously cutting-edge. Emotions confused her at the best of times, but it was hard to be frightened in such a familiar environment. Instead, she had a sudden urge to leap up and examine the new equipment.

"There she is!" a pleasant female voice said. "Don't be frightened. You're going to be fine."

Valerie tried to sit up, but the nausea rose quickly. She lay her head back down and tried to focus. The letters E-Galaxy were displayed on the ceiling above her head, in gold. Below them, ran a sentence in a smaller font: Will your love stand the test of time?

"Don't try to get up yet. You'll feel woozy for a few minutes. Take it easy."

The voice came from a pretty middle-aged woman in a white lab coat. She was slender with mocha skin, long brown hair and hazel eyes. She looked harmless.

"Can you tell me your name?" she asked.

That was easy. "Valerie Revel."

"Do you know what year it is?"

"2015." Were they testing for a concussion?

"That's the year you just came from. Do you know which year it is here?"

"Oh!" Valerie remembered now—she remembered all of it. "2260?"

"Perfect! My name is Petra. Do you know why you're here, Valerie?"

Valerie felt her heart lurch. "Yes—I remember. Is he here?"

The brown-haired woman tilted her head. "Behind the sliding glass doors, right over there. But before we go any further, I need to remind you that you can go back home any time, free of charge, in the next 30 days. We guarantee that."

Valerie glanced anxiously at the doors. E-Galaxy was sandblasted into the glass.

"Do many people do that?" She had to ask.

Petra smiled. "No one yet. Our matching technique is almost foolproof. And of course, we have centuries to pull from. The only thing we can't check for is severe homesickness. But if that happens, we can try sending the two of you back to your time. Haven't had to do it yet, though."

Valerie rose gracefully to her feet. "Thank you. Thank you so much. May I see him now?"

"Of course, dear. He's been waiting for you. I hope you like flowers, because that room seems to be full of them."

Valerie didn't care about flowers or anything, except covering the distance to the glass doors, which were opening. She could see him now on the other side—the soft dark hair, the rugged, kindly face and brilliant smile she had come to know via her computer and E-Galaxy, after months of searching through all time for the man who was really meant for her.

She was through the opening in three seconds.

***

Jack Connelly followed his constable out of the shabby foyer, and firmly closed the door to Valerie Revel's apartment building behind him. No trace. No damn trace anywhere. Where the hell was she?

He looked up at the sky. City lights blocked out most of the stars, but here on the edge of town, a few bright ones peeked through on a black velvet sky. Lucky stars?

Caught by a fey moment, he made a fervent wish. *Valerie Revel, be happy wherever you are.*

It was a cool night, but crossing the parking lot, Jack Connelly felt an uncommon chill.

"All those missing girls," said his detective constable, shivering. "Year after year, all across the country, there are hundreds of girls we never find. Where do they go?"

"I don't know, Marco," Jack said. "It's almost as if they were sucked up into the sky."

THE BENCH RESTS

By Rosemary Aubert

He'd only come to the courthouse to bring his wife her lunch.

Which had been confiscated at Security, of course.

He should have foreseen that. He checked the impulse to shake his head in self-disgust. Yet again, he'd neglected to weigh the new against the old, the probable against the dead certain.

Walking slowly down the long, slippery hallway that led toward the up escalator, he tried to concentrate. What exactly had his wife told him about lunchtime? That her testimony might be finished by then? It had been two or three years, but he still remembered that the schedule of the court was as wily as a bronco. No knowing what time she'd really be done.

He mourned the loss of that confiscated lunch, though. He could still make a pretty mean sandwich. He'd even remembered not to include anything that smelled strong. At the last minute, he'd added a nice apple. He'd hoped that the required noise of crunching wouldn't embarrass his wife if she had to eat in the company of strangers.

Suddenly an old memory flitted through his brain. He was seated on the bench. The court clerk in her smart black robe was directly in front of him, down a level, so that he was looking at the top of her head. He could see that she was pretending to annotate the day's docket. But what she was really doing was silently unwrapping a chocolate bar. The smell of it wafted up to his nostrils. He could stop the proceedings and get her to surrender it....

"Judge Marshall! Come for a little visit? It's so nice to see you."

The voice cut through his daydream like a shiv. He turned and almost banged into a young lawyer with an armful of files. It surprised the old judge to see cardboard folders, pieces of paper sticking out of them willy-nilly in a messy display of mismanaged paperwork. He thought they'd have done away with all that paper by now—put the records on the Internet or something.

"You've got yourself quite a pile of documents there," he said to the young man, stalling for time to remember his name.

"Merkovitch," the lawyer said, as if he knew what the judge was thinking. "I'm Dalton Merkovitch. I worked with you on the Blane case—for three years, actually."

The judge nodded as if he recalled the whole thing. All he really remembered was that Blane was a loser who had got what was coming to him for having killed his best friend in a fit of rage. He glanced at Merkovitch. Prosecution or Defense? He tried a fishing tactic. "Well," he said, "I guess our man's done a bit of time since you and I laid eyes on each other, eh?"

Merkovitch nodded, smiled.

Prosecution, the old judge decided. He nodded and smiled, too.

Squinting just enough to make out the number over the nearby courtroom door, but not enough to make Merkovitch pity him, he gave the door a good push and let himself into the courtroom.

It still smelled the same. The heat of the old, cranky boiler system. The sweat of fear. The mustiness of papers long trapped in boxes and drawers. The hint of camphor from the mothballs that kept the legal robes from being eaten.

It sounded the same, too. Right down to the audible breathing of the entranced spectators, shifting in their hard wooden pews. Some of them were mere gawkers, but not all. It had long simultaneously amused and appalled Judge Marshall that spectators in murder cases always sat in two distinct groups. Family and friends of the victim. Family and friends of the accused. Like witnesses at a wedding of the damned.

"Judge Marshall—a pleasure! Come in!" This in a hushed whisper from the guard at the door, who wasn't supposed to say anything—just usher people in. The judge raised his hand in a small, silent salute. The courthouse was full of well-meaning lackeys like the doorman. There was no way in the world he was going to remember the name of any of them.

He tried to slide soundlessly onto a bench at the back. No such luck. The little metal pull on the zipper of his jacket scraped along the wooden seat. The sound reached the ears of the sitting judge, who turned her eyes on him for just a second, enough to embarrass Judge Marshall into sinking down onto the seat in a slouch.

But in a minute, he decided that the snooty-looking lady judge hadn't recognized him and wasn't likely to glance his way again. He sat up straighter and took the liberty of having a good look around.

The first thing he saw was that he was sitting with the family of the accused. The man in the prisoner's box was surrounded by glass walls, guarded by two strong-looking young officers, and possibly even shackled to the floor, though nobody but the guards would know that. Yet it wasn't hard to see that the offender was a handsome boy with a distinctive look that Judge Marshall thought marked him as a southern European—Spanish or Italian. He'd taken as many ethnic sensitivity training workshops as the next judge, so he knew that you weren't supposed to even think about such things.

But a lifetime in the law, first as a family lawyer, then in criminal law, then as a prosecutor and finally as a judge, had taught him to take note of everything. And he noticed that the man in the box looked exactly like the people sitting in the three spectator rows ahead of him. There must be 30 of them.

Wait a minute! *Roma*, that's what they looked like.

He was puzzling over whether that might mean anything, trying to remember things he'd lately read about the prejudice against that particular group, when he felt that someone was studying him as intently as he'd been studying his neighbors.

Dismissing ridiculous old ideas about the evil eye, he looked up.

And he saw his wife glaring at him right from the witness stand!

He'd forgotten that he'd promised her that he wouldn't remain in the courtroom during any portion of her testimony. He had very little idea of what she intended to say. They'd agreed to keep it that way. Well, it was too late now. He shrugged his shoulders.

But she didn't see the gesture. Her eyes were back on the prosecuting attorney as he shuffled his papers, stalled for effect, spoke.

"One final thing, Mrs. Marshall. When you entered your garage on the evening in question, were you alone?

"Yes. My husband always goes grocery shopping with me. But he lags behind. Talking to people in the elevator and things like that. I just go ahead and wait for him in the car."

"Thank you." The lawyer smiled slightly, then dipped his head in the direction of the defense table, as if he were turning over his witness for cross-examination with the greatest of confidence.

The defense rose. Yet another young man. They all seemed like children, even the lady judge. Even the grandmothers of the accused were younger than old Judge Marshall and his wife. He almost let out a sigh, but he caught himself in time.

"You told the court you were headed out to do your grocery shopping the night my client was arrested, did you not?" the defense began. He had a grating sort of voice, the kind Judge Marshall knew his wife hated.

"Yes." She closed her lips tight after that one word.

"And you also stated that you and your husband usually do your grocery shopping together? Isn't that what you told my friend here?" He nodded toward the prosecutor, who did not respond.

"Yes, but…"

Judge Marshall tried hard to avoid eye contact. The reason his wife didn't want him in court while she was testifying was because she felt he'd exercise some sort of undue influence on her. He thought that was batty, but she maintained that after nearly 50 years of marriage, she could tell what he was thinking by the way he was looking at her.

What he was thinking was this: That the night his wife had seen a dark-haired man running through the parking garage beneath their condo, he had been sick in bed. He knew for certain that he'd stayed home that night because he'd watched the season finale of *The Great Race*. In fact, much as he would have hated to admit it, he'd really not been that sick. He'd just wanted to see who'd win. The show had been half over when his wife had walked out the door. He was sure of it, because the winner hadn't been revealed yet and he remembered feeling relieved that he could watch the most important part of the show without her interrupting him by talking while he was watching, which was a bad habit of hers.

"Mrs. Marshall…" the lawyer said, swaying a little. Judge Marshall wished the man would stand still—wished he could tell him to do so, as he had so often told lawyers in the old days. "Mrs. Marshall, are you sure you allowed yourself to be unaccompanied during those moments in the garage on the evening in question? Don't you think it was rather late to be in an underground garage alone?"

"I beg your pardon?"

His wife's tone was sharp. Judge Marshall knew what that meant. Her toes had been stepped on.

"I'm asking you whether you are sure there were no other witnesses present in the parking garage that late at night."

"You think I'm too old to go out at night?"

An audible gasp spread across the gathered court the way the leak of air from a kid's balloon would spread across a condo party room.

The head of the presiding judge snapped around. "Just answer the question," she warned.

By the look on his wife's face, Judge Marshall knew the exact thought that was going through her head. *Nobody can tell me what I'm too old or not too old to do.*

"Maybe I can rephrase that a little," the lawyer said. He glanced toward the jury, and for the first time, Judge Marshall took a look at the lucky 12. There was a pretty good mix of male and female, young and old. A witness like his wife was a sure bet with a jury like that. They would believe whatever she said. The old people would identify with her as an equal. The young people would be reminded of their grandmothers—or maybe their ancestors.

"You state that you entered the parking garage at about 8:30 p.m. You state that you saw a young man who fit the description of my client running through the garage at that time. Is that correct?"

"Yes."

The defense attorney grinned. Judge Marshall could only see the lawyer's face because the man had turned around to face his client. The accused himself seemed suddenly frightened. He tried to twist around as if to seek some kind of support from the 30 look-alikes behind him. The lawyer turned back to face Mrs. Marshall. "Madam," he said, "your testimony puts my client in the garage one full hour before the crime was committed, doesn't it?"

Justice Marshall saw the look of shock on his wife's face. "But—?"

The prosecutor rose as if to make an objection.

But even the jury seemed to understand that there was nothing to object to. He sat back down. He frantically searched through the papers in front of him with such energy that Her Honor had to ask him to be quiet.

"I s-saw him running," Mrs. Marshall stuttered. "It was him."

For a wild instant, Judge Marshall thought his wife was pointing in his direction, but of course she was really pointing to the prisoner.

"My client doesn't deny being in the garage, ma'am. You're aware of that fact, are you not?"

"Yes. But—"

"In fact, it is his contention that he left prior to 9 p.m., the time at which the murdered woman made a frantic phone call to her girlfriend."

The defense lawyer paused. Judge Marshall knew the pause was meant to give the jury time to consider what they'd just heard—to come to the only possible conclusion, which was that his wife had just destroyed the State's case. In the silence, Judge Marshall could hear all those old familiar sounds again. The breathing of the people in the court, the useless riffling of papers that could prove nothing, the sigh of relief of a killer about to be let off.

And of course Judge Marshall knew it was not the prosecutor who had made a mistake. It was his wife. If the murdered woman had been alive at 9 p.m., she would have been alive at the beginning of *The Great Race*. How long did it take to strangle somebody, then to run down seven flights of stairs? About as long as it took to find out who had won the race.

He'd been a judge for a long time. A lot of case law began to reel itself out in his mind. The State versus this one and that one.

Would he stand up, like someone out of those old *Perry Mason* shows and set the record straight?

Would he take aside that nice guard who had greeted him at the door and tell him that he needed a word with Her Honor?

Would he send some sort of signal to his wife to alert her to her error and get her to change her testimony?

Thinking hard as he was, he missed what happened next. But he soon figured that either the judge or the prosecutor had called for the lunch recess. Because the jury filed out, and then his wife left the stand and made her way toward the table where the prosecutor stood. There was some sort of exchange between the lawyer and his wife, but

Judge Marshall couldn't hear anything. The lawyer's back was to him, and his wife was so short that he couldn't even see her face, hidden as it was by the broad shoulders of the prosecutor.

What Judge Marshall had once liked most about sitting on the bench was that he could take all the time in the world to make up his mind about most things. Send a man to jail for life? *I'm giving it some thought.* Call a mistrial and begin all over again at a cost of a couple hundred thousand dollars? *I'll let you know.*

But of course, he didn't always have that luxury. Sometimes he had to make up his mind in a single instant.

Now seemed such a time.

What he decided was to keep his mouth shut. He hadn't tried to influence a witness in 40 years—not since his last day as a practicing lawyer—and he wasn't about to start now.

The accused was led out of the court, and his relatives filed out, too. Judge Marshall was the last one of the spectators to leave.

Just as he got outside the door, he heard a familiar whisper. The door guard was standing there. He had a paper bag in his hand.

"Security sent this up to you," the man said proudly—like one who is pleased to offer impeccable service of some sort. "They said you might be needing it."

Mrs. Marshall's lunch!

The judge took it. He reached out and shook the man's hand. In the old days, he would have said, "Good man," or "Well done." These days such remarks were considered patronizing. "Thanks," he said to the guard. "Thanks a lot."

He took the lunch and walked slowly toward the down escalator. He thought the best thing was just to sit downstairs by the door for a while. For almost the whole of his career in this courthouse, there had been back door, side doors and more than one front door to use as exits, but since 9/11 that had changed.

Now there was only one exit. If his wife decided to go out—or even to come looking for him—sitting by the exit was his best chance of seeing her—or of her seeing him.

But he didn't think that would happen.

He figured that the lawyer would take her back to his office—the Office of the Prosecution in the secure area on the first floor—and that together they would somehow try to undo the damage she'd done to the case.

Judge Marshall decided to wait for half an hour. Then, he would go home.

And if she wanted to explain what had happened, how she had made such a terrible mistake, then she could tell him.

Otherwise, he would just keep his own peace.

Concentrating as he was on these thoughts, he jumped when someone was suddenly standing in front of him, blocking the light from the exit's barred window that had been installed right after 9/11.

"It was 8:30. You and I have gone grocery shopping every Thursday at 8:30 since we moved into that condo. Plus, I probably would have checked my watch to make sure the store would still be open."

"If we did the same thing every week for years," Judge Marshall said. "Why would you need to check your watch? Besides, that store's 24/7—has been for five years."

"Don't talk to me like I have Alzheimer's," she said.

That grim possibility had never occurred to the judge, but it did now. He looked at his wife. *Nah.*

She had just made a simple mistake that was all.

"Everybody's wrong once in a while," he said. "Want some lunch?"

She glanced at the paper bag where he'd placed it on the seat.

"Why don't you sit down for a minute?" He picked up the bag and patted the empty place beside him.

Mrs. Marshall sank into it. She'd always been a small woman. That was one of the things he loved about her. In the old days, he used to call her "my pocket wife" the way he called his favorite book "my pocket Criminal Code." She seemed smaller than she'd ever been. No, he reminded himself. That was stupid.

"I told that lawyer right from the start that I was in that garage. He looked in all his papers but he can't find where he wrote it down. He thinks I'm the one that made a mistake. He thinks he can still fix things if…"

She looked up at him. He could see she was fighting the urge to ask him for help.

"It's a good sandwich," he said. "No onions."

She accepted half the sandwich and took a bite. She chewed carefully, swallowed, shook her head.

"When people do the same thing every week of their lives, how can they make a mistake about what they did?"

Judge Marshall didn't answer. He was thinking about the Blane case, the one that Merko kid had worked on with him. He remembered there had been some sort of time mistake there, too. It wasn't that unusual for several witnesses to an event to give differing times for the same occurrence. One of the things that working in court for 50 years—heck, for 50 minutes—soon taught a person was that eyewitnesses were often the worst kind. And the more eyewitnesses there were, the more conflicting stories might be told.

In the Blane case, Judge Marshall had seen a discrepancy right from the word go. Of course, it wouldn't have been his place to say anything to the witnesses, though he might have held some sort of a hearing with the lawyers if it had become necessary.

But it hadn't been necessary. The erring witness had suddenly remembered that on the night in question, she had been on the way to her sister's birthday party. An easy-to-remember event like that—the jury had believed her. The erroneous testimony had been rescinded. The record had been corrected.

But what did that have to do with his wife?

She was picking at her sandwich as if she had no appetite.

"Something wrong with the sandwich?" he asked.

"No."

"Not fresh enough?"

"What?"

"I used the lettuce we bought last night."

"Last night?"

"Oh, come on," he said with mock impatience. "Now are you going to tell me that you can't remember that we went grocery shopping last night?"

"That's right," she said absently. "It's Friday today. Thank God."

"Thank God?"

"Yes. No matter what happens to me this afternoon, there won't be any court tomorrow."

"Nothing's going to happen to you this afternoon," he said. But it was a sort of lie. Because at the very least, there would be some sort of re-examination, and that would give the prosecutor plenty of time to grill his wife.

"You know," she said, "all the years you worked in court, all the cases you tried—"

"Yes."

"You never talked about them when you came home."

"So?" Was she going to tell him that he should have shared his experiences so that she could have learned how to be a better witness? That didn't make any kind of sense.

"So I got used to thinking that you had this—I don't know—this other life—like some sort of mystery existence or something." She stared into the air in front of her for a minute. Then she smiled. Judge Marshall felt a pang. The smile looked awfully sad. "But the fact is, when you retired, I could figure out that you must have been the same way in court as you were at home."

"Meaning?"

"Always doing the same thing at the same time. Routines. That's why we always shopped on Thursday. You said routine was important. You said if you do the same thing at the same time as often as you can, you—"

She stopped. Again a look of shock crossed her face. But only for an instant.

"I remember."

"What?"

"I remember it wasn't 8:30 at all. It was 9:30."

Judge Marshall popped the rest of his half of the sandwich into his mouth. In order to avoid saying anything.

"You weren't with me because you were sick. When it got to be almost 8:30, I asked you if you were ready to go, and you said you didn't think you could handle it. I told you I'd wait half an hour to see whether you might feel better, and I did wait, but by the time I got my cloth shopping bags together and checked with you to decipher the list you wrote in your terrible handwriting, and found my own keys to the car, it was past nine. I remember that I thought it was great the way you didn't tell me it was too late to go out by myself."

Judge Marshall laughed.

But his wife became agitated again. "How am I going to convince them?"

"Of what?"

"How can I make them believe that this time I know what I'm talking about?"

He could have offered to speak to the prosecutor and offer himself as a witness. He could have told his wife about *The Great Race*, admitted that he'd not been as sick as he'd pretended to be.

He could have quoted those cases he'd thought of up there in the courtroom when he'd realized she was making some kind of fool of herself.

But he didn't.

He hadn't worked in the courts for 50 years without realizing that justice, like every other game in town, is a crapshoot.

Before she'd gotten into this mess, she'd told him to stay out of court when she was on the stand. Because she knew that he could influence her. And even without his legal training, without his having told her year after year what he had been doing all those days in court, she had understood that it wasn't fair for her to use any recollection except her own.

That hadn't changed. She was the witness. Not him.

And she was a cute little old lady. A jury who didn't believe her deserved to be responsible for letting a murderer go free.

Judge Marshall reached into the paper bag on his lap.

"Look," he said, "an apple. Let's share it."

"Like Adam and Eve?" his wife said.

"No," he answered. "Like you and me. Every man for himself."

About Rosemary Aubert

Rosemary Aubert is the author of seventeen books, among them the acclaimed Ellis Portal mystery series and her latest romantic thriller *Terminal Grill*.

Rosemary is a two-time winner of the Arthur Ellis Award for crime fiction, winning in both the novel and short-story categories. She's a popular teacher and speaker as well as a member of the Crime Writers of Canada and the Mystery Writers of America. She conducts a much-in-demand writer's retreat at Loyalist College in Belleville, Ontario each summer.

Her short stories, essays, poems and reviews have been widely published in Canada for many years. She has had four volumes of poetry published. Rosemary is an active member of the Arts and Letters Club of Toronto where she promotes Canadian writing and encourages other writers like herself. Her latest novel is number six in the Ellis Portal series: *Don't Forget You Love Me* (Carrick Publishing).

http://www.rosemaryaubert.com/
Amazon Author Page
Facebook
Mesdames of Mayhem

THE 14th OF FOREVER

By Donna Carrick

"I'm just saying, as pagan fertility festivals go, this one really sucks."

"You wouldn't feel that way if you were dating."

"Maybe not," Mallory, said, "but on behalf of all the single guys and gals, I think we could do without the fat cherub and his nasty red arrows. Anyway, what are you and Celia doing tonight?"

It was only half a beat. No one else would have noticed, but Mallory knew him. She sensed a stiffening of Jerome's shoulders when he answered.

"Lucky me," he said, "I get to save my money this year. Celia's out of town, staying with her mom in Cornwall."

"And the kids?"

"They went with her. We figured at their ages it wouldn't hurt them to miss a week of school."

Jerome crept onto the shoulder, planting the cherry on the Crown Vic's roof. Daytime traffic was a bitch on the 401, especially given the winter conditions, and cops were an easy target for rush-hour motorists. He took his sweet time exiting the vehicle.

The scene had been cordoned off with pylons, funneling westbound traffic to the left. The victim had politely fallen onto the far right westbound collectors' lane.

That meant they didn't have to shut down all four lanes, but the right one and on-ramp were a bust.

The drop from the Don Mills overpass wasn't overly dramatic. She'd initially bounced off the roof of a 2008 Grand Caravan. She might have even survived, except for her frailty...and the Ford Escape that caught her on the rebound.

A Uniform waved as they approached.

"I'm Detective Mallory Tosh, and this is my partner Detective Jerome Christie."

The constable flashed a crooked grin. "Tim Beckwith. Nice to meet you, Detective." He nodded at Jerome. "What's happening, Chris?"

Chris was Jerome's nickname, a handle he detested. He smiled at the constable.

"Same old, Tim. How's our victim?"

"Still quite dead."

Jerome chuckled and Mallory rolled her eyes at the constable's bit of gallows humor.

It might have looked like a simple traffic accident, but in Toronto all "sudden deaths" are first handed off to Homicide. Only when foul play is ruled out and the death signed off by the city Coroner as fully explained can the case be closed.

"Bad time of day for it," Mallory said, nodding at the bottleneck that had already formed under the Don Mills bridge.

"Shit, Mal," Jerome said, "is there ever a good time of day to end up like that?"

The forensic photographer was hard at it, recording the bundle of fabric and blood from every available angle.

Crime lab techies in bunny suits, shod in white-paper booties, combed two and a half lanes for any evidence of wrongdoing.

"Jumper?" Mallory said.

"Looks like," Jerome nodded.

"I told you, my friend. People really don't like Valentine's Day."

***

Sherman Grady was not your Joe-average accountant. Despite his well-known dexterity with numbers, he harbored a romantic soul.

He replaced the receiver, having confirmed the flowers would be delivered to his wife by noon. The accompanying note would read: *Yours till the 14th of Forever.*

Next, he made sure their reservation was secured for 6:30 at the David Duncan House. He'd booked it months in advance, knowing how difficult it was to nab a table anyplace decent on Valentine's Day.

His mind was not operating at its usual capacity lately, so he felt better having nailed down the plans.

He thought back to his wedding, 30 years ago today. She'd been a stunning bride, a rare blend of beauty and modesty, confidence and poise. Long blond hair that fell in natural honey-colored waves over ivory shoulders.

Sherman had been a handsome enough young man in his own right – arrow-straight bearing and a quick smile. He knew how lucky he'd been, how his charm had come to his aid in winning her undying love.

They'd sworn it then, and his promise was as meaningful today as it had been on Valentine's Day 30 years ago.

Yours till the 14th of Forever...

Sherman wasn't given to displays of emotion, at least not outwardly. He liked to think he carried himself with professional grace. Certainly, it stood him well in the current corporate climate, with colleagues running around in a constant state of suppressed panic, everyone watching the heads roll and doing the math...

Life, he thought, *is a game of chicken. When you see that proverbial light at the end of every tunnel, you've got to stare it down and pray it's not an oncoming freight train.*

He was good at that, good at maintaining an aura of quiet calm in the face of chaos. It was this quality that had helped him stay employed these past 30 years and still kept him in professional demand.

When he'd asked for her hand, he'd told her he would provide, that he would keep a steady job, and he had, despite the corporate shenanigans and shake-ups.

He'd done it by coupling an analytical mind, exceptional business skills, a computer-like genius for math with a warm smile and undeniable charm.

Despite his normally cool demeanor, he couldn't help but raise an eyebrow when his phone rang and the call display showed the extension for Human Resources.

"Hi, Judy," he said. "What can I do for you?"

It might have been anything. Five of his coworkers had been packaged off the previous week. As the company's only accountant, he'd felt relatively safe, especially since he reported directly to the CEO, but one never really knew.

"Sherm," she said, an edge of nervousness in her voice, "can you come to my office?"

"Of course, Judy. What's up?"

"Just come here, Sherman, right away, please."

Stay calm, he told himself.

He made his way down the hall, past the empty boardroom. It reminded him of the old joke: *How do you create a successful small business? Well, first you start with a big business...Ha-ha!*

The elegant boardroom used to be nearly impossible to book, being used daily for back-to-back meetings by every department.

These days though, it seemed the only meetings held with any regularity were the ones in Judy's office – the ones where the final handshake took place.

Sherman peeked into Thomas' office on his way down the hall.

"Still on for lunch?" Tom asked.

"Still on," Sherman agreed. "Can't chat, though. I'm off to a meeting with Judy."

"Oh, cripes," Tom said. "Well, good luck!" Then, as an afterthought, he added, "Been nice knowing ya!"

Sherman chuckled, more to calm his own nerves than because the joke was funny.

The door to Judy's office was closed. He knocked before opening it.

"Come in, Sherm," she said. "Have a seat."

He looked around the room at the unfamiliar faces.

Instead of sitting, he asked, "Judy, what's happening?" He wasn't jittery, exactly – his professionalism wouldn't allow for that – but he was noticeably anxious.

Judy stood and came around the desk.

"Sherm," she said, taking his elbow and guiding him to a seat at the round table before settling down beside him, "these are Detectives Mallory Tosh and Jerome Christie of the Toronto Metro Police Services. Please, Detectives, sit down." She waved at the empty chairs.

Mallory threw a look at her partner. Out of respect, it was usual to stand to deliver unfortunate news, but the silly HR person had positioned it so they didn't have much choice.

Mallory nodded, and she and Jerome sat across from Sherman Grady.

"Mr. Grady," Mal began, "we're here about…."

"Oh, my God," Sherman sputtered, "is it Valerie? Has something happened to Valerie?"

Sherman was, after all, good at math. He and Valerie had no children, no other close family members or dependents. Valerie had not been herself this past year. She'd been showing signs of early-onset dementia. Since her 55th birthday last year, she'd taken medical leave from her job at the bank, citing "stress" as the underlying condition.

And it was stressful for her, to find herself losing her ability to handle numbers quickly and efficiently, and subsequently coming under the scrutiny of the bank's management.

He'd taken her to the family doctor, who'd prescribed a cholinesterase inhibitor and a mild dose of memantine to minimize the memory loss and confusion.

Most days weren't too bad, but lately she'd begun leaving the house after he did in the morning. If he couldn't reach her on the home phone, he'd usually get her on her cell, but sometimes she'd forget to put it into her pocket.

Just last week, on Wednesday, she'd called him from the supermarket. She couldn't remember why she'd gone there, and was panicking. He'd had to take a time-out from his spreadsheets to pick her up and drive her home.

The doctor had her lined up for testing at the Memory Facility in North York, but that was still a month away.

Jerome flashed a look at Mallory.

She understood, and let him take the lead.

"Why do you say that, Mr. Grady?" he asked.

It might seem unkind, but they couldn't let it pass. After all, every sudden death was considered questionable until they had ruled out the possibility of foul play.

Grady had immediately assumed something had happened to his wife. The detectives didn't know him. They weren't aware of his lack of other family, his wife's medical history or his proficiency at math.

For all they knew, he might have a much darker reason for suspecting "something" had happened to Valerie.

"She…she hasn't been herself lately. She's been…easily confused." Sherman fought to regain his composure.

"Sherm," Judy said, taking his hand, "I'm so sorry."

Mallory shot a look at the HR manager that said "Stand down, lady."

"I'll let you three talk privately," Judy said. "I'll be in the break room if you need me, Sherman."

When the door had closed behind Judy, Mallory spoke.

"In what way has your wife been confused?"

"I can't really explain it," Sherman said. "She used to be so sharp. Lately she doesn't always know what day it is. I had to remind her yesterday that today is our anniversary. We were married on Valentine's Day and we always celebrate with a nice dinner. She used to get excited, but now she doesn't remember."

"When did you last see your wife?" Jerome asked.

"This morning, when I left for work. Around 7:00. Please, tell me what's happened."

Mallory studied Grady's face, taking in the guarded but growing panic.

"We're sorry to tell you, Mr. Grady," she said, "but your wife has been involved in an accident."

"What?" Sherman said, rising to his feet. "What happened? Is she all right? I have to get to her. Where is she?"

"Please, sit down, Mr. Grady," Jerome said. "Mrs. Grady, at least we believe it's Mrs. Grady, died this morning in a traffic accident. It happened around 7:15."

"But you're not sure it's Valerie?" Sherman said, his voice registering hope.

"We're fairly certain it's her, Mr. Grady," Mallory said.

Sherman thought once again of his wedding day, 30 years earlier. Although he struggled for composure, he was unable to stem the tears that threatened to spill from his eyes.

"I'll have to identify her," he said. "You'd better take me to her."

"Mr. Grady," Jerome said, his voice kind but firm, "it was a very bad accident. We'll be using her dental records to identify her. She's with the Coroner's Office now. I'm afraid you won't be able to see her till they release her to the funeral home."

"What do I do?"

Detectives Tosh and Christie had attended their share of grieving loved ones. They had broken the bad news more times than they could count.

It always came down to the same question: *What do I do now?*

What do I do this morning? This afternoon? This evening? Tomorrow?

It was the human fall-back position, to take action, to fight the inevitable.

They always needed to be doing *something*.

It didn't matter that nothing they might do, no conceivable action on their part, would change the facts.

Their loved one was gone.

Death is final.

Just the same, for the living, it was important to be doing *something*.

"We'll need you to come down to the division with us," Mallory said. "You'll need to sign the requisition for the dental records. You'll need to identify her belongings – her coat, purse, clothing."

"She was carrying her purse?"

"Yes, sir," Jerome said.

"I'll tell Judy I'm leaving now," Sherman said. "She'll let my boss know."

"There's no need, Mr. Grady," Mallory said. "Ms. Hanover knows you'll be leaving with us, to identify the belongings."

***

Sherman stared at the coffeemaker in the visitors' lounge at 33 Division. He'd often seen the police cruisers driving on Don Mills or York Mills, on their way to their base on Upjohn, but he'd never been inside the building.

The two detectives had left him sitting there for what seemed like hours, but was probably closer to twenty minutes. Although he hadn't taken his eyes off that coffeepot for more than the quarter-second it took to blink, he could not have described it, nor, if pressed could he even have told you it was, in fact, a coffeepot.

It simply didn't register. It was there, in his sightline, but the image didn't penetrate via the optic nerve to travel to his brain.

It was just there.

And he was there.

This was really happening.

Twenty minutes, thirty, it hardly mattered. Time had no essence. It was merely something to be tolerated, passed through, withstood.

Of course, that could be said of many things in life.

They needed to be withstood.

Sherman could not have described his thoughts, as he sat there staring at the coffeepot, back arrow-straight, hands on his knees, a proper schoolboy waiting for instructions from his teacher.

His mind had somehow detached itself from his body. He had the eerie sense that he was watching himself, that the real Sherman was hovering somewhere near the ceiling lights, poised to fly away without notice, abandoning him in that strangely sterile room.

"Would you like a cup of coffee, Mr. Grady?"

It took a second before he realized she was speaking to him.

"Huh?" he said.

He turned to see Detective Mallory Tosh enter the room, followed by her partner, Christie. The detectives were carrying what appeared to be evidence bags.

Sherman's stomach churned as he recognized Valerie's winter coat. It had cost a small fortune – a birthday gift when she'd turned 55 late last year – but it was lovely. A stylish cashmere, with snug lining, perfect for Canadian winters, and a beautifully tapered cut that flared at the hips, enhancing her still regal figure.

Valerie had clapped her hands when she opened the box, and they were both astonished at how well he'd guessed her size and fit.

That had been months ago, back when his wife still clung to a semblance of mental normalcy.

"I wondered if you'd like a cup of coffee," Mallory repeated. "You were looking at the coffeepot."

"Oh," he said, "no, I didn't realize I was doing that. But yes, I guess I would appreciate a cup. That's very kind of you."

Mallory looked at Jerome, who raised a brow in acknowledgment. Neither would say it out loud, but they'd discussed it many times before, how the grief-stricken, the "loved ones", always seemed to follow a script. Their behavior might vary wildly from case to case, depending on their own unique personalities and experiences, but they each held onto a basket of words they could dip into during times of crisis.

Kind was one such word.

The deeper the grief, the more profound the shock, the more firmly the family member would cling to the notion of kindness in others.

"Not at all," Mallory said. "Let me get that for you." She passed the bag she was carrying to her partner.

"We have to ask you," Jerome said, "whether you recognize these items. Take your time. We need to leave them in the bags, but I'll put them here on the table. Please just look at each one. Let me know if you need me to turn the bags over."

"Yes." Sherman left the affirmation to rest on the ensuing silence.

The detectives allowed the gap to build, hoping for a follow-up comment from Grady.

When he did not elaborate, Jerome said, "Do you recognize any of these items?"

Mallory placed a ceramic mug in front of Sherman.

He lifted it to his mouth before answering.

"Yes," he repeated. "That's Valerie's coat. I'm sure of it. I bought it for her last fall. And that's her favorite purse – cream-colored to match the coat. Was she carrying her ID?"

"That's right, Mr. Grady," Mallory said gently. "That's how we knew to contact you. She had her ID in her purse, along with your office and cell phone numbers as an emergency contact."

Grady's perfect posture seemed to disintegrate before their eyes. He slumped in his chair, wrapping both hands around the hot mug for comfort.

"Oh, my God, it's really her. It's really Valerie, isn't it?"

"Yes," Jeremy said, "we're afraid so."

"Do you know why she might have been walking along Don Mills this morning?" Mallory asked.

"She's had a few of these episodes lately. Her dementia seems to be increasing. Last week she left the house and went to the supermarket, but came to her senses and called me on her cell. I picked her up and took her back home."

"But why Don Mills? Was it normal for her to walk there?"

"No. I don't think she's ever done that before. But I work near there. It's possible she was trying to get to my office."

"That would make sense," Jeremy said. "The accident happened at 7:17 this morning. That's a very short time after you left her at seven. Would she have been able to dress herself and walk to the Don Mills overpass in that short of a time?"

"Is that where it happened?" Sherman asked. "Did she fall from the bridge at the 401?"

"Mr. Grady," Mallory said, forcing him to meet her eyes, "she would not have fallen. There's no way anyone could fall from that overpass. The safety railing is too high."

Sherman digested the fact, struggling to avoid the obvious conclusion.

"Are you saying she…Are you saying… Did my wife jump off the bridge?"

"We can't say anything with certainty at this point," Jerome said. "We're just trying to nail down the timeline. Do you think Mrs. Grady – Valerie – do you think she could have walked to the overpass in the short time since you left her?"

"She was already dressed when I left," Sherman said. "Until last summer she still worked at the bank, the one at Don Mills and York Mills. She was a creature of routine – habit, if you like. Even though she was no longer able to work, due to her dementia, she still liked to get up with me in the morning, dress and have breakfast."

"You say she worked at the Don Mills and York Mills bank?" Mallory said. "Is it possible, Mr. Grady, that she thought she was walking to work?"

Sherman paused.

"Yes, that's certainly possible. We live…lived…I mean, our place is a condo in one of the high-rises at Sheppard. I usually take the car, and since she's been ill, I keep her keys with me. I used to drop her off at work every morning and pick her up at night, but it wouldn't be difficult for her to walk there."

"Was your wife well physically?" Jerome asked. "She looked frail to us, but of course, under the circumstances, it's hard to tell."

"Valerie has always been fit, and proud of her figure. The past few months, though, I think she sometimes forgets to eat. She has lost some weight. You could say she's been frailer than usual."

"Had your wife been diagnosed?" Mallory asked.

"Not yet. The family doctor prescribed a cognition-enhancing drug, and set up an appointment at the North York memory clinic. They had planned to assess her to see if the problem is…was Alzheimer's. The appointment was scheduled for April."

"Meanwhile, you were coping with the problem?"

"Yes. We were coping."

A young woman with a ponytail and a short tweed skirt came into the lounge area.

"Detectives," she said, "can I speak with you for a moment?"

Tosh and Christie followed the woman, leaving Sherman to once again study the coffeepot at 33 Division.

***

Some time later, the detectives returned. Christie carried a box of pastries, which he set on the table near Sherman.

"Mr. Grady," he said, "have a doughnut."

"No, thank you."

"Mr. Grady," Mallory said, "it's going to be a long day for you. Please, we insist, you need to eat something. If not a doughnut, then we'll have someone bring you a sandwich if you like."

Grady let out a sigh. "The doughnut will be okay," he said, but didn't reach for the box.

Mallory opened the lid. "What kind?"

Finally, Sherman chose an old-fashioned, chewing slowly and without tasting.

"Did your wife have any friends?" Jerome asked. "Was there anyone she remained in contact with socially, maybe someone she'd worked with at the bank?"

"What do you mean? Why do you ask? We have a few friends, like everyone. People we get together with occasionally for dinner or drinks."

"That's it? We've been trying to get a handle on her state of mind, whether she was depressed, whether she'd been considering harming herself."

Grady sat up straight in his chair.

"My wife," he said, "was a very sick woman. She wasn't well enough to engage in any kind of a social life. We maintained a few friendships together, but she didn't have the strength to see people without me."

"What about before," Mallory asked. "I mean before she got sick. While she was still working. Was there anyone she was close to then? Anyone she might still want to see?"

"You think she was trying to see a friend? Not coming to my office, but to her old workplace? I suppose that's possible. There was a lady…I can't remember…I think her name was Sheila. They used to have lunch together regularly."

Jerome nodded at Mallory. "Yes," he said. "That would be Sheila Matheson. We have someone speaking with her now."

The change in the room was barely perceptible. Mallory, though, picked up on it immediately. She'd been raised in a family where being sensitive to mood changes was a valuable survival skill.

Jerome sensed it too, but would have been hard-pressed to describe what exactly was different.

Sherman didn't bat an eye. He made no move, no comment. And yet the very air that surrounded him had become somehow charged – electrified – with a current of anxiety.

It lasted for less than a second. Sherman recovered, took a sip of his coffee, and said, "Yes, that's right. Sheila Matheson. That was her name."

"The reason we asked," Jerome said, "about Mrs. Grady's friends is because..." He paused.

Mallory picked up the sentence where he left off.

"A couple of passing motorists," she said, "reported seeing someone on the bridge with your wife."

"Of course they weren't sure," Jerome said. "They were heading east on the 401, at highway speed. Still, a handful have called in and said they saw a woman in a white coat, followed by a man dressed in either brown or black. They said it almost looked like they were together, even though he was a little behind her."

"A man?" Sherman said. "They must be mistaken. Why would Valerie be out walking with a man at that hour of the morning? Especially as sick as she was. It must have been a stranger. Someone who happened to be walking there at the same time."

"That's possible," Mallory said. "The only thing that seems odd is why a man would just keep going. Why wouldn't he stop and call 911 on his cell phone? Or flag down a passing driver to get help?"

"If I was walking behind a lady and saw her climb over that railing, I'd try to stop her," Jerome said. "If I couldn't stop her, then for sure I'd try to get help."

"Do you think someone pushed her over the railing?" Sherman said. "That's just crazy. Why would anyone want to hurt Valerie?"

"I'm sure it won't amount to anything," Mallory said. "It's just something we have to follow up. Besides," she added, "your wife might have waited for the man to pass before... Maybe he didn't know what she was about to do."

"But as far as you know," Jerome said, "your wife wasn't seeing any friends socially, I mean, without you present."

"No," Sherman said. "She really wasn't well enough for that."

"Very good," Mallory said. "Our people will ask around at the bank, but it looks like this was an accident resulting from early onset-dementia."

"Are you well enough to drive, Mr. Grady?" Jerome asked. "We can take you to your car, or if you like we can have someone chauffeur you home, and we can deliver your car for you."

"It's a short drive home from my office," Sherman said. "Please, take me to my car. I'll be okay."

"Is there anyone who can stay with you?" Mallory asked.

"No. But I'm really tired. I'll get some rest. There will be arrangements to make. When will my wife be released to the funeral home?"

"The autopsy should be completed by Wednesday. Unless we tell you differently, you'll be able to make arrangements any time after that."

Sherman nodded and drank the rest of his coffee.

"What am I going to do?" he asked, staring into the mug.

***

Home at last, Sherman poured himself a strong drink. He wasn't much of an imbiber, but the past five hours had left him knackered. He still had the feeling his soul was floating somewhere outside of his body, like he was disconnected from himself.

He fondled his wedding picture in its ornate frame and remembered once more how beautiful she had been, how much they had loved each other.

The sense of loss was nearly overwhelming.

***

Robert McQuade and Sheila Matheson sat together nervously in the visitors' lounge at 33 Division. They didn't speak – they didn't have to. They'd discussed the problem many times before. Each knew almost by heart the story they intended to tell.

***

Sherman nursed his drink. He hadn't slept the night before, and felt himself drifting into that sweet release, but forced himself to remain awake, at least a little longer.

Time was neither linear nor circular, in his experience. Instead, it was a game of hopscotch. Once you'd lived through a moment, you could relive it easily and at will.

Sometimes, though, time got the better of you. Sometimes it dragged you back and forth, hopping like a madman over the chalky pavement, reliving moments, days, weeks you would rather relegate to the past.

Recalling sights, smells, feelings you longed to forget.

Anything could act as a trigger for the game.

A particularly poignant piece of music.

The way a dress clung to a woman's hips.

Anything.

"Elizabeth," he said, for the hundredth time, cradling their wedding picture against his chest, the one with the heart-shaped wreath of red roses as a backdrop, "why did you have to die?"

Everything had gone to shit, the day they'd discovered she had stage four ovarian cancer. All of their sweet plans, their gilded dreams, blasted into the stratosphere in that horrible moment of clarity.

The children they would never have, the travel they would never enjoy. The old-age comfort they would never share.

How deep their love had been, even in that awful moment!

If he could have captured it, preserved it under glass, confined it to a spreadsheet – but it was nothing more than memory now.

Nothing more than a bitter-sweet mental album filled with images of a life that wasn't meant to be.

And oh, the grief! The grief that never seemed to end.

In his darkest hour he had turned in desperation to her sister, Valerie, who shared her figure, her honey-blond hair, her voice and physical beauty.

And Valerie, haunted by her own sorrow at her sister's death, had turned to him.

They'd married, as had he and Elizabeth, on Valentine's Day, a tribute to his sense of romance and his commitment to finding happiness beyond grief.

It seemed, at the time, the best solution for both of them, to pick up the lost threads of love and use them to forge a new love, a new life.

After all, they'd known each other for years. It seemed to make sense.

After mere months, Sherman realized his mistake.

Valerie may have *looked* like Elizabeth, but that was where the resemblance ended.

Where Elizabeth was modest, elegant and poised, Valerie was demanding, impossible to please, at times almost a hateful shrew.

She belittled him, mocked his source of livelihood, his love of numbers, his lack of interest in earning more money.

Her job at the bank paid slightly more than his and she never let him forget it.

The final insult, though, had come early last year, when he discovered she'd been having an affair.

Out of respect for his own beloved Elizabeth, and knowing he was doomed to never find a love like that again, he'd remained wedded to her sister those past 20 years. He'd used every ounce of his outward calm, his charm and wit to hold that marriage together, despite her insults, her sudden bursts of rage, her appetite for material things.

But an affair?

That was simply too much.

Sherman valued fidelity and trust above all things.

That was what made him such an exceptional accountant.

He found out the truth quite by accident, that Valerie had been stepping out with a coworker by the name of Robert McQuade. He was at a local restaurant for lunch with his colleague, Thomas Braithewaite. Unknown to either of them, Valerie was also there with her friend, Sheila Matheson, from the bank. They didn't see each other, but Sherman caught the unmistakable shrill of Valerie's mean laughter, and immediately paid attention.

The women spoke softly, but he was able to hear. Thomas didn't think it strange — he never did say much over lunch. The men habitually ate in silence.

"He rang my bell, baby," Valerie said.

"Is it serious?" Sheila asked.

"I think it might be. But in any case, it's clear, I've got to leave the accountant."

"When will you tell him? Where will you go?"

"I'll figure it out," Valerie said. "Life's too short for this pretense. I deserve to be happy for real."

And she was right, after all. Everyone deserved to be happy, didn't they?

Too late for Sherman, though. Too late for Elizabeth.

Until that moment in the restaurant, he had never really *hated* another human being.

Unable to finish his lunch, he told Thomas he had a stomach bug and hightailed it back to the office.

That night he sat up planning, "crunching the numbers", working it out in his mind.

First, make sure the insurance was up to date.

Then, investigate easy-to-access drugs that can cause cognitive disorders. Study the dosage required, administer and begin the long-term care process.

Finally, when everyone could see what a caring husband he really was, end this farce, once and for all.

That morning, he and Valerie rose together as usual. She was no longer capable of making breakfast, so he did it, taking care to leave out the usual dose of pharmaceuticals. It wouldn't do to have any trace of unprescribed pills in her digestive tract.

He helped her dress, and convinced her to drive with him to work, saying the bank had called, and they needed her help. He promised to drop her off there.

She was so confused.

After parking at his office – he knew no one would be around at that hour – he swiped in. Instead of entering the building, though, he went back to the car for Valerie.

"Come on, dear," he said. "I'll walk you to the bank."

He wasn't wearing his usual coat. He'd left it in the car. Instead he was wearing an old brown overcoat that had belonged to him when he was a younger man. He also wore a brimmed hat, which he pulled down low to conceal his face.

Sherman walked behind her, speaking to her only when there was no one in hearing range.

"Why do they need my help?" she asked. "I'm not feeling well."

"It's okay, dear, they only need you to balance an account. You'll be home again soon."

Luck was with him as they approached the Don Mills overpass. There was only a small handful of cars on Don Mills, and no other pedestrians yet. The winter sun was habitually late to rise, and in the semidarkness under the streetlights, he knew that even if he was seen, no one would recognize him.

Not wanting to miss the opportunity, he acted as soon as they were on the bridge.

"Sweetheart," he said, grabbing her from behind, "go to Hell."

And now, he thought, savoring the last sip of whiskey, all that remained was to wait out the funeral and cash in the insurance policy.

And hope to hell that dolt Sheila Matheson didn't suspect anything.

***

"What's our next step?" Jerome asked after Robert McQuade and Sheila Matheson had left the Division.

"These are just stories," Mallory said. "Without evidence, they don't mean anything."

"The standard autopsy procedure falls short of giving us what we'd need."

"My money's on cremation. I'm betting he'll wait till the body's released, then make the arrangements quietly."

"Yeah," Jerome said. "He wouldn't rush it – might tip us off."

"Arsenic shows up in the ash after cremation."

"I don't think it's arsenic. At those levels, a blood count high enough to cause flat-out dementia, I doubt whether she'd be able to walk."

"You're right. But if not poison, then what?" Mallory asked.

"Let's call Samden at the Coroner's Office. Put a bug in his ear, ask him to run every test he can think of for any substance known to cause profound dementia and memory loss."

"Good idea," Mallory said. "And be sure to wish him a Happy Freakin' Valentine's Day."

About Donna Carrick

Donna Carrick is an award-winning author, whose Kindle novels have achieved over 100,000 downloads. She's active in the Canadian writing scene, is an executive member of Crime Writers of Canada as well as a member of Sisters In Crime, Toronto Chapter.

Her novel *The First Excellence* won the 2011 Indie Book Event Award for excellence in fiction. Her story "Watermelon Weekend," featured in the Mesdames of Mayhem crime anthology *Thirteen*, (Carrick Publishing) was short-listed for the Arthur Ellis Award.

With her husband and business partner Alex Carrick, Donna co-founded and operates Carrick Publishing, dedicated to helping Indie authors excel in their creative goals.

An office manager, wife and mother of three, Donna divides her time between the hectic pace of Toronto and the relative peace of Ontario's spectacular Georgian Bay. Life is never dull with husband/author Alex Carrick, their children, their beloved golden retriever Daisy and Dora the Cat.

http://www.donnacarrick.com/
http://www.carrickpublishing.com/
Amazon Author Page
Facebook
Twitter

BEAT THE CLOCK

By Catherine Dunphy

There he was again.

Winona bent over the cart of books that needed to be reshelved—God, how she hated this part of her otherwise great job at the library—and worked at being invisible. Not easy, given that she took up a lot of the aisle and didn't believe in wearing basic black. Or gray. Or anything that matched.

She sighed as one of the library's many—many— Maeve Binchy novels toppled off the trolley and hit the carpet with a thud. A muffled thud, but a thud nonetheless. She glanced over at the slight young man buried in medical books, ready to smile at him apologetically, but he was oblivious to everything save the text he was so urgently reading.

Strange, she thought, very strange.

She told Jason about it at home that night.

"He's there every day, from the minute we open to just before lunch. I swear he never even gets up to stretch."

"Sure he isn't napping under that tower of books? Wouldn't be the first one." Jason waggled his bushy eyebrows, inviting a laugh.

Winona didn't take the bait. "Sometimes, I swear I can hear him flipping the pages. Thwap, thwap, thwap. It's as if he's trying to find something—and he can't."

"Probably swotting to get into med school."

Jason was starting to talk like something out of his grandmother's collection of *The Boy's Own Annual* he was reading. But as he lowered his long, lanky body beside her on the couch and kneaded her plump shoulders just the way she liked, she leaned back against him and dropped the subject.

***

The next morning Winona dressed with extra care, draping a chartreuse length of scarf over her polka-dotted, size 18, pink sateen dress. Even Jason noticed.

"Going for the glare factor?" He smirked, whipping out his retro shades. "Naw, you're going for his attention, aren't you?"

"You know me too well," Winona grabbed her man's hand and pulled him out the door.

They were both heading to the library. Twice a week Jason took a break from working on one of his many start-up apps and cheerfully took over the loathed shelving-and-sorting chores, freeing her to roam the computer where she was—let us not be modest—a bloody superstar. Ask her and she shall find it—either in the stacks or on the Internet or, usually, both. Plenty of happy members of the Millartown library swore by her fast-fingered sleuthing. Last night, she had made up her mind. Whatever that worried young man was seeking, she would help him find it.

"I think you should leave him be," Jason said at the door to the library.

His raised hand cut off her protest. "I know you want to help him, but you can be a bit of a busybody. Some people fly solo in this world. It's their thing."

"Jason, it's my job." She flounced in ahead of him. "And I'm good at it."

"True." Then he grinned. "In good part because you are one nosy broad."

Still, she waited until Jason was back in the stacks before she approached the boy. No, she now saw, not a boy. Faint lines stretched from the corners of his eyes, the furrow between his pale brows was permanent and, when he finally looked up at her, his dark eyes were anguished.

Winona instantly regretted her garish outfit, rare for her. Here was a man—older than her, maybe in his mid-30s—who was in pain.

"I want to help you," she blurted. *Idiot.*

He waved a tired hand over his laptop, his yellow notepad and the pile of books. "I don't think you can."

She sat down in the chair opposite him. "Why not? It's my job."

She picked up one of his thick medical texts. "These are practically obsolete the minute they are printed and bound." She tapped the back of his open laptop. "I've got access to all kinds of sites and Listservs that the public doesn't. What is it you're looking for?"

He closed his computer, grabbed his jacket and, without another word, got up and strode out of the room. Winona stared after him, open-mouthed, before she noticed he'd forgotten his yellow notepad. She picked it up. HLH, she read in crabbed handwriting. A rare but potentially fatal medical condition. Usually occurs in *children*—he had underlined the word so fiercely that he had cut through the paper.

Her hand flew to her mouth. That poor man—he's the father of a dying child. She hurried back to her office and fired up her computer.

Hemophagocytic lymphohistiocytosis. Excessive immune activation that brings with it deteriorating organ functions, she read.

Horrible, she thought, and continued reading. Deadly if not treated, worse in adults than kids, usually, especially in the familial form but terrible for kids, too. Only about a quarter of the people diagnosed with it can expect to live another five years.

She shuddered. The man was desperate. No wonder.

***

The following day, she arrived for work and immediately went to look for him in his usual spot. He wasn't there. Nor was he there the next day.

"I have to find him," she wailed to Jason that night. "He was probably just doing the regular searches. Johns Hopkins. The Histiocyte Society. They're the experts, but they are so careful. They recommend genetic testing—duh—but it's a little late for that."

Jason put down the *Boy's Own* he was reading. "You probably should cool it, Win, but you're not going to leave him alone, are you? So tell me, what did you find?"

"They've got a clinical trial going. Using some new drugs to tame the autoimmune system before doing the rest of the treatment. Jason, it seems to be working."

"So it can't be a secret."

Winona nodded. "But you have to go deep to find out they're coming to Canada. Not here. Toronto. But Jase, if he moves fast, he's still got time to sign up for it. The cut-off's in four days. I've got to find that guy."

Jason yawned and picked up his book.

"You try the hospital?"

***

She called in sick the next day. It was one of Jason's workdays, so he could cover for her. Still she didn't want anyone to see her, so she gave the library a wide berth and took the back roads to Millartown General. It was a bustling place and getting bigger, thanks to Jason's grandmother. Her very generous donation meant last year's fund-raising campaign for a new hospital wing had been a success. Winona frowned. She should have brought Jason with her. Most days, she forgot he was the sole heir of the town's wealthiest family and how that opened doors. Wide.

She straightened her shoulders, patted down her cowgirl skirt, adjusted her cat-ear headband and walked through the revolving doors.

"Children's ward?" she asked the receptionist.

The middle-aged woman, whose nameplate read Chrissie, looked startled, then beamed up at her.

"I didn't know the kids were having a clown in today. It's the fourth floor. Go right up."

Admittedly she had lathered on the blusher that morning, but Winona wasn't about to take offence.

"Whatever it takes," she muttered, stepping aside to let an orderly pushing an empty gurney leave the elevator. The man ducked his head in thanks as he set off toward emergency. She rode the four floors thinking hard about what to do next. Three days. He only had three more days.

The doors opened onto a cheerful nursing station with balloon wallpaper and busy nurses in Mickey Mouse smocks. Winona approved. Nobody paid her the slightest attention, which was good but also not good. How was she going to find this sick child?

"The children are watching television. We didn't expect you." The accusing voice belonged to a stern woman with a clipboard. Winona sighed. A bad-tempered control freak was in charge of this place. They really were everywhere.

She assembled her biggest, fakest smile and explained she had been hired to bring cheer to just one patient—not an entire ward. "I'm with the Histiocyte Society." She raced past the name. "They didn't identify the child. Well, perhaps they did, but I deleted their email." Winona was babbling but a flood of words was often an effective distraction. She inhaled deeply. "I'm sure there are not many children here with HLH."

The head nurse glared at her as she punched numbers into her cell phone. "In fact there are none, as I think you know."

Two security officers appeared almost instantly.

"Someone else hit the meds cupboard?" one of them asked the nurse.

"Or tried to." She snapped her phone shut, looking pleased with herself. "This lady is leaving. Please escort her out and make sure she is not allowed back in again."

"Wait, please. There's a sick child here. I can help. I know—"

As Winona was frog-marched out through the lobby, she passed the same orderly, this time with an elderly woman on his gurney. She looked again. The orderly was the man from the library. Winona gasped and tried to wrest free of the guards' tight grasp.

"Let me go," she hollered as people turned to stare then hurriedly looked away. The orderly stopped.

"It's me, from the library," Winona yelled at the man. "I know about HLH. I can help you."

His face closed down. He said nothing as he quickly steered his startled patient to the elevator.

Winona slumped on the bench outside the hospital's front doors. She felt spent. Useless. Too tired to mop the trail of tears trickling down her rouged cheeks. There was so little time left. Just hours, really. He had to work up the application, make it strong, get it to shout out to anyone reading it that his child—not someone else's—had to be part of the trial. Could they find a doctor who would vouch for his kid at such short notice? Was there a doctor here in Millartown with the creds and connections to cut through all the damned red tape?

She grabbed her bag and pulled out her laptop.

A take-out cup of coffee appeared before her.

"You look like you could use this." Chrissie from reception folded herself down on the bench beside Winona and took a long sip of her own coffee.

"Thanks." Winona took the cup and placed it on the ground in front of her. There was no time for this.

Chrissie got down to business. "I heard you in there." She gestured back at the hospital, then searched Winona's face intently. "Don't have long on my break so I'll get to the point. I've seen you in the library." She held up a hand to ward off Winona's surprised reaction. "You do help people."

Chrissie leaned in closer.

"Listen up. That orderly, Lou, his shift finishes at 11. But he doesn't go home. There's a lab—a small one no one uses anymore—in the old part of the hospital that's going to be demolished. Seventh floor, end of the hall. He's there every night by himself until three, four in the morning trying to find something—anything—to cure her."

She got up, crumpling her empty coffee cup.

"And don't ask me how I know, okay?"

Astonished, Winona could only nod as the woman hurried back inside.

***

Jason had been asleep for hours when she crept out at 2 a.m. The lone nurse in emergency didn't look up from *US Weekly* as Winona, wearing the only subdued gray clothing she owned with an officious-looking laptop bag over her shoulder, walked purposefully past her and down a long corridor to a back elevator. Her heart was pounding as she waited for it. This time there were no security guards around, just a tired cleaner. The seventh floor seemed to be mainly dark, empty offices. Light streaming through a closed door at the end of the hallway told her the location of the lab.

Through the door window, she could see Lou, his back to her, bent over an antiquated Bunsen burner. In her excitement, she flung open the door, sending it crashing against the wall of the small lab. He jumped as if scalded, knocking vials, test tubes and jars onto the porcelain tile floor, where they exploded into pieces, their contents dribbling away.

"Oh God, I'm sorry," she babbled.

His face was flushed. In his gloved hand, he had a long and ugly shard of glass, the remains of the hot shattered vial he'd been holding over the burner. It glittered red and lethal, and Winona involuntarily stepped back from him.

"You have ruined everything. I was so close." His voice was raw and furious. The muscles in his neck twitched as he kicked aside some of the glass. His leather heels crunched on the granular liquid that had seeped onto the tiles as he moved toward her.

"I didn't mean to." A wave of fear washed over her. Winona fought to keep panic out of her voice. "I just wanted to help you."

"Help me?" His cry echoed through the empty hall. "I already told you. No one can."

Then Winona heard his despair and grief. She put her hand on his taut arm.

"I am so very sorry. About everything."

His slim shoulders drooped as he turned away from her and leaned on the counter. He looked down at the shard of glass he was holding and, shuddering, dropped it. Winona saw again the desperate, sad man from the library.

"I've lost her. I've lost Jess."

Winona winced. It was because of her. Because she was loud and clumsy and had made him spill and lose whatever elixir he thought might save her. She had to make it up to him. He had to hear her out; he had to get his girl into the trial. "No, no. You haven't. There's still time."

He whirled back toward her.

"Don't you get it? I can't save her. It's over."

"Maybe not, Lou. Maybe you should hear what she has to say."

Chrissie stepped carefully into the room, her voice calm and flat, with one arm outstretched as if calming a trapped animal.

"I told her to come, Lou. Maybe she's found something to help Jess."

Chrissie smiled at Winona. "My kid brother. A bit obsessed, actually totally insane, to be doing all this—" her hand indicated the lab and Lou's shattered work "—but he's one of the good guys. Trust me."

She stroked his gaunt cheek. "Lou's been sneaking in here for months experimenting to find a drug combo to save his girl. Don't think he's slept in a year."

Lou stared at the floor at the remnants of his concoction. His breathing was ragged; his shoulders heaved. "Chrissie, I was so close. I can't do it all again. There's no time."

Winona retrieved her laptop with shaking hands, propped it on the lab counter and hurriedly clicked her way to the site she wanted. "Here. A trial for a new treatment for HLH. In Toronto. There are still two days left to apply. But you need to get medical experts to vouch for you. Fast."

Chrissie looked over her shoulder. "We can do that."

She laughed at Winona's obvious surprise. "Lou used to do medical research in the children's hospital down east. He knows plenty of docs."

***

Morning light was beginning to push through the dark night when Winona slipped out of the hospital. Chrissie had cajoled, begged and finally ordered Lou to look at the application. The siblings had been engrossed in creating their plan of action when she left. She was feeling less guilty, maybe even a little bit pleased with herself as she returned home.

"I think he's going to do it. He's going to be able to save his daughter after all," she told Jason over breakfast. To which he high-fived her. Euphoria and a lot of caffeine propelled her through the workday. But that night, when she realized she hadn't heard anything from Lou or Chrissie, she began to worry that they were having trouble with the application. The deadline was at five o'clock the next day. She could only get to sleep after she decided she would run over to the hospital at lunch to make sure everything was all right.

It seemed as if her head had just touched the pillow when a thunderous boom shook the walls of their apartment.

"What the—?" Beside her, Jason sat bolt upright.

Winona ran to the window and saw faraway flames shooting high into the night. "That's the hospital."

She threw on some clothes and ran out the door, Jason right behind her. They leapt into Jason's battered Honda and drove until, rounding a corner, they saw the huge flames and heard their roar. The hospital's old administration wing was a black and hollow outline against the sky, lit up by the red glow.

Firefighters were battling the flames and the billowing smoke. Winona could hear the crackle of the walkie-talkies of emergency personnel calling for backup.

She grabbed the arm of a firefighter with a clipboard. "I know someone who's in there. I'm sure of it. Is he okay?"

The man gave her a stern look. "Lady, it's an empty building. I need you to step back out of the way." Then he stopped. "What floor?"

Winona quaked. "Seven."

"Jesus, that's where it started." He barked some orders into his walkie-talkie and turned on his heels, leaving them standing forlornly on the sidelines.

"He's there, isn't he?" Jason said finally.

Numb, Winona nodded. "He must have been trying another drug experiment after I ruined the first one."

He put his arm around her. "Not your fault. You hear me?"

They stood like that until they saw firefighters wheel a gurney with a covered body out of the building.

***

Two weeks later, a pale and visibly aged Chrissie met a subdued Winona for coffee. Silently, the grieving woman handed her a sheaf of papers. Tears welled in Winona's eyes when she realized what they were: Lou's application for the study. She looked up at Chrissie, who was watching her intently.

"The Fire Marshal's Office says the fire started in the lab." Chrissie took a deep breath. "They don't think it was an accident."

She sighed and her hands cradled her cup as if for warmth—or courage. "Ever since they got the diagnosis last year, he'd been obsessed. They had to postpone the wedding. He didn't want to but Jess kept getting worse. He took the job at the hospital to be near her. He—"

"Wedding?" Winona interrupted.

"It was supposed to be in June. Big one. Traditional. But by then she was so sick and all he wanted to do was save her. I know. What chance did he, one guy, have to do that? None. But he couldn't stand by and watch her die. It was killing him. That's why he was reading all the medical books and trying all the experiments."

"Jess was a woman?"

"Pardon?" Chrissie looked at Winona as if she were speaking another language.

"Not a child?" Winona couldn't let the thought go.

"Well, of course she was a woman. Thirty-two years old. I don't..." Chrissie's voice trailed off as Winona gasped and covered her face with her hands. She had given him hope, then ended his dreams when he read the fine print. The study was only for children. Not for his Jess.

Chrissie tapped the sheaf of papers lying on the table between them. "Look, he had finished the application.

That's why I am here, to thank you. You got him to try something other than his wild goose chase to find a miracle cure. "

Winona's heart caved in. She thought about the young, desperate man in the library. She still had his yellow pad of notes, with the word *children* so violently underlined, in her desk. Now she understood why. There was nothing for his Jess. Winona's aching heart fell even further.

Chrissie stood up heavily to go. "Jess died that night, too. "

Shock ran through Winona. And then, selfishly, a growing sense of reprieve. Lou must have given up when Jess died. Maybe, just maybe, she wasn't to blame.

Chrissie sounded so very tired. "It happened a couple of hours before the fire. His name isn't on the visitor's log, but one of the nurses said Lou was with her at the end, holding her hand."

Chrissie's sad smile was a replica of her brother's.

"I want to believe they were together when she died. He deserved just that one small comfort. But I guess I will never know."

About Catherine Dunphy

A National Newspaper Award winner for feature writing, Catherine Dunphy was a staff writer at *The Toronto Star*, Canada's largest newspaper, for more than 25 years.

She is the author of *Morgentaler, A Difficult Hero*, which was nominated for the prestigious Governor General's Award in 1997. As well, she has written two books of young adult fiction related to the much-heralded Canadian television series, *Degrassi High*, which has been shown throughout the world.

She has also written screenplays for the Canadian television series, *Riverdale*, as well as created a four-part CBC radio mystery series called *Fallaway Ridge*. She currently writes for magazines and teaches print journalism and magazine writing at Ryerson University in Toronto.

In case you are wondering, she hates having her picture taken – and has always been a mystery reader/addict.

Mesdames of Mayhem

TROUBLED TIMES

By Lisa de Nikolits

"I was six then," Auntie Ethel said. "In 1921. When Father died."

"What did he die of?" I asked.

"Heart, lungs. I don't know, Beth." She shrugged. "He was fairly young, in his mid-40s. He married late and Beatrice Anne was a young wife in her early 20s. I was a honeymoon baby."

"Was she very sad about your father's death?"

"I can't say for sure, but I don't think she was. She was still young and she had inherited a fortune. A fortune, I might add, that she had no interest in worrying about, apart from insisting that she would neither scrimp nor save, and she certainly stuck to her word on both counts. By the time she moved in with us, she hardly had any money at all. But luckily my Ed was always a generous and kind man."

"What did she spend her money on?"

"Holidays abroad, jewelry, high teas, and maids to tidy up after her. Nothing with any kind of investment value, although she did have some good pieces of jewelry."

"How long did she live with you?"

"Not long at all. She shared a flat with a woman named Rita for most of her life."

"Were they lovers?" The thing I liked about my great-aunt was that I could speak my mind with her, and there weren't many people I could say that about.

"No, no, dearie," Auntie Ethel said patiently. "Rita was a secretary of sorts to my mother. She was her confidante, her companion. Poor Rita, she was such a plain woman, whereas Beatrice Anne was an extraordinary beauty. Rita never married, but everyone knew that she was madly in love with the pastor of her church. He was a good-for-nothing fellow. Everyone knew that too, everyone except Rita. Poor Rita. She had remarkably sloping shoulders that you couldn't help noticing. Mind you, I'm not being an awful gossip. It was quite mesmerizing just how sloping those shoulders were."

"And she was in love with a charlatan."

"For the most part, he used his looks to keep his shirts ironed, his suppers cooked, and his house cleaned. He was a very handsome man. He looked like Robert Mitchum."

"God rest his soul." I grinned at her. "I've got no idea who Robert Mitchum is, Auntie Eth."

"Well, never mind. So there was Rita, living with Beatrice Anne—"

"Did you call her Beatrice Anne to her face?" I interrupted, not meaning to be rude.

"Oh yes, dearie, she insisted on it. She didn't want people to think she was old enough to have a daughter my age. She chopped 10 years off her age when she turned 40, went right back to being 30. Until she hit 57. Then she admitted to being 50, and by the time she was in her late 60s, she owned up to her real age, saying that it no longer mattered what people thought."

"And by that time she had lost all the family money."

"She had, indeed. But it wasn't really her fault. You must remember that she was born into money and married money. She was educated by governesses who all agreed that economics and numbers were too unspeakably unfeminine to even think about. Young ladies were concerned with etiquette, needlepoint, poetry and music—all the finer things in life."

"Must have been nice." I imagined myself in an elegant drawing room, dabbling in watercolors while a large dog lay asleep in front of a roaring fire.

"You would have died of boredom, dearie."

I poured another cup of tea for Auntie Ethel and passed her a lemon cream cookie.

"Thank you." Auntie Ethel said and sighed.

I leaned toward her. "Are you okay?"

"Yes, I'm fine. Sometimes I can't help thinking that if Beatrice Anne had been slightly more aware of the financial side of things, that it would have been easier for the entire family."

"Did she have money when she lived with Rita?"

"She did, but it was dwindling fast."

"Was that why she came to live with you? Because she ran out of money and Rita left her?"

Auntie Ethel was about to answer when the door was pushed open and my mother edged in sideways, carrying a large bouquet of flowers and a cake in a white box.

I jumped up to take the cake and squeezed next to the bed while my mother navigated her way into the small room and air kissed each of Auntie Ethel's soft, powdered cheeks.

I set the cake down on the small coffee table while my mother sank into a chair and held the flowers in my direction.

I took them, filled a vase with water at the tiny kitchen sink, and arranged the flowers.

"That's lovely, dearie," Auntie Ethel called out. "Leave the flowers on the bookcase. Come and have some cake."

"Looks like cake is the last thing she should be eating," my mother commented. She leaned back in her chair, fanning her face with a magazine. "You used to be such a skinny thing, and now you're quite chubby," she said to me.

"Where were we?" I asked Auntie Eth, ignoring my mother.

"We were talking about Beatrice Anne and Rita," Auntie Ethel reminded me.

We were there to celebrate Auntie Ethel's 94th birthday, and, bless her, she still had her wits about her.

"Oh, that old story," my mother said. "The old family fortune lost by one too many high teas, etcetera, etcetera. Not to mention what a supposedly great artist Beatrice Anne was."

It seemed odd that I had never heard the story of Beatrice Anne before, when my mother clearly had.

"Beatrice Anne was a great artist," Auntie Ethel said quietly. "If you asked her, she would say she that had never studied and that she had never been taught. But, in fact, she had been taught and she had learned, from the governesses and then from the finishing school at Wiesbaden."

"Wiesbaden?" I jolted upright.

I had taken a gap year after high school and backpacked across Europe, visiting the big cities and working tables to make money. When I hit Germany, something inexplicable urged me to visit Wiesbaden. On a whim, I bought a train ticket and set off in the cold gray mist to check out the town.

I found the place to be fairly unremarkable. And there was no epiphany as to why I had felt the need to visit.

But now, in light of this mention of Wiesbaden, I wondered: Had Beatrice Anne, for reasons known only to her, wanted me to go there? Had she wanted me to visit the very place where she'd studied art? I imagined her in a rowboat on the Rhine, craning her neck gracefully away from flirtatious boys. Perhaps, like me, she had a secret love.

"I've been to Wiesbaden," I blurted out, but had nothing more to add. My mother looked at me as if she were surprised that I was there at all, which was her usual expression when it came to me.

Auntie Ethel patted my hand and continued. "Beatrice Anne was a *great* artist." She emphasized the word *great* ever so slightly and gave my mother a look. My mother, smoothing an invisible crease out of her trousers, didn't notice. "But it is interesting to note that she did not paint at all in the years after Rita. She did not so much as pick up a pencil or a brush. But the day she before she died, she did two things. The first was to ask my Ed to go out and get her a nice piece of art paper and some oil paints. The other was to phone all her friends for a good chat.

"After she had made her calls, she went out into the garden and she painted the avenue of roses that led from the garden gate to the front door. She didn't paint them from the front door of the house to the gate. Instead, she stood on the sidewalk and painted them leading up to the house. She always loved a good rose garden. As soon as she finished, she went straight to bed. In the morning, Ed went to take her a cup of tea, then came and told me that he could not wake Beatrice Anne. We knew immediately that she had died."

"What happened to the painting?" I asked.

"It got lost along the way," Auntie Ethel said. "So much gets lost over time."

"How are things here?" my mother asked Auntie Ethel. "Any new complaints about the objectionable Mr. Thomas?"

"He's still cutting corners," Auntie Ethel said. "We've been eating tuna casseroles for weeks now. I'd bet my last dollar that he got a deal on tuna from one of his lowlife friends and pocketed the money he saved."

"At least tuna casseroles are nutritious," my mother said.

Auntie Ethel looked at her levelly. "When was the last time you ate a tuna casserole?"

"Still," my mother said.

"And other little things," Auntie Ethel said. "The toilet paper is quite terrible these days, not that one wants to talk of such things, but it is one of life's necessities. I never thought that it would be a concern at my age."

"I'll get you the good stuff," I assured her.

"Do you want me to talk to Mr. Thomas?" my mother asked,

Auntie Ethel shook her head. "Please don't. I don't want him to think I'm a troublemaker. It would only get worse for me. Never mind. I'll be fine."

"Well, if you change your mind, I'll be happy to talk to him," my mother said. "Would you like more tea?"

Auntie Ethel beamed. "That would be lovely."

While they busied themselves, I looked around the room at the faded floral cushions on the bed and the brown ceramic mugs carefully arranged on top of a small fridge. Butterflies, roses, teddy bears and thick white art paper warped by water and time.

It was, I thought, a holding pen for a person whose life was drawing to a close, but it was cheerful for all that—

a neatly-made bed, sunshine, a place for every tiny treasured thing that bore witness to a life fully lived. All pruned and snow-globed into a small cell, with a bathroom adjoining.

That led me to wonder where life would find me, at 94, which, of course, led me to Ryan, an orderly at the home where Auntie Ethel lived.

It's where I met him, and since then, he's never been far from my thoughts.

***

"God's truth," Ryan said, his gaze on the floor somewhere around the area of my left foot. "I stayed overnight at my buddy's house because I didn't want to drive drunk. The next morning, when the cops pulled me over on my way in to work, I didn't realize I was still legally drunk." I looked at him across the food court table and didn't say a word.

"I lost my license for three months, but that's okay. I deserved it." He ran his fingers through his unruly dark hair, the hair I loved to run my fingers through, too.

But I didn't give an inch. I looked down at my slice of pizza, still not saying anything. He grabbed my hand and held it tight.

"The thing is," he said, "being in the courtroom yesterday, being humbled like that, well, it gave me time to think. I walked and walked after I finished up there, and course, while I walked, I thought of you, about our future."

I looked at him, wondering what I had seen in him. Then I cataloged the lies he had told me, still unwilling to see the truth.

I had been prepared for disappointment right from the start. Even so, the sucker punches still hurt when they landed.

I sighed. I was grateful, given this most recent development, that I had kept our relationship hidden. The look on my face must have told him he had better come up with something better than hints at a hope-filled future. He gave a half nod and continued.

"You make me want to be a better man, a different man. You make it possible for me to be the man I've always wanted to be." He let go of my hand and I felt a wave of emptiness wash over me. "I want to give you something. I found it, and although I didn't buy it, it will tell you how I feel about you."

He pushed something toward me, something glittery and beautiful and shiny. I gasped.

It was a vintage art deco watch—a long rectangle of sparkly lines and curves and angles. It was extraordinarily beautiful.

"You found this?" My voice sounded incredulous.

He pulled back and glared at me. "You think I lifted it? From whom?"

From one of the old ladies at the home, I wanted to say, but I couldn't. Despite my misgivings, I took the watch and fitted it onto my chunky wrist. The watch smiled at me as if I had been born with it. It shone with an elegance and charm that had thus far been entirely absent from my life.

"I wish I had found a ring," Ryan said, significantly, and I looked up at him.

"You know how I feel about you," I said. "But I have to trust you if we're going to build a life together."

"What's not to trust?"

"Ryan! You've just lost your license! How's that for a prime example? And you've told me that Mavis has complained about you more than once and that you could lose your job."

He shrugged. "There are always more jobs." He blew his hair out of his eyes. "And one day the band will make it big. You'll see." His voice took on an accusatory tone. "You should have more faith."

I opened my mouth to say that if they wanted to make it big, they should try turning up for the gigs they had been booked for, instead of getting wasted and forgetting where they were supposed to be. I had tried being the band's manager for a couple of weeks, but I soon realized that it wasn't good for my relationship with Ryan. I gave up and joined the other girlfriends in watching, admiring and enthusiastically partaking of the partying that went hand-in-hand with the band.

The trouble with Ryan was that he was so darn beautiful. Even Auntie Ethel had commented on him, saying she always enjoyed it when the long-haired boy was around, singing and pretending to play guitar on the mop.

"Where did you find this?" I asked, turning my attention back to the watch. It was hard to focus on anything else. "Does it work?"

"It does work. You have to wind it up. And I told you, I found it. But you don't believe me. I thought you'd be happy. I'm not sticking around if you're just going to grill me. I don't need this shit."

He got up and glared at me. I watched him march away through the food court, and my eyes filled with tears.

I checked the time. I had to get back to class. I was studying to be a dental hygienist; all I wanted was to finish the course, get a good job, and have a little apartment with Ryan. If only he would straighten up just a little, be more punctual at work, play a few good gigs and party less, we could have a really good life together.

If only...

***

"I have to go," my mother said, and snapped me back to the present.

"Goodbye, Auntie Eth," Mother said. "I hope you've had a good birthday."

"Very lovely," Auntie Ethel said. "Your Beth's a good girl. She visits me often, not just on birthdays."

Her compliment fell on deaf ears, and my mother smoothed her trousers. "I'll put the rest of the cake on the sideboard," she said. She gave me a look as if to say I should have known to do this myself, and I blushed.

"I can stay longer," I offered. Auntie Ethel's happy look lifted my spirits.

"Come to the car," my mother ordered. "I found a new Shirley Temple movie for Auntie Eth. I forgot to bring it in."

Auntie Ethel looked as if heaven had just dropped into her lap.

I followed my mother outside in silence, racking my brain to try to say something of interest.

"My course is going well," I eventually offered, and she gave a slight grunt of disapproval.

"Why you'd want to spend all day looking inside people's mouths, I have no idea," she said. "All that saliva and plaque...Ugh!" She gave a small shudder. "And you've got a degree in English literature, all paid for! You should do something with that."

Given that we had already had this conversation more than once, I did not reply.

"Have you had any episodes lately?" she asked. I looked away in shock, wondering why she would ask me that.

"Of course not," I said. "Why?"

She studied my face. I was staring at the ground, but I could feel her probing. When my mother looked at me like that—really looked at me—it was like the fingers of a blind person skimming braille—she could read messages I didn't even know were there.

"You've got that look about you," she said eventually. "Is something worrying you? You usually have episodes when you're upset."

"I'm not upset about anything," I said.

"Try to stay out of trouble," she advised. "And try not to hurt yourself, either."

She unlocked the car, reached inside, and handed me a plastic bag.

"Make sure you set it up for Auntie Ethel," she said. "You know she still struggles getting the DVD to work."

"I will," I said, and I was going to say something about how nice it had been, the three of us together, when my mother got into the car, snapped her seat belt into place, and drove off without so much as a wave.

***

I stood there in the late evening heat of the Indian summer, trying not to think about what my mother had said. Of course I wasn't having episodes. I was perfectly happy, and I didn't know why she had to come and ruin everything.

I dug the watch out of my jeans and looked down at it, turning it over in my hand and loving the sparkles that flashed in the sunlight.

"Granny Jean's really losing it," I heard a voice say. I turned around to see a mother and daughter heading toward a nearby car.

"She's been losing it forever," the daughter replied, checking her phone as she spoke.

"She hasn't been losing jewelry forever," the mother retorted. I swung around in shock. Jewelry? I hoped they would say more but if they did, I couldn't hear it because they got into their car and drove off.

Jewelry? Surely this wasn't just a coincidence? Granny Jean loses and Ryan finds. I put the watch back in the pocket of my jeans, feeling slightly sacrilegious. Something that beautiful demanded to be treated with more respect than being stuffed in and yanked out of a pocket.

***

"Who is Granny Jean?" I asked Auntie Ethel when I was back in her room,

"Not sure, dearie," Auntie Ethel said. "There are a lot of us here. I stick to myself. I don't need new friends, not at my age."

"What happened between Rita and Beatrice Anne?" I asked. "You were going to tell me before Mother arrived."

"Beatrice Anne drove Rita mad," Auntie Ethel said, "and one of the bones of contention was that Beatrice Anne would persist in listening to horrible ghost stories every night on the radio with the volume turned up high. She would shriek alarmingly and most distressingly during the entire broadcast. And, at each utterance of anguish, Rita would rush into the adjoining room, her nightgown billowing voluminously, fearful of finding a terrified Beatrice Anne lying dead on the floor, only to be hushed and admonished for interrupting. Poor slope-shouldered Rita would always leave in an angry huff only to be roused some hours later by Beatrice Anne in need of an aspirin and a hot drink to calm her ghostly frightened nerves."

I loved the way Auntie Ethel told a story. She had always been my person of refuge, even when I was a little kid. My mother dropped me off whenever I had an episode because she said Auntie Ethel could deal with me when no one else could. I don't remember having episodes, only fuzzy memories of people being angry with me. But I do remember lying snug and cozy, tucked in a warm blanket, with colorful night lights swirling softly overhead while Auntie Ethel told me stories. She was a born storyteller, visiting orphanages and hospitals to tell tales to the kids there. She was given a community service medal by the mayor, and there was a framed article on the wall about it.

I was lucky to have Auntie Ethel, and that's why I visited her as often as I did. No one else was in my corner like she was, not even Ryan.

"So, no," Auntie Ethel said musingly, "it was not a successful living arrangement at all. No one knows what really happened in the end. The prevailing rumor was that Beatrice Anne was set to run off with the pastor until he learned that she had lost all her money, and then Rita found out about the whole thing. Which would explain the end of their friendship. But all we know for sure is that it ended in blows, and that Rita packed her bags and left that same night. No one knows where she went. She simply vanished, and all Beatrice Anne would say was that she couldn't remember what the argument had been about or what had happened. Then she came to live with us, and she said she never wanted Rita's name mentioned again. Anyway, dearie, I am getting rather tired. I think I am ready to watch my Shirley Temple film now, if you don't mind."

"Of course I don't mind," I said. I loaded the DVD into the machine and got the movie running.

"I'm just going to the vending machine," I said to Auntie Ethel, but her attention was firmly on the TV. She barely nodded as I left her room.

***

I went around to the nurses' station, thinking that the supervisor, Mavis, one of Ryan's least favorite people, would be able to tell me where to find Granny Jean. Mavis knew everything and everyone.

I was about to approach the desk when Mr. Thomas, the manager of the retirement home, came out of his office. He was the one responsible for Auntie Ethel having to eat tuna casseroles for weeks on end and wipe her poor bottom with cardboard. I felt a wave of hatred that brought an ugly heat to my face. I quickly pressed my back against the wall so he wouldn't notice me.

"Mavis!" he yelled. "I don't feel good. I'm going home."

Mavis barely looked at him. She nodded and turned to answer the telephone.

I sidled over to Mavis. As I watched Mr. Thomas leave, I saw him drop a small ringed tag with a key attached. I rushed over and picked it up and I was about to call out to him when I changed my mind and I watched him head out.

I turned the key over in my hand. Main Office was neatly written on the label.

I had the key to his office! It occurred to me that I didn't have to ask Mavis anything. I could find what I was looking for in Mr. Thomas's office: the room number to Granny Jean's humble abode and what's more, I could see if I could find any evidence of tuna fish and toilet paper being bought on the cheap.

Mavis slammed the phone down and strode past without noticing me. I seized the moment, unlocked Mr. Thomas' office, and slipped inside, taking the key with me.

The office was neat and uncluttered, except for a large pile of winter coats in the corner. The desk surface was bare except for a calendar, a pot of pens, and a telephone.

I decided that the filing cabinet was the best place to start. I pulled open the top drawer and found it full of computer cables and electrical outlets. The second drawer contained unopened reams of paper. The third was stuffed with old gym clothes that stank of rancid sweat, and I couldn't close it quickly enough. The fourth drawer held a mother lode of treasure. I knelt down, unable to believe my eyes.

There, solidly packing the whole drawer, were bags of weed and bricks of hash.

The soothing fragrance wafted up to greet me and my mouth watered. I froze, at a loss what to do next, when I heard the unmistakable sounds of Mr. Thomas shouting Mavis's name from down the hallway.

I turned and threw myself under the pile of coats, crawling into the center, curling up quickly and lying dead-still.

I heard Mr. Thomas turn the doorknob and rush inside. He headed straight for the bottom drawer of the filing cabinet and pulled it open. He gave a loud sigh of relief when he saw his stash was untouched.

I could hardly breathe. My cave was hot and almost airless, but I couldn't risk moving an inch in case the coats slid off. I wouldn't be able to explain being in his office, not to mention hiding in a huge pile of smelly winter coats. The coats were scratchy in the way an old feather pillow annoys your cheek in the middle of the night and it wasn't long before I was drenched in sweat.

Mr. Thomas closed the filing cabinet drawer, and I heard the squeak and groan of an office chair. Oh God, he was sitting down. Who knew how long he would be?

I heard him pick up the telephone receiver and punch in a number.

"It's me."

There was silence.

"Yeah, well, I wouldn't have called, but I wanted to see if you can come and pick up the stuff tonight."

More silence.

"I know, I know we said the weekend but I'm here now and I just thought..."

Silence.

"Okay, no, don't worry. No, there isn't a problem. We'll stick to the plan."

He put down the phone.

"Mavis!" he yelled. "Get in here."

I heard the sound of Mavis's shoes on the carpet.

"Where are the spare keys to my office?" he asked her, pulling desk drawers open as he spoke.

"At your home," Mavis answered calmly. "You always said it was safer to keep them there."

"Oh, yeah, right." I could feel him thinking, while more sweat pooled in the small of my back.

"You still can't find your keys?" Mavis offered helpfully.

Mr. Thomas snorted. "Wouldn't be asking you if I could, now would I? I'm going home to get my spares. You keep an eye on the office while I'm gone. Think you can manage that?"

"It might just be in my repertoire of manageable responsibilities," Mavis replied, but the sarcasm was lost on Mr. Thomas.

"Good girl. I'll be about an hour."

I heard them both leave and close the door behind them. I didn't want to risk moving until I was certain they were gone, but I finally couldn't stand it any longer and crawled out from under the pile of coats. I gulped in gigantic breaths of precious cool air.

I sat on the carpet, my chest heaving. I was still catching my breath, but I was also furious at Mr. Thomas. How dare he deal drugs on the premises when he was supposed to be looking after my beloved great-aunt?

I had no idea what to do. There was no way I could hustle that many blocks of hash out without anyone seeing me. Besides, was that what I really wanted to do? I didn't want to encourage Ryan to fall deeper into a life of crime; I wanted to steer him away from it. But could I take a brick, just one—you know, just for recreational purposes—and hide it under my sweater? But how would I explain it to Ryan? What about taking one of those big bags of weed? Whatever I was going to do, I'd better do it fast. And what about the real reason I was there—to find out which room Granny Jean was in?

I crawled behind the desk, opened the filing cabinet and lifted out a brick of hash. I stuffed it into the waistband of my jeans and pulled down my T-shirt. I tiptoed over to the door and cracked it open, willing it not to creak or make any kind of noises. I could hear Mavis's voice—she was arguing with sweet old Mr. Arbuthnot, who said that the vending machine had eaten his money yet again.

"You're not supposed to be eating candy after your dinner anyway," she said.

I clearly heard Mr. Arbuthnot's expression of disdain at her comment.

"Why's there a vending machine, then?"

"Like I tell you every time, it's for the visitors."

"I want my money back. Make it give me my money back."

"It probably just needs a good shake. Come on, I'll help you."

This was exactly what I needed to hear. I watched her walk away with Mr. Arbuthnot, and then I quickly slipped out of the room and walked down the hallway away from the direction of the vending machine. My T-shirt was stuck to my back, and my hair was wet with sweat. It suddenly occurred to me that Mr. Thomas would check his stash as soon as he got back, and sure as eggs is eggs, he'd spot the missing brick. I wished I hadn't taken it. I wanted to run back and replace it, but I couldn't risk it. Mavis was sure to return soon, and I was lucky to have gotten out scot-free.

I snuck out a side door and bumped into Granny Mary, leaning on her walker and sucking hard on a fag. She looked startled and guilty.

"Can I have one?" I asked her. She immediately relaxed and dug into her dressing gown.

I drew hard on the cigarette, feeling dizzy but calmer.

"Don't tell Mavis," Granny Mary said. "She thinks I've given them up. What's the point at my age? Take away my one pleasure."

"I won't say a word," I promised. The brick of hash was digging into my stomach. It was hot outside, and I wondered if the drug's pungent fragrance would soon be making it presence felt. I really should have thought things through better.

I took another drag and said goodbye to Granny Mary. I walked around the side of the building, crushed the cigarette and entered the front lobby. I signed myself out, making it look as if I had gone before Mr. Thomas had left for the first time, before he realized he had lost his office key.

I jogged across the garden, and went down to the bus shelter. Catching sight of a pay phone, I decided to call the cops and leave any anonymous message about Mr. Thomas's stash. I dug into my pockets for some spare change, and it was then that I realized what an idiot I had been—my purse was still in Auntie Ethel's room, along with my wallet and my phone and everything. Now I was really stuck. The brick of hash was still stuck to my stomach.

Just then, a bus pulled up, and the doors opened.

"Getting in?" the driver asked me.

I nodded. "If I've got enough money." I pressed the brick against me while I rooted in the pockets of my jeans, coming up with a dollar.

"I'm short," I said to the driver and turned to leave. But he shrugged and motioned me up.

I thanked him and made my way to the back of the bus, sitting down with relief. I looked out the window, gnawing at my lip, not sure what to do.

***

I got home and fortunately my roommate was there to let me in. She wasn't interested in my story of having left my bag at the retirement home. I buried the brick of hash behind some sweaters and searched through all my jackets, looking for spare change. I found $10 in loonies and quarters, all of which weighed a ton, and I threw them into a little beaded cocktail purse I had bought for one of Ryan's fancier gigs.

"I've got to go back and fetch my bag," I told my roommate, who barely shrugged as I left.

***

I took a bus back to the retirement home and stopped at the pay phone I had passed earlier.

I called 911, deepened my voice as much as I could and affected a British accent. I probably sounded really weird.

"You should search the cabinet in Mr. Thomas's office in the retirement home at Benlamond Avenue," I said. "Glenwoods, the retirement home across from the Baptist church, just north of Kingston Road. He's got drugs in there, very bad drugs, and he shouldn't be in charge of looking after our loved ones." I repeated all the details three times and hung up.

I signed in at the visitors' desk. Fortunately for me, there had been a shift change, and I wasn't questioned as to why I was returning after so short a time.

When I opened Auntie Ethel's door, she was fast asleep in her chair, the Shirley Temple movie long since having ended.

Closing the door, I went in search of Mavis and found her on the phone. When she had finished her call, I asked her where I could find Granny Jean.

"Most likely watching TV," she said, pointing to the common room.

"Um, what does she look like?" I asked, knowing the question sounded stupid.

Mavis gave me a funny look. "She's got bright red hair. You can't miss her."

"Thanks."

As I was about to enter the common room, I saw a couple of policemen at the front door, heading for Mavis. I decided that the faster I could engage Granny Jean in chatter, the better.

I spotted her immediately. She was sitting on the saggy brown sofa, staring open-mouthed at the TV channel that was reporting on traffic and weather conditions.

I sat down next to her. "Hi."

She didn't blink or turn to face me.

"Do you want me to change the channel?" I asked.

Again, she didn't move.

I realized I wasn't going to get any help from Granny Jean in solving the mystery of Ryan's found treasure.

***

There was no sign of the policemen on my way back to Auntie Ethel's room, but I could see that Mr. Thomas's office door was open. I assumed the police were inside.

I suddenly froze with fear—what if they found my fingerprints on the cabinet, or on the plastic wrap of the drugs? Once again, I was filled with anger at my own stupidity. And once again, I regretted taking that brick of hash.

I quickly walked back to Auntie Ethel's room and found her awake, getting ready for bed.

"I get so tired these days," she said. "An early night for me, dearie. Thank you for the visit. I always love to see you."

"Let me help you with your nightie," I said, easing it over her head. "Where are your bed socks? We don't want your feet to get cold."

"You're such a good girl." She put one hand on my shoulder. "Tell me, dearie, is everything all right with you?"

"Oh yes," I said. "I've got a boyfriend. I've been meaning to tell you about him, but it's too late now. You must get some sleep, but I'll come back tomorrow and tell you all about him. I know you'll really like him."

I helped her get under the covers.

"I'll like anybody who takes good care of you, dearie."

"Oh, he does," I assured her. "Look what he gave me. Don't get the wrong impression. He doesn't have any money, really, but he said he found this and wanted me to have it."

I dug the watch out of my pocket and Auntie Ethel sat straight up in bed and stared at it as if she had never seen anything that beautiful before. She was speechless.

"I know," I said. "It's so beautiful, isn't it? I wasn't sure if I should keep it, but he said he found it, and I trust him."

"It looks to be a very valuable piece," Auntie Ethel finally said. "I would love to meet your young man, Bethie."

"And you will." I picked up my purse and turned out the light. "Now you sleep tight, and I'll see you tomorrow."

***

I walked past the office, alarmed to see that more police officers had gathered outside. I increased my pace, signed myself out quickly, and once again found myself waiting for the bus.

I dug into my purse, pulled out my cellphone and called Ryan.

"It's me," I said. "Listen, Ry, I've done a bit of a stupid thing but before I tell you anything, I need to know something. Where did you find the watch? I have to know, before I tell you anything."

He sighed. "Remember that gig we did for that rich girl's birthday party? The one where they had that huge tent in the garden, and we were only allowed in the house to use the washroom next to the kitchen?"

"Yes, I remember." It had been one of their best gigs ever. It was during one of our most difficult periods, when I'd been desperately afraid he was going to leave me. It seemed that all we did was argue. And believe me, there was no shortage of gorgeous girls, lining up, showing off their smooth, flat bellies and making eyes at him. He always promised me I was the only one who mattered to him, but how could I be sure? And my mother was right—I *had* gained some weight, eating comfort food because I'd been so miserable. So, yes, I remembered that gig very well.

"The next day," Ryan continued, "I heard something rattling around where I keep my spare strings and my capo and stuff. I opened it up and found the watch."

"Where do you think it came from?"

"No idea. All I know is that I packed my picks and my capo and my strings, and it wasn't there, and then the next day it was. I've been keeping it, to surprise you. First, I wanted to see if anybody reported it, but nobody did. I didn't want to give you something stolen. I even asked a buddy of mine, a PC on the force, to give me the heads-up if he heard that any shit had been stolen. And then I screwed up, and I lost my license. I wanted to make things good with you, since I knew you'd be pissed off, and you were. I gave it to you then."

I was silent.

"I swear to God, Beth, I'm telling you the truth. It's such a lame-assed story. Don't you think if I was going to lie about it, that I would've made up something better?"

He had a point there. He could sense I was relenting.

"Maybe that girl gave it to you," I said, "the birthday girl. Rich like that, maybe she thought it would make you like her."

"Whatever. You know I'm not interested in her. What happened with you? C'mon, tell me."

"I'm at the phone booth, the one at the bottom of Glenwoods. Can you come and get me?"

"Yeah, sure. Oh shit, I can't drive, I keep forgetting. Listen, I'll take a cab, okay? Don't move. Sit tight and wait for me."

I hung up and crouched down to hide under a tree.

While I was waiting for Ryan, more cop cars pulled into the home, their lights flashing with importance.

I felt like I couldn't breathe. Why had I taken that brick, why had I touched the others, and why, oh why, had I called the cops?

After what felt like a decade of waiting, I finally saw Ryan's cab pull up.

I ran up to him and dragged him to sit under the tree with me. Then I told him the whole story.

"You stole a brick?" He sounded amused. "That's righteous, Beth. Listen, don't worry. If the cops find your prints, then just tell them the truth, you were in fuckwit's office trying to find something. Oh shit. What were you trying to find?"

"Evidence he was buying crap toilet paper and cheap tuna fish," I promptly replied. He looked baffled, but nodded.

"Yeah, sure, you were looking for that, and then you found the hash, and you touched it. But you immediately called the cops. Fuckwit isn't likely to count his hash, and who'd believe him anyway? The less there is for the cops find on him, the better for him. It'll lessen his sentence.

Don't even think about it. I know a buddy who'll sell it for us, get us some nice coin."

I suddenly felt hot tears pouring down my cheeks. I wiped my nose on my arm. "Gross. Sorry. I just got such a fright, is all."

He moved closer to me and put his arm around me. "I love you, Beth. Sometimes you drive me nuts, but I love you. I'm doing my best for us. Can you see that?"

"Yes," I said, still crying. "I do. Listen, I want to go and check on Auntie Eth. I kinda just left her."

"I'll wait here," Ryan said. "I'm not on the roster, and I don't want anyone wondering why I'm there."

"Keep this," I thrust my purse at him. "I won't be long."

***

I walked up the long green lawn and entered the building. The cops were now clustered around the coffee machine, joking with each other.

"Excuse me, miss," one of them called out. "Can we help you?"

"It was my great-auntie Ethel's 94th birthday today," I said, "and I forgot something in her room when I left. I won't be long. Why are you all here?"

"Someone reported an incident," the constable said.

"Everyone okay?" I thought it best to act surprised and curious.

"Everyone's fine," the constable said. "I'll let you go, then."

I smiled, hoping he wouldn't wonder about my teary, swollen face.

I got to Auntie Eth's room and opened the door quietly.

The room was dark, and I crept in. I knew every inch of it intimately. Auntie Ethel was right when she told my mother I visited often. I did.

I crept closer to the bed and saw that she was fast asleep, with one hand on the coverlet, close to her face. Her breathing was shallow but even, and her mouth was slightly open.

I patted her warm back, but lightly. I didn't want to wake her.

"I love you," I whispered. Then I crept back out, as quietly as I had come.

***

Of course, I had no way of knowing that Auntie Ethel opened her eyes as soon as I had left the room. She hadn't been asleep at all.

She had been lying there, wide awake, filled with sadness, wondering why I had stolen the watch from her, when she had planned to give it to me along with all of Beatrice Anne's jewelry.

She knew I wasn't feigning ignorance about not knowing where the watch had come from—she had shown it to me only one time when I was very young. But, true to my style, when I was having one of those "moments," I had no recollection of ever having seen it.

She wondered what was troubling me, because I only ever suffered my thieving fugues when I was stressed or worried about something. I stole when anxious or upset then I'd deliver my offerings to whoever was causing my distress, while having no memory of the theft or the gift giving. Then I'd have to suffer the confusion and embarrassment of trying to explain to both parties what had happened.

Auntie Ethel thought about Ryan, that beautiful chaotic boy, and figured he must be the reason for my current agitation. She had no proof but she was sure he was the new boyfriend I had referred to. Even at a glance, she could see that Ryan was unreliable at best.

She knew that she would be leaving the world soon, and that there was nothing she could do to help me. There was no point in talking to my mother; my episodes had always made her angry, as if they were something I was doing on purpose to punish her.

With no solution at hand, Auntie Ethel lay awake all night, thinking and worrying.

The worst of it was that she blamed herself. If she hadn't stolen the watch from Rita all those years ago, that terrible argument would never have happened. Now I had to live with inheriting the worst of the family madness.

Ethel had taken the watch, Rita's prized possession, on a whim on one of her visits when she found it dropped close to the floorboards the morning after a particularly harrowing ghostly evening. Ethel was going to give it back to Rita, who was still shaken from Beatrice Anne's antics the previous night. Instead, she quickly slipped it into her pocket, hardly aware of what she was doing, driven by compulsion and craven need.

It was all Ed's fault. He had been stepping out on her, she knew he had. He was kind and generous to a fault, but he was not the faithful sort. She had been convinced that he was going to leave her, and he was all she had.

So she pocketed the watch. When she got home, she dropped it into Ed's desk drawer and the incident faded from her memory entirely. She didn't recall that she had taken it even when Rita and Beatrice Anne had their violent falling-out. Her memory was jogged only when she was cleaning out Ed's things after his fatal heart attack.

She had stared at the watch in horror, seeing, in her mind's eye, her quick magpie stoop to grab it up and whisk it away. She felt shame and humiliation about what she had done.

Too late. Too late to make it right between Rita and Beatrice Anne. Now, too late to help me.

Her fault. Her bad blood flowed through my veins, blood tainted by weakness and fear. It was all her fault, and she couldn't think of a way to make it right.

About Lisa de Nikolits

Photo Credit: Bradford Dunlop

Lisa de Nikolits is the award-winning author of four published novels: *The Hungry Mirror*, *West of Wawa*, *A Glittering Chaos* and the *Witchdoctor's Bones*. Her fifth novel, *Between The Cracks She Fell* was launched in Fall 2015. All Inanna titles.

Lisa also has a short story in *Postscripts To Darkness, Volume 6*, and she is delighted to be in *13 O'Clock* by the Mesdames of Mayhem (Carrick Publishing, 2015). She has also been featured on online short story, flash fiction and poetry sites.

lisadenikolitswriter.com
Amazon Author Page
Facebook
Twitter
Mesdames of Mayhem

NICK OF TIME

By Rosemary McCracken

Tierney Pratt Financial's holiday luncheon is always a big hit with our clients. Not even a snowstorm, like the wicked one we had last December, keeps them away. Two days after that blizzard, everyone on our guest list turned up at the York Club dressed to the nines and primed for a good time.

We spent an hour chatting over cocktails. When lunch was announced, I waited until all our guests had gone up to the buffet. Then I filled a plate for myself and took a seat beside Roger Durrell, an elderly client of Stéphane Pratt, my business partner. Roger and I had exchanged pleasantries at the office and at other social events, but we'd never spoken at length.

"What a pleasure," he said. "I'm dining with the best-looking woman in the room."

Flattery makes me uneasy. Still, I was glad I'd had my blond hair styled that morning and I was wearing my smart new Suzy Fong number.

Roger sported a jaunty Christmas bow tie so I asked if he was all ready for the holiday season.

"I am," he said, "but it will be different this year. My first Christmas without Emma in nearly 50 years."

With a jolt, I remembered that his wife had passed away a few weeks before. Stéphane and I try to mark all the important events in our clients' lives—weddings, the births of children and grandchildren, christenings and bar mitzvahs. When one of our clients loses a spouse, we send flowers and try to attend the funeral or memorial service. But when Emma Durrell died in mid-November I was on vacation with my Mr. Right Now.

"I'm so sorry for your loss," I told Roger. "I was away when your wife died or I would have been at the funeral."

"Emma tried to kill me."

I was shocked, and he clearly read it on my face. "She suffered from dementia," he said, placing a hand on my arm. "I kept her at home as long as I could, but she no longer recognized me. One day she came up behind me holding a carving knife. I locked myself in the bathroom and called our niece on my cell."

He held out his hands in a gesture of helplessness. "I had to put Emma in a home."

There were tears in his eyes.

***

After our guests had left, Stéphane and I repaired to the bar. We ordered a bottle of wine and recapped the party's highlights.

"Another triumph, boss lady!" He clinked his glass against mine.

"It was a good party." Then I told him what Roger had said about his wife.

Stéphane ran a hand through his spikey hair, making the platinum highlights sparkle in the light. "It's always difficult when one spouse has to place the other into care."

"It's also difficult knowing your spouse tried to kill you. Roger has to live with that for the rest of his life." His story had hit me hard.

Stéphane took a sip of wine. "Emma was incapacitated for some time before she went into the nursing home. When I visited the Durrells last summer, she couldn't follow the conversation. She got progressively worse."

"She must've been pretty confused if she tried to stab Roger," I said.

"She probably thought he was someone else."

The Durrells became Stéphane's clients shortly after he joined my practice five years ago. "Roger and Emma had separate investment accounts," I said.

"Oh, yes." Stéphane grinned. "Emma had family money. She was Charles Turner's daughter."

Toronto's Turner Centre for the Arts was named after Charles Turner, the wealthy industrialist. Emma must have come into a considerable sum after he died.

"Her estate won't be settled for months," I said.

"*C'est vrai.* The will is still awaiting probate."

I nodded. Probate, the process of having the courts rule that a will is valid, is just the first step in settling an estate. After that, its executor will usually spend another year completing forms, writing letters and paying debts before receiving a tax clearance from the government. Estates are time-consuming to settle, and the estate of a wealthy woman like Emma Durrell would involve considerable work.

"Who's the executor?" I asked.

"Emma's lawyer, Brian Shapiro. Her beneficiaries are Roger, of course, who gets the family home and three-quarters of her financial assets. The other quarter is divided among four charities."

"No children?"

"No. There's a niece but she wasn't named in the will. Roger gave her Emma's jewelry. He said she was helpful when Emma's health declined."

"The niece is…?"

"Nadine Turner, daughter of Emma's younger brother."

"How's Roger doing now?"

"He's looking forward to some travel this winter."

***

Mr. Right Now comes to Toronto every few weeks on business. On his visit the following week, Devon Shaughnessy and I were in festive holiday spirits, and we dined out every evening. On his last night in town, I took him to Neptune, the fish eatery in the theatre district that the restaurant reviewers were raving about. My lobster bisque and Dover sole were every bit as delicious as they'd reported.

While we waited for our dessert, I excused myself to visit the ladies' room. On my way back to our table, I spotted a familiar face. Roger Durrell's. He was dining with an attractive redhead in her late thirties. A good 10 years younger than me.

I pulled up at their table. "Hello, Roger."

"Why hello, Pat." He turned to his companion. "Pat Tierney is the Tierney in Tierney Pratt Financial. Pat, this is Julie Harrison."

Julie and I bobbed our heads.

"Julie and I are flying down to Florida on Boxing Day," Roger said. "A charming little resort in the Keys."

Julie put her hand on his and smiled.

I wished them a great holiday and made my way back to Devon.

"Good for Roger," Devon said when I'd filled him in on Roger and Emma, and on Roger's vacation with the redhead. "He's making up for lost time."

I rolled my eyes. Men!

***

On our coffee break the next morning, I told Stéphane about Roger's upcoming holiday. He cocked an eyebrow and sat down across from me at the kitchenette table.

"Roger's had a difficult year," he said. "He needs a vacation."

"His wife died less than a month ago."

He leaned back and laced his hands behind his head. "Roger just received a $100,000 payout from Emma's life insurance policy. He'll have to wait a few more months until Shapiro can make an interim distribution."

A hundred grand would cover his vacation with Julie—and more.

Stéphane grew thoughtful. "Roger thought he'd have control of Emma's money when she became ill, but she'd restricted his authority to her personal care. Not her finances."

I was surprised Roger hadn't known that his wife had given him authority over her care but not her money. But it happens. Emma had drawn up the power-of-attorney documents with Brian Shapiro and left them with him. Stéphane had asked for copies when he started managing Emma's money.

"I let him know exactly what powers he had and what he hadn't." He shrugged. "The Durrells lived on Emma's money, and she kept a tight rein on it even after she was incapacitated. She gave directions that, during her lifetime, her money would maintain the family home and pay for her care. Roger received a modest allowance."

"How modest?" I couldn't help but ask.

"Twenty-five grand a year." Enough, but not a lot.

"What line of work was Roger in?"

"He did a bit of this and a bit of that over the years. Tried to start a business at one point but it never got off the ground."

"He must've felt pussy-whipped," I said.

Stéphane tried to suppress a smile.

"How much does he come in for down the road?"

He named a seven-figure sum.

I whistled. "Roger's about to have a whole lot of fun!"

***

Three days into the New Year, Nadine Turner visited our offices. From my office, I heard her introduce herself to Rose, our administrative assistant, and ask for Stéphane.

I came out of my office. Nadine was a knockout. Chestnut-brown hair swept into a chignon, high cheekbones, emerald eyes and a good figure displayed to advantage in a well-cut pantsuit. I put her age at 35.

"Stéphane will be back on the tenth," I said. "In the meantime, can I help you? I'm Pat Tierney, his partner."

She looked at me appraisingly. "Maybe you can."

"Your uncle must be in Florida now," I said when we were seated in my office.

The smile fell off her face. "Roger couldn't wait to get his hands on my aunt's money. The house in Rosedale, the expensive cars, the trips—Emma paid for it all. Now she's gone, he's living it up with a woman young enough to be his daughter."

I waited but I knew where she was headed.

She turned sorrowful eyes on me. "I hadn't heard anything about Emma's will so I contacted Stéphane. He told me to speak to Brian Shapiro, my aunt's executor. Shapiro said Emma hadn't included me in her will. He wouldn't even give me a copy."

She took a tissue from her handbag and dabbed at her eyes. "My mother died when I was seven, and Emma and I became very close. She wanted to see me provided for. She told me she was leaving me half of her money."

Emma had raised Nadine's hopes and let her down—big-time.

"I understand Roger gave you her jewelry."

She gave a little snort. "Most of it was costume stuff, except for a pearl necklace and a couple of rings with small stones."

She sat up straight in the chair. "I can't believe my aunt wouldn't honor her promise. I'd like to see her will."

Brian had sent Stéphane a copy of Emma's will. It was in our office safe.

"Right now, Mr. Shapiro is the only person authorized to show you the will," I told her. "But as soon as it is probated, it becomes a public court record and you can apply for a copy. You may want to have an estate lawyer make the request."

"I can't afford a lawyer."

I thought of the Turner family money. Nadine's father would have inherited some of it.

She pulled her chair closer to my desk. "Emma wrote that will when she was no longer herself." Her voice took on a hard edge. "Roger made her do it."

***

As soon as Nadine left, I telephoned Brian Shapiro. He acted for several of our clients, and I'd worked with him on a number of occasions. "Poor girl," he said after I told him about Nadine's visit. "Her life hasn't turned out as it should've."

"There's the family money."

"Her dad lost his shirt when TeleWorld tanked."

At its height, the telecommunications giant's market cap accounted for a third of the entire value of the Toronto Stock Exchange. When its stock crashed, it took a wide swath of investors and pension funds with it. Not even the wealthy and privileged like the Turners are immune to the fallout from corruption and bad management.

"Then he killed himself," Brian added.

I took a few moments to digest that. Nadine had been a teenager when her father took his life. Couldn't have been easy for her.

"Does Nadine work?" I asked.

"Went to all the right schools, then got a university degree in something like art history. Wouldn't give her the lifestyle she wanted."

"How does she support herself?"

"Last I heard, she had a clerical job at a film studio."

She really had been counting on money from her aunt.

"Emma Durrell didn't leave her niece a dime," Brian said. "Nadine can complain all she likes but there's not a damn thing she can do about it."

***

It was a quiet day, with many of our clients still on vacation. I prepped for a client meeting the next morning, but my thoughts kept returning to Nadine. And to Roger in Florida with a younger woman. I wasn't surprised when Rose buzzed me saying he was on the line.

"You're back home," I said to him.

"Got in yesterday. The weather was on the cool side, but the food was excellent. That's what Emma liked about that resort."

"Stéphane is away this week."

"Your receptionist told me that," he said, "but I'm sure you can help me."

Stéphane had sent Roger an email asking him to sign a form that is now required under Canada's anti-spam legislation. We need written approval from our clients to contact them online. It's meant to crack down on unwanted email, but as far as I'm concerned it's just more red tape to deal with.

"He told me to sign and date the form, then scan it and email it back to him," Roger said. "I have no idea what 'scanning' means."

"I'll bring the form over and you can sign it." I figured that would be easier for both of us.

"It's not too much trouble?" he asked.

"No trouble at all. I'll come by around five thirty."

***

The curtains on Roger's red-brick home were drawn when I pulled up across the street. There were no vehicles in the driveway.

"No one's home," Devon said.

"There's a lamp on in the front room. See the sliver of light between the curtains? The car is probably in the garage."

I grabbed my leather case, then reached over and touched Devon's silver head. "Won't be long. I've been looking forward to dinner at Penelope's all day." The Greek restaurant on King Street was one of our favorites.

I rapped the brass knocker on the front door. When no one answered, I grasped the door knob and turned it. The door opened.

The hall was in shadows, illuminated only by lights in the two rooms on either side of it. "Roger!" I called. "It's Pat Tierney."

Silence greeted me.

"Roger?" I called again. "Are you here?"

From where I stood, I could see that no one was in the living room to my left. I approached the other room.

A long mahogany table stood in its centre. Roger was seated at its head, tied to the back of his chair, a gag in his mouth. Nadine stood over him, holding a sharp kitchen knife inches from his throat.

His eyes spoke volumes—terror, bewilderment, pleading for help.

Nadine turned her head to face me, her wavy chestnut hair tumbling around her shoulders. "Pat Tierney, the perfect financial advisor." She sneered. "Nothing you wouldn't do for a wealthy client, is there?"

"Put the knife down," I said.

"Sit. And put your case on the table." She moved the blade closer to Roger's throat.

Without taking my eyes off her, I sat and set my case in front of me. Nadine flung it into a corner of the room where it landed with a thud. She sat down across from me, the knife still in her hand. At least it was farther away from Roger's throat.

I needed to get her talking. Maybe Devon would realize something was wrong. "What did you do to Emma?"

"Why should I tell you?"

"You gave it a lot of thought. Not everyone would have planned it as well."

She laughed. "It's not over because you turned up." She held up the knife.

"What gave you the idea?" I asked.

"My aunt was in the early stages of dementia. She was taking Extra Strength Tylenol for her arthritis so I started slipping her more."

"The extra dose really slowed her down," I said.

"Put her in a world of her own but it didn't kill her. She was a tough old bird."

"Smart. You didn't want to introduce another compound that could be identified in an autopsy."

Nadine eyed me warily. "A little more in her system would look like an accident."

"Extra Strength Tylenol is sold over the counter in Canada. Very convenient," I said.

She smiled. "I didn't have to worry about prescriptions."

"You couldn't visit Emma every day, and she was less confused when she didn't have that extra dose. On one of those days, she tried to stab Roger. How did you turn her against him?"

"A few hints here and there."

"But your plan backfired when he placed her in a home."

Nadine's green eyes blazed. "The one Roger insisted on cost a fortune."

"It would eat into the inheritance you thought you'd get," I said. "Something had to be done."

"I visited her with more Tylenol, but she kept hanging on. One day, I'd had enough. I held a pillow over her face."

She had the grace to lower her eyes for a few moments. "Roger called that evening to say she'd died in her sleep."

Roger's face had turned an unhealthy shade of red.

I heard a sound in the room behind us. Julie Harrison appeared in the doorway, carrying two bottles of wine. "My God!" she cried when she saw me. "How did you get here?"

"You didn't lock the front door," Nadine said.

"This wasn't part of the plan," Julie said to Nadine. "What'll we do about her?"

"Calm down, babe, and pour us a glass of wine. Then you can tie her up. Later she'll meet with an unfortunate…accident."

Julie went over to the sideboard and uncorked one of the bottles.

"Julie was on assignment in Florida for the past week," Nadine said. "Serving Tylenol cocktails."

"You're taking Tylenol?" I asked Roger.

He nodded and glared at Julie.

"Roger wasn't easy to work with," Julie said. "He's a health nut. Watches everything he eats and drinks. I only managed to slip him some powder twice."

She placed a glass of wine in front of Nadine. "I'll get more cord downstairs," she said and left the room.

Nadine turned to Roger. "Your time has run out, old man. Once we take care of Pat, you'll write a new will that leaves everything to me. Only fair because you swindled me out of my family's money."

She took a sip of wine and turned back to Roger with a smile. "You'll handwrite your new will, Roger. Holograph wills don't need to be witnessed. Then Julie and I will decide what we'll do with you."

Roger gave a roar that blew the gag out of his mouth. "Snake!" he cried. "We put you through school after your father lost his money. We bought you your condo."

In the middle of Roger's outburst, Julie returned with several lengths of cord.

"Take the knife, Julie, while I put a sock in his mouth." Nadine handed her the knife.

Rapping sounded on the front door. Julie glanced in that direction and I saw my chance. I sprang from the chair and head-butted her. She stumbled and dropped the knife. I ran to the door and unlocked it.

Julie leaped on my back as the door swung open and Devon stepped in. I fell backwards, landing on the floor on top of her.

"Thank God you're here, Devon!" I said as I scrambled to my feet.

"I'll say!" Roger said.

Nadine had the knife. She glared at me and crouched, poised to attack.

I picked up the glass Julie had given her and threw the wine in her face. She yelped and dropped the knife on the floor. I lunged for it, seizing its handle. Nadine threw herself on me and reached for my hand.

"No!" Devon pulled her off me. He dragged her, arms and legs flailing, to a chair.

"Sit still, Nadine." I held up the knife.

She eyed it and stopped squirming. I held it to her throat while Devon tied her wrists behind her.

"Watch out!" Roger shouted.

We swung around to see Julie wielding a large crystal candlestick. Devon knocked it from her hand. He grabbed one of her arms and edged behind her to get her other arm. She elbowed him in the stomach. When he fell back, she bolted out of the house.

Devon bound Nadine's torso to the chair. I untied Roger.

"You got here in the nick of time, Pat," Roger said, flexing his hands. "You and your friend saved my life."

He turned to Nadine. "It was Emma's decision to leave you out of her will. She said it was time you stood on your own two feet."

He motioned for me to come closer. "Pat, would you go the room across the hall? There's a manila envelope in the top drawer of the desk."

When I brought him the envelope, he took out a document and turned to its last page. "Take a look." He held it out to Nadine. "Emma's will is dated three years ago when she was sound of mind."

Nadine looked at it, then turned her head away.

Roger folded the document and put it back in the envelope. "You said time had run out. You were right, my dear, it has." He smiled. "For you."

About Rosemary McCracken

Toronto journalist Rosemary McCracken writes the Pat Tierney mystery series. *Safe Harbor*, the first novel in the series, was shortlisted for Britain's Debut Dagger Award in 2010. It was published by Imajin Books in 2012, followed by *Black Water* in 2013.

"The Sweetheart Scamster," a Pat Tierney short story in the crime fiction anthology, *Thirteen*, (Carrick Publishing) was a finalist for a 2014 Derringer Award. A second Pat Tierney short story appeared in *World Enough and Crime* (Carrick Publishing 2014).

Jack Batten, *The Toronto Star*'s crime fiction reviewer, calls Pat "a hugely attractive sleuth figure."

http://www.rosemarymccracken.com/
http://rosemarymccracken.wordpress.com/
Amazon Author Page
Facebook
Mesdames of Mayhem

LIFE IS A BIG HEADACHE

By Sylvia Maultash Warsh

At my age, I know more people that are dead than alive. These days, when someone dies, I find myself reliving scenes from the past, and if I'm lucky I picture that person sitting at my kitchen table *kibitzing*. If I'm not so lucky, I only remember the last goodbye, a pale corpse lying in a hospital bed, the person I loved gone, gone. This is what I remember of my *Mameh* and *Tateh* (may they rest in peace), because I was there when they breathed their last, and the image will be printed in my brain till I go to my own grave.

You would think this is bad enough, but *now!* If you live long enough, you see everything. How will I get the picture of Abe's poor cold body out of my skull? You can't understand unless I describe what happened.

It was a Thursday. I drove to the Dominion store to do my grocery shopping. *Mameh* used to cook on Fridays for the Sabbath so I keep the schedule but I make enough for most of the week. She would roll over in her grave that I don't light candles on *Shabbos* anymore. Just for me, what's the point? The sun will set without my help.

At least my days at the factory are over. I retired from sewing piecework on the machine five years ago this month, May 1979. I could sew a zipper into a pair of pants with my eyes closed. *Mameh* used to say I had "*goldene* hands"—I made her a few dresses in my day. But I can also change the oil in my Grand Am. I love cars. I'm not what you would call your typical little old Jewish lady. First, I'm too big. I was taller even than my brother, Saul, may he rest in peace. He used to joke there was Cossack blood in me. I shrank a bit, after 70 years, but I'm still too tall for ladies' wear departments. No matter, I sew my own clothes. Also, I can fix anything in the house, including the toilet. How many little old Jewish ladies can do that?

So, back to the story. I parked the car and *schlepped* my groceries through the back door. Inside, I climbed the few back stairs to the first floor, when I remembered I should check for the mail. I walked toward the front staircase. Then I saw him. My heart jumped into my mouth! Abe was lying there upside down at the bottom of the stairs. I screamed, "Abe!" But it echoed in the empty building—nobody was home. He lay sprawled headfirst, one foot on the step above pointing up.

I bent over him to take his pulse—stupid, because I knew he was dead, his skin gray and clammy. I ran upstairs to my apartment to call 911. At the same time, I called Danny. I couldn't tell him what happened; I just said, "Come home, it's your father," and hung up.

You don't stop loving a man after 40 years, even if you can't live with him. While I waited for the ambulance, I stroked his gray hair like he could feel it. What a handsome man he used to be. I could barely look at his twisted body, his mouth hanging open. I took his hand, but somehow I couldn't cry. Maybe it was the shock, but it felt like I was in a movie. This wasn't Abe but some actor—Walter Matthau—and he wasn't really dead.

Though Abe is my ex, I delivered brisket and *cholent* on Friday afternoons that he could eat for a week. He also lived free in the basement of the sixplex which my *Tateh* bought in 1955. Abe's the father of my only son—I should kick him out? Even if he didn't contribute his share of the gas and power? He didn't have money left over after the liquor store and the racetrack. Old Age Security only goes so far. And how much could he make at the flea market on weekends? He used to have a storefront to try to sell all the *dreck* he bought, but he barely scraped by. After we divorced, he let the store go and made house calls to fix people's televisions. At this he was good, and in those days people kept their TVs longer.

Then he started losing at cards and at the track. The first few years when he tried to win me back, he told me I was his luck. With this he thought to persuade me. He repeated what my *Tateh* used to say: "Luck is like a string of pearls—if one breaks, all scatter." But I was tired of his failures. If I wasn't luck for him before, what would change? I told him he was the opposite for me. Bad luck. Finally, he saw I meant it and left me alone.

I'm okay for money because long ago I opened a secret bank account when I saw how the money flowed from his hands. And of course I get rent from the three apartments left. I'm not greedy. I let Abe have the studio in the basement and Danny the apartment on the second floor across from mine. I should ask rent from my own son? He doesn't make much as a book editor. At least he doesn't drink or play the ponies. I don't understand from editing, but it must be important because he meets writers. My Danny is the first in the family to go to university, so I'm proud.

***

First came the firemen, then the ambulance. Both asked the same question: "What happened?"

I told them, "I wasn't here. I just found him like that."

Then the police came and asked more questions. "When was the last time you saw your husband alive, Mrs. Rosenthal?"

"Ex-husband. Last Friday."

The constable looked up from his notebook. "You live in the same building and you didn't see him for a week?"

"Young man, how often do you see your neighbors? He went his way, and I went mine."

He stifled a smile. I didn't tell him that apart from delivering food, I avoided Abe because it hurt seeing him, remembering what we had once and why we didn't have it anymore. I never figured out what he was trying to wipe away by drinking. Himself, maybe. What he saw in the war when he was overseas. Such a long time ago.

It wasn't hard to avoid him because I liked nine-to-five, and he was a night owl. I would just turn on the TV after supper—*Miami Vice* or *The A-Team*—when I heard the outside door. Sometimes I looked out the living room window to see him walking to the bus stop. I'm not stupid—I know he avoided me, too. He had the good sense to feel guilty.

The constable went on. "What do you think happened?"

All the while Abe lay there, one foot sticking up, waiting for the medical examiner. I turned so I shouldn't have to see him.

"I'm sorry to say this, but Abe was a drinker. He probably lost his balance and fell."

He nodded, kept scribbling in his notebook. "Was he depressed?

I gave him the fish-eye. "You mean did he throw himself down the stairs? No!"

"Did he have health problems?"

"At 73, everyone has health problems." I kept my tongue and didn't say that his insides were probably pickled from the years of booze.

Danny rushed in. When he saw his father lying there, he turned white. He took a step toward the body, but stopped, his hand flying to his mouth. A cry strangled in his throat. Then he turned to me, buried his face in my neck and sobbed. I love my Danny, but it was embarrassing. They don't make them like they used to. All my life I wanted someone to lean on. People take one look at me and assume I am self-sufficient. But in this respect, I'm like everyone else. When I was young, I thought Abe would take care of me. But him I couldn't trust, never mind lean on. Now my son was crying like a girl.

Finally the medical examiner, a thin bald doctor, arrived. I felt better after he explained that by law he had to come out where someone died at home. So he wasn't there because the young *pisher* policeman thought I pushed Abe down the stairs.

The doctor asked me questions about Abe's health: Did he have high blood pressure? (Yes) Did he have trouble with his balance? (Only when he drank) and so on. He wrote down my answers in his little book. He crouched over Abe, listened to his chest with a stethoscope, lifted up his eyelids. He wasn't going to take the firemen's word that Abe was dead. He went to the top of the stairs, looked around, scribbled some more.

"Did he ever have a stroke?"

"No."

"It's possible he had one before falling down the stairs. An autopsy will tell."

I panicked. "No! Please! Don't cut him up. We're Jews. We don't cut our people up."

He looked up from his little book. "Do you have any reason to believe this was not an accident?"

"You mean did someone kill him?"

He waited. "If there are any suspicions, we'll have to do an autopsy."

"No," I said, trying to talk calm. "It was an accident, this I am sure. Only let me bury him."

He gave the okay and the ambulance boys lifted Abe onto the stretcher. (Under 40, they all look like boys.) Before they could pull the cover over him, I put up my hand.

"Please," I said. "A minute."

Next time we saw him he'd be in a coffin. Danny kissed him goodbye on the forehead. I bent down to his cheek one last time. That's when it hit me. No smell! His mouth was open and I should've smelled booze. I stared at his face like he would wake up and tell me something. If he wasn't drunk, maybe the doctor was right and he had a stroke. It was possible. So why didn't I believe it?

***

The police finally let the tenants into the building. The Babcocks from one first floor apartment, then Mr. MacPherson from the other one, crept in the front door like a baby was sleeping. Mr. and Mrs. Babcock, young, well-groomed—how much water they used in the shower!—ran a shoe store in a fancy shopping mall. Mr. MacPherson, a bachelor in his 50s, taught shop at a high school and sold insurance on the side. His cheeks were always reddish, like he stood out in the wind too long. His sports jackets hung lopsided.

"I'm so sorry," he said, taking my hand.

I stood in the hall aimless, still thinking about Abe and why he smelled like nothing.

"Are you all right?" Mr. MacPherson said, his black shaggy eyebrows pointed together.

"Thank you," I said.

But my head was somewhere else. There was another problem. Why was Abe on the second floor anyway? He avoided me like the plague. If there was an emergency in the apartment, he called Danny.

"Mrs. Rosenthal?"

"Mr. MacPherson." I was getting a bad feeling about Abe. He was sober and he was on the wrong floor, stroke or no stroke. Could've been a robbery? He had no money for someone to come in and steal. Maybe that was it. He owed some bookie money. They came to collect and he ran up the stairs to me like I could help. He must've been desperate...

"Please, call me Mac."

The man said this every time I spoke to him.

"Let me take you up to your apartment," he said.

I looked over to where Danny was talking to Robert, the other tenant in the basement. Always neatly dressed in the most up-to-date clothes, this Robert. He said he was a student, but if you asked me, he was long in the tooth for books.

Mr. MacPherson picked up my bags with one hand. With the other, he took my arm, like I was made of china, and escorted me up the stairs, past where Abe lay broken an hour ago.

***

That night, Danny and I sat together in the living room like two stupids, staring at the TV with the sound off.

He wasn't usually home in the evening—why should he be, a handsome 36-year-old bachelor?—so I didn't often have the pleasure of his company. But I was relieved when finally he got up, tears in his eyes, and kissed me good-night.

I turned the sound on for the late news, but somehow I couldn't listen. Pierre Trudeau opened his mouth, then Ronald Reagan, but the words flew away. The clock ticked. I sat. No point going to bed. I couldn't sleep.

I opened the door to my apartment and listened. Nothing. Everyone was in bed. I crept down the stairs like a burglar to the basement, then along the hall to Abe's door. All these years I delivered him food, I never went inside. He would stand in the doorway, sheepishly holding the pot or the pan, thank me, invite me in. I always refused and hurried back upstairs, glad to escape.

Now I unlocked the door with my key and went in. (So what? I'm the landlady, I got keys to all the doors.)

When I turned on the light, I grabbed for my chest, I shouldn't have a heart attack. *Oy*, what a horrible little room he had! How could I forget? The old brown couch pulled out into a bed, but I could see from the pillows he didn't bother and slept on it like it was. Some cupboards for a kitchen, a tiny fridge, a hot plate. A toilet with a bath, you could hardly turn around. Empty whiskey bottles here and there. If the place wasn't small enough, boxes sat in every corner. I knew what they were. Job lots—a store cancelled an order, so Abe bought the goods in bulk, cheap. Dresses the wrong color. Phones out of style. Only he couldn't always sell. Always the impulse to buy, but the luck to sell? *Feh*.

I should've given him one of the regular apartments. Would've been a few dollars less in my pocket. So why didn't I? It was hard to admit, even to myself, but I was punishing him—he destroyed all the dreams I had for us. I remember when he used to call me his queen, because my name is Regina. In his mouth, "Reggie" was sweet like honey. So what happened? Life. Only after 20 years did I give up on him. And yet, it wouldn't have killed me, once we were old, to be kinder.

I sat down on the couch, miserable, catching a whiff of his sweat, not unpleasant. On the coffee table sat a bottle that could've been soda, only it was green. FreshBios. The label listed the ingredients: spinach, aloe, green tea and vitamins. He suddenly tried to be healthy? Also on the table, racing sheets with horses' names circled. He never changed. What money he didn't drink away, he threw at the horses with both hands. *Ach!* Now that he's dead, don't think bad thoughts.

I got up and walked to the medicine cabinet with its cloudy mirror. For 70 I wasn't so bad. Wavy hair, still brown (once a month I touched up with a kit). All my own teeth. Still vain enough to pencil in eyebrows.

Nosy, I opened the cabinet. So many pills. Some I was taking too. For blood pressure; cholesterol; attacks of nerves. Here was one I didn't know he was taking. Digitalis. *Mameh* used to take it for her heart. Maybe it *was* his time. My *Tateh* used to say, "If one is fated to drown, a spoonful of water will do." But Abe had more than a spoonful of water. No! It wasn't fate! He should've lived longer. Maybe he fell, but maybe he didn't. And he was trying to come to me for help.

I closed the cabinet and saw myself again. Stupid old cow! If I didn't do something, who else was going to care?

***

The next morning, I called the number on the card the *pisher* constable gave me.

"I was just going to call to give you the all clear, Mrs. Rosenthal. The medical examiner determined your husband's death was an accident, so they'll release the body today. You can make arrangements for the funeral."

I was stunned. "Not so fast, Mr. Policeman. It's a mistake! He was on the wrong floor. He wouldn't go up to the second floor so he shouldn't see me."

"Maybe he went to see your son."

"He knew Danny would be at work."

There was a pause you could drive a truck through.

"The M.E. said your husband—"

"Ex-husband."

"—probably had a stroke. It's always hard to let go..."

"I let go a long time ago. But it's not right. What if he didn't fall? What if someone pushed him?"

"I know it's a shock, Mrs. Rosenthal. It's normal to be...Is there someone you can talk to, a friend? A clergyman?"

"I'll talk to a stone," I said and hung up.

***

The funeral was on Sunday at the graveside. I still had no tears. Why couldn't I cry? The rabbi from the funeral home recited the prayers for the dead. Danny said the mourner's *Kaddish* for his father. Since we were divorced, I wasn't expected to mourn. So why this weight on my chest?

Only a small group stood near the grave on the cloudy May day: the tenants from the building; my widowed cousin, Lola, who I saw once or twice a year, and her daughter; Mr. Sullivan, Abe's partner from the flea market, and Seymour, who helped out; some of Abe's old poker buddies; and two people from Danny's office. I invited them all back to the apartment for tea. I wasn't going to sit *shiva* for a week for an ex-husband, but one day I could spare to remember him.

Lola's daughter, Marsha, stood talking to Danny in my living room. I could see from the way she looked at him that she liked him. They weren't first cousins, and I would be thrilled if Danny would finally settle down. But he was very picky, and whenever I asked, he would say the right one didn't come along yet. He didn't have that look in his eye for Marsha.

Danny excused himself from the cousins and brought me over to his boss, Mr. Dufour, a skinny man in his 60s with long hair like a hippie. Beside him was Paula, a plain girl of 30 with bad teeth, who, Danny said, was the publicist, whatever that meant.

We stood around saying not much, so I was relieved when Mr. Sullivan approached—a tall man, maybe 50, with big shoulders like he could carry you. When he smiled, his cheeks rose up like a devilish squirrel, so cute I wanted to pinch them. Behind him followed Seymour, closer to my age, short and pudgy.

"Thank you for coming, Mr. Sullivan."

"Dear lady, just call me Paddy. I was gobsmacked when I heard about Abe! He was like a father to me, he was."

"He could find the best goods," Seymour said. "He knew people."

Sure he knew people. Guys who called him when shipments "fell off a truck." He had a busy circle of such acquaintances, even when we were together. The garage, like the living room, used to be filled with boxes of unpredictable goods: reading glasses, kitchen gadgets, speakers.

"You should come out to the stand, Mrs. Rosenthal," Seymour said. "Shouldn't she, Paddy? Abe had some nice pieces of china. Some crystal. He would've liked you to have them."

Paddy smiled, again the cheeks puffing out, this time eyes watery with tears. "Of course, of course. Sure you're always welcome."

"I don't really need anything," I said.

"This isn't *need*, Mrs. Rosenthal," Paddy said. "By golly, they're yours, anything you like. We'd be mighty honored with your presence. Sure it'll be a fine day when you come."

His voice sang with some leftover Irish accent. The ends of his sentences stayed high, with a bit of breath at the end. Like he had more to say, but was too polite to say it.

He went on. "Abe knew how to pick them. Yourself included. Oh, but you're grand!"

He looked me up and down, and I blushed. It was a long time since someone gave me such a compliment. Here was a gentleman. And I loved the flea market. I never went because Abe was there.

"Please, have something to eat." I pointed to the table at the other end of the living room, where Mr. MacPherson stood helping himself to my apple cake. He sent me a smile, shy, like a teenager.

Paddy approached him and shook his hand like they were old friends. It's a small world.

Danny was talking to the Babcocks and Robert, the basement tenant. They chattered with him like they never did to me. Young people!

Abe's four poker buddies came up to me, all old and shrunken. One called Joe said, "He didn't come to the game anymore. Hard up for cash. It wasn't the same without him. He was such a *kibitzer*."

"*Abe?*" I said. "A *kibitzer?*" He never joked with *me*.

Another old guy said, "There was no bullshit with him. What you saw was what you got."

This I didn't dispute. It depended on what you saw. "Did he owe any of you money?"

They looked at me with their eyes bulging out. "Mrs. Rosenthal," said Joe, "we would never ask for..." His face went red.

"I wasn't offering," I said. "Just curious."

They glanced at each other, nodded politely. They were small and gnarled, like goblins. I didn't think any of them were capable of throwing Abe down the stairs.

"What about his bookie?" I said. "Did Abe owe *him* money?"

Joe shrugged. "Who doesn't owe Irv money?"

"Irv? Where I can find him?"

Joe stared at me. "You want to pay *him* back?"

"I have a tip on a pony."

"*Oy*, you shouldn't start. Besides, it's not a place for a lady."

I almost smiled. I was a foot taller than him and could probably knock him over.

"Tell you what," he said. "I'll place the bet for you."

"Thank you very much, but I can take care of myself."

"Mrs. Rosenthal..." He looked at me, serious. "I would never forgive myself if something happened to you." He sniffed the air. "Abe raved about your apple cake."

He nodded to his buddies, and they made for the table with the food.

I felt someone beside me. Mr. MacPherson, in one of his lopsided jackets.

"I couldn't help overhearing, Mrs. Rosenthal," he muttered. "I know where you can find Irv."

I turned to see his blue eyes, his cheeks with tiny red veins. "You know Irv?"

He looked down at the floor. "Not really. I'm not a bettor, but every now and then I would accompany Abe to the tavern for a wee dram." He peered at me like a guilty schoolboy. "It's on Queen Street. I could take you there."

"That's very kind, Mr. MacPherson."

"Mac."

"Mac. But I don't want to trouble you. If you give me the address, I can go myself."

"No trouble, believe me. Like the man said, it's no place for ladies."

"Mr. MacPher...Mac, I'm a big girl. Please, just the address."

He wrote it down on a piece of paper.

***

Out of respect for Abe, I waited till Tuesday to go down to Tony's Bar on Queen Street. I put on a dress I made years ago, happy it still fit. A shirtwaist in a navy-and-green plaid with big pockets. When I put up the collar, I looked like Doris Day, only a few more wrinkles around the eyes and no blonde. Maybe a little stiff from arthritis. Okay, not so much Doris Day.

Before I left, I dug up the switchblade Abe gave me while we were still married. Of course from a job lot, boxes of knives illegal because you could flick up the blade with one hand. For a change, they sold fast. I put it in my pocket just in case.

I parked at a meter on Queen Street late in the afternoon. Tony's was dark, like the inside of Jonah's whale, but the whale probably smelled better. Here was musty from damp walls and old beer. Also wall-to-wall lowlifes.

I stood at the door, pretending to fix my hair while my eyes got used to no light. By the bar, men drank and argued, cigarettes between their fingers. A few men sat at tables. Smoke so thick you could hang a broom.

All the men watched me walk up to the bartender at the end of the counter. A few whistled. They should get some light in there so they know what they're looking at. If it wasn't so soon after the funeral, this might've given me a lift. Meanwhile, I fingered the knife in my pocket in case anyone should try something.

"I'm looking for Irv," I said to the bartender.

He pointed to the back where a sign said Washrooms, with an arrow pointing downstairs.

The eyes followed me, so I sashayed past like I was 40. I didn't go downstairs, because voices came from behind a closed door on the left. I opened it a bit to look in.

What a surprise—Abe's poker buddies sitting around a table playing cards. With them sat a big middle-aged man, straight brown hair plastered back. Joe, the head goblin, saw me and went red.

"Mrs. Rosenthal!"

I stepped inside. The big man dangled a cigarette from the side of his mouth. "You must be Irv. I'm Abe Rosenthal's wife."

He immediately put his cards on the table face down. Shrewd brown eyes watched me. "I was very sorry to hear about Abe. My condolences, missus. He was a good man."

Just then, a phone rang on a small table beside him. He answered it, while pulling a sheet of paper from somewhere. Joe and the other goblins didn't take their eyes from their cards.

"Yeah, okay, Paddy," Irv said. "Power House in the fourth. Citizen in the fifth."

The same Paddy?

He went on with some numbers that made no sense to me, then hung up. The sheet disappeared.

"What can I do for you, Mrs. Rosenthal? Joe, get the lady a chair."

I raised my hand to nix the chair. If I sat down, I wouldn't be able to run so fast. "If you don't mind me asking, did Abe owe you money?"

"Everyone owes me money!" Irv said with a smile and slapped Joe on the back in fun. Joe started to cough, but waved his hand to show he would live.

"A lot of money?" I asked.

"Enough."

"Enough to want him dead?"

Irv tilted his big head. "Mrs. Rosenthal, please, I got a reputation. You can't go accusing me of such things. Word gets around."

The goblins all shook their heads. "We won't say nothin'," Joe mumbled.

"Besides, I heard it was an accident," Irv said.

"Do other people have accidents when they can't pay?"

He took the cigarette out of his mouth. "Look, missus, I'm a fair man. Usually I don't take bets from guys who're hard up. I made an exception of Abe because, well, me and him go back a long way. But I got sick of chasing him. I got better things to do. So I wrote off what he owed me and didn't take his calls. I don't deal with his type anymore—you should excuse me. My customers now are plumbers, accountants, even judges. That kind."

Did I believe him? The goblins looked nervous around him. Or maybe they were just embarrassed I found them.

"Mrs. Rosenthal, if I bumped off every *putz* who owed me money, I'd be out of business."

The phone rang again, and I left.

***

I moped around the next day. I didn't believe Irv. If he let deadbeat customers off the hook, why should anyone pay?

At least Danny came for dinner from guilt that I was alone. I was alone before, too, except that Abe was in the basement. Did that count? Unlike his father, Danny never really liked my cooking. He preferred Indian and Chinese.

Even while he ate my leftover apple cake for dessert, he had needles in his behind, *shpilkes*, like *Mameh* used to say about me. I knew he would scram as soon as he could.

Before he ran away, I asked him, "Did your father confide in you? Maybe someone threatened him?"

Danny gave me a sour look. He didn't like talking about what happened. Maybe he had the same picture in his head that wouldn't go away, Abe upside down on the stairs. The picture made me keep asking.

"Maybe he argued with somebody? A bookie named Irv?"

He put down his fork. "Ma, it was an accident."

In other words, shut up.

Later that night, Paddy Sullivan phoned me. After the niceties, he said, "By the way, Mrs. R., I hate to ask. But if you'd be so kind as to get me a copy of Abe's death certificate, I'd be so grateful. For the lease. It's in Abe's name, and I don't want to renegotiate. If I show the landlord the partnership papers and the death certificate, he'll let me keep paying the same rent."

I never heard of such a thing, but then nobody ever died on me in one of my apartments. The funeral home gave me extra copies of the death certificate. Even after the divorce, I was still Abe's executor and his beneficiary. I inherited all of his nothing. Sure, Paddy could have a copy.

***

I didn't cook on Friday—what was the point, just for me. Danny went out. I made some eggs for supper, and that was enough. I was disappointed in myself that I couldn't find the truth—what really happened to Abe? Maybe the truth was in front of my nose. Maybe he came upstairs to tell me something (what would be so important?) and he got dizzy and fell. Maybe I was just a stupid old woman who watched too many detective stories.

During a commercial on *Magnum, P.I.*, it hit me. I never asked Robert, the other basement tenant, if Abe had visitors. From the second floor, I wouldn't know.

I rushed down the stairs to the basement and knocked on his door. No answer. I started to leave when the door opened. I must've woken him up; he was in his robe, hair a mess. Young people these days! They don't make them like they used to.

"I'm sorry to disturb," I said. "I just wanted to ask you something."

Instead of inviting me inside, he stepped into the hall and closed the door. So he had company. *Mazel tov!*

"Did you ever see if anyone came to Abe's apartment?" I asked.

He shook his head.

"Never?"

He blinked. "I'm not nosy, Mrs. Rosenthal."

"I never said..." Why was it so hard to talk to young people?

"I did hear him arguing with someone. But it was on the phone. Twice, maybe three times."

"What did he say?"

He screwed up his face thinking. "I couldn't hear much, but I think it had to do with money."

"Did he mention an Irv?"

"I don't remember."

He crossed over his arms to signal he was finished. He waited till I started moving away before he went back in.

I'm ashamed to say I peeked inside when he opened the door. I wish I didn't! Instead of a nice girl in her underwear, who did I see walking with no shirt, but Danny! *Oy vey!* Where did I go wrong?

I ran up the stairs and locked my door. Then I sat in the dark, sipping a glass of Manischewitz wine, thinking how lucky Abe was he didn't live long enough to see this.

***

All night I couldn't sleep. I tried to keep my mind off Danny and that I would never have grandchildren. So I thought about who could be on the phone with Abe. Someone he owed money to. Irv would deny it up and down. No use asking him. But I knew who else to ask.

Saturday afternoon, I drove to the flea market, deep in the west end. The place was like a huge barn, with so much merchandise, stalls one on top of the other, you didn't know where to look first. I headed for where Abe used to have his stand, but it wasn't there.

Someone shouted, "Mrs. Rosenthal!" Seymour waved from down the aisle.

Paddy grinned at me while talking up a customer. The stand was much bigger than Abe used to have. I recognized the old wooden sign painted in red letters: Rose Valley Merchandise. Rosenthal in German means "rose valley." Long ago, Abe gave a sign painter a stereo in exchange for the lettering. Abe was gone, but the sign was still there, above the portable TVs, radios, phones, blenders, coffeemakers, mugs, you name it, all piled around the edge. In front sat a dark wood cabinet, the kind *Mameh* used to like (me, I prefer modern). I expected to see fancy dishes behind the glass. Instead, stood bottles of FreshBios, like the one I saw in Abe's place.

"Grand to see you, Mrs. Rosenthal!" said Paddy, finished with the customer who bought *bupkes*. "Looking gorgeous today, you are."

I blushed.

His hand was warm when he shook mine. Seymour stood watching that nobody should take anything.

I took the envelope with the death certificate out of my purse and gave it to him.

His eyes got watery. "That's too kind of you, Mrs. Rosenthal, too kind."

I realized from this whole mess with Abe dying and people acting too polite that I don't like sentiment. It embarrasses me. "Nice stand," I said.

He looked with a critical eye at his merchandise. "Oh, but we're going into a smaller space soon. Now that Abe has...left us."

I didn't want to ask him how was business, since it was a Saturday afternoon and customers were scarce.

"This is a good seller?" I asked, pointing to the bottles of green stuff.

His face lit up with such a smile. He opened the glass door and took one out. "A discerning lady such as yourself would see the benefit of this miraculous product. A bottle every day for two weeks, and all your aches and pains will vanish." He took the cap off and held it out.

What could I do? I had to take it. He watched while I took a sip. It didn't taste so bad. Like grass where the dog peed on it.

"Very nice," I lied, a little white one.

His chest puffed up like he would talk about his children. "There's no doubt in my mind—in a few years, this will replace food. Jaysus, why cook? All the nutrition you need is right here. I buy it from a company in California. Sure and it's their number one seller. Don't let it go no further, but I'm going to buy a franchise."

That sounded expensive. I didn't see people lining up for it here.

"I'm getting out of the junk business, I am. Stepping up in the world."

So why was I surprised?

"I tell you, the future is in health drinks. And the franchise has tremendous promotion. Even ads on the radio. When people know I've got it here, they'll come flocking!"

Another *luftmensch* who built castles in the air. Good luck to him.

"So what would you like, Mrs. R.?" He led me inside the stand where I saw the better stuff: crystal vases, wine glasses, fancy dishes.

"Really, I don't need anything," I said. I already had too many *tchotchkes*.

"There must be something. Your apple cake would look lovely on this." He lifted up a white cake stand with flowers and a gold border. A beauty. Okay, to make him happy.

Enough schmoozing. I lowered my voice. "So how much do *you* owe Irv?"

His face fell flat. "Who says I owe him?"

"You play the ponies, you owe money."

He stared at me, trying to figure out how I knew. "I'm paying him back."

"Irv takes installments?"

He looked away, nervous. "I paid most of it."

"How much did Abe owe?"

He shrugged.

"Does Irv...hurt people who owe him money?"

He looked at me funny. "You think Irv...?"

"Would he?"

He lowered his voice. "Wouldn't surprise me. Begobs, he's dangerous. I'm scared myself."

"Shouldn't we tell the police?"

"Leave it be, for your own sake, dear lady."

His mouth puckered, nervous. Then a few customers showed up in front of the stand. Paddy turned to go. "Mind yourself, and stay away from Irv. I wouldn't want anything to happen to you."

***

It rained the next few days, and my ceiling sprung a leak in the living room. I was too busy cleaning up to think about Abe, happy to get my mind off that *meshugas*. While I was putting a pot under one of the drips, Mr. MacPherson showed up at my door. It was one of his rare days off.

"Mrs. Rosenthal, I wonder if you could do me a favor. Mr. Sullivan is coming by in an hour to pick up this envelope, and the school just called—I have to run to a meeting. Could you possibly give it to him? He's quite anxious for it."

"Of course."

"I'll put a note on my door."

I took the envelope, stupidly excited. I knew Paddy had a pretty wife at home, but I fixed my hair, put on the shirtwaist and my little heels.

Only then did I really look at the envelope. It had a window where Paddy's name peeked through, typed on pale green-patterned paper, like a check. But the address stumped me. C/O of Rose Valley Merchandise. Abe's company. The return address was an insurance firm. It was a check for Paddy! Insurance money? From Abe's company? I turned the envelope toward the light to see if I could read anything through the paper. Too thick.

I boiled water in the kettle, but not for tea. *Mameh* used to steam the stamps off envelopes to save on postage. I held the envelope over the kettle, the steam rising up. I had to fill it twice and work for 10 minutes before the flap would open.

The envelope was damp and bumpy when I took out the check. I stopped feeling guilty when I saw the amount. Impossible! Ninety-five thousand dollars! My heart beat loud in my ears. I couldn't believe what was going through my brain. Was it possible? I didn't have time to think before footsteps came up the stairs.

I opened the door and there he was. Tall and handsome and...

"Oh, there you are, Mrs. R! Looking grand, as always. Fierce weather we've been having, isn't it just?"

I waved the check in his face. "What does this mean?" I shouted.

He grabbed it. The cute cheeks went white. "What do you mean opening my envelope?"

"Why are you getting money for Rose Valley, after Abe is dead?"

His face changed in front of me. The eyes sparked, like a fire. "Who do you think you are, butting in...?" Then he thought better of it. "If it's any of your business, we had partnership insurance."

That was why he needed the death certificate! "So much for a *partner?*"

"Don't you think I've got expenses?

"This is how you're buying the franchise."

He blinked, the fire raging behind his eyes. "I worked hard all my life and finally I have a chance to make something of myself, get away from that crappy business."

"So Abe had to die?"

"It had nothing to do with me. He had a bad heart. Finally got him."

"Why was he on the steps?"

Then the lamb became a wolf. "He was coming up to get the dinner you always cook for him. He told me you're a grand cook. He started up the stairs and..." Paddy clapped his big hands together. "Gone, just like that!"

Then I knew he was lying. "So you were there!"

Suddenly he had his hands on me and shoved me into the apartment. "Jaysus, you couldn't leave well enough alone!"

My heart beat so fast I thought it would explode. I looked up at Paddy's white face, the eyes gone hard.

"He was bleeding me dry! I told him I wanted out. But he kept buying, and the creditors came after *me*! Irv wouldn't touch Abe, but he has no such sentimental feelings for me. He sends goons out with baseball bats. I had no choice."

I caught my breath. "You could do what I did. I divorced him!"

His mouth twitched. "It was too late for that."

"You wanted me to think Irv killed him. But it was you!"

"You have to understand— he didn't suffer. I'm not a bad man. I put his heart pills in his FreshBios. A lot of pills. He didn't fall down the stairs."

He was not convincing me of his goodness.

"So he was already dead when you...put him there."

His eyes were wild. "He was a weight around both our necks, admit it."

I opened my mouth to say *No*, but nothing came out.

"Look, Mrs. R., I'll give you some of the insurance money if you'll just..." He held the check out to me.

I shivered at the thought of money sprouting from Abe's grave. I ran to the phone in the kitchen. Before I could dial 911, he grabbed my arm. The phone fell from my hand. The look in his eye! My blood ran cold. I took a glass from the counter and smashed it over his head. The surprise made him let go, and I ran to the door.

I pulled it open. "Help!" I yelled. "Help!"

But no one was home in the middle of the day. I ran two steps out the door, but he was right behind me. He yanked my arm hard, almost from the socket. I screamed from the pain. Then I couldn't scream anymore because he put both hands around my neck and squeezed.

I couldn't breathe! This was how I was going to die? I scratched at his fingers to loosen his grip, but he was too strong. He had such a look of concentration. In a flash, I remembered the knife and reached into the pocket of the dress. I couldn't see, but I pressed on the button like Abe showed me in another life. I felt the blade flick up. Before I could black out, I stabbed it hard into the back of his neck. He groaned; at the same time, his hands let go of me. I could breathe again.

He gasped and staggered, one foot on the landing, the other on the stair. My blood was racing. I wasn't such an old woman to give up. While he tried to balance, I lifted one leg and gave him a kick.

Down he went. Down the stairs, like a stone. I panted, terrified he would get up. But he lay quiet, upside down like Abe, his head at a funny angle, with the knife sticking out of his neck.

I held on to the rail, shaking. That could be me, another corpse on the stairs. My heart was racing so fast I had to plop down on the top step. Now I felt every one of my 70 years. It was a miracle I was still alive. *Tateh* used to say, "Life is a big headache on a noisy street." I was glad I still lived on that street.

Then, from nowhere, a picture came in front of my eyes: Abe and me when we were young and shining with happiness, our whole lives ahead of us. Where did it all go? Nothing turns out like you expect. How empty the building was without him! A sting came to my eyes, and finally the tears flowed down like a river.

About Sylvia Maultash Warsh

Sylvia was born in Germany and came to Canada as a child. She earned a BA and a Masters in Linguistics from the University of Toronto. Her short stories and poetry have appeared in Canada and the US.

Sylvia is the author of the Dr. Rebecca Temple series. *To Die in Spring* was nominated for an Arthur for Best First Novel. *Find Me Again* won an Edgar award. *Season of Iron* was shortlisted for a ReLit Award. Her fourth book, *The Queen of Unforgetting*, an historical novel, was chosen for a plaque by Project Bookmark Canada. Her latest, *Best Girl*, a Rapids Reads novella, came out in 2012.

Her short story, "The Emerald Skull," featured in *Thirteen*, (Carrick Publishing) was nominated for an Arthur for Best Short Story.

Sylvia is currently working on an historical novel. She lives in Toronto where she teaches writing to seniors.

http://www.sylviawarsh.com/
Amazon Author page
Facebook
Mesdames of Mayhem

HIDDEN

By Jane Petersen Burfield

There was the bell, and the banana, and the artichoke. I circled the objects with satisfaction. Next up, cake and ruler. As I studied the puzzle book page for hidden objects, I remembered the first time I ate an artichoke. It was in a sweet little restaurant up the hill in Hampstead, North London. Julian had insisted I try it as an appetizer when he heard I had never tasted one before. I remember savoring the sauce, licking my fingertips as I nibbled on the leaves. Julian laughed and kissed my buttery hand.

I quickly refocused on the picture. Okay, there's the cat, and the fountain pen. Where's that ridiculous ruler? Ah, beside the mushroom.

Julian loved mushrooms. We would go for a walk in the woods and I would pick freshly erupted ones beneath the trees. The mushrooms smelled like the lush earth they grew in. At home, I would make him a champignon omelet in our tiny kitchen.

The ticking clock made me a little anxious, so I returned to the book. I found the star, the hourglass, and the syringe.

When Mum became ill, Dad was not able to cope, and they called me. So I went to look after her, while Dad went to a rugby game with friends.

The weekend I was away, Julian invited my friend, Sonia, for a walk in the woods. He said he'd been lonely. They went to our little restaurant for a mushroom soufflé. And he brought her home again.

To *my* home.

I looked down at the book on my lap. I concentrated on finding the last few hidden objects. There the magnifying glass. Next, the spade. A clock and some daisies. I circled them all as I waited. I hated waiting.

Most mushrooms you find in the woods are safe. But you have to be careful about which ones you pick in the woods. Some can kill you.

I forced my eyes back to the page. And as the clock ticked, I kept searching, looking for the final object, a key.

Waiting until the jury returned.

About Jane Petersen Burfield

Killing someone softly with words is greatly appealing to a North Toronto matron like Jane. After raising three wonderful daughters in a 4th generation family home, she is ready for more adventure. Finding a way to use fashion, vegetables and small animals in her stories to bring about justice, albeit rough justice, is her challenge.

To her utter amazement, Jane won the Bony Pete Short Story Award in 2001 for "Slow Death and Taxes", the first short story she wrote. After several more years of success with the Bloody Words story contest, she decided writing was a misery-making but delightful challenge. She has had short stories published in *Blood on the Holly* and *Bloody Words, the Anthology*.

Jane is honored to be a member of Mesdames of Mayhem, and looks forward to the creative buzz that comes from an association of women writers. She hopes you enjoy her story about a woman creating her own justice.

Facebook
Twitter
Mesdames of Mayhem

MIRROR, MIRROR

By Cheryl Freedman

Snow White was six years old when she went missing for the first time.

Her disappearance caused quite the commotion at the palace, and the fuss spilled over to me, which was a Good Thing. Not that I wished the princess or her father, King Orfeo, any ill will, but my business is finding lost people and things, and Snow White's disappearance definitely fit that bill. Besides, I didn't yet realize that the child wasn't all sweetness and light and that she had, in fact, a rather nasty streak in her.

I'm Goslin, founder of Goslin's Location Agency ("Specializing in Missing Royalty and Strayed Magic Items"). I'm intimately acquainted with the royalty part of the business, being the daughter of a human mother who was (and technically still is) a princess and a father who's the ogre who kidnapped and later married her, this being Mother's idea as she was singularly unimpressed by the quality of her would-be rescuers. I inherited Mother's looks (attractive, if I say so myself), royal rank (often useful), and fairy godmother, Dilnavaz (of questionable value at the best of times, and at the worst of times...well, let's just not go there). From Daddy, I inherited a mouthful of sharp teeth, which are great for intimidating most deadbeat clients and recalcitrant witnesses, but otherwise, force me to adopt a mysterious close-mouthed smile and a bad temper, which I'm working on...really.

I'd been in a foul mood for several days. Business was slow, and I was trying to decide how to deal with a deadbeat client without, well, beating him to death. To make matters worse, my partner and would-be card sharp, Marlowe, was driving me crazy with his nonstop muttering and swearing as he tried to finesse some sleight-of-hand card trick, something made infinitely more difficult when one lacks opposable thumbs, which Marlowe does.

Marlowe I inherited from nobody, and his background and lineage make mine seem perfectly normal. Marlowe is not human or even humanoid, although he may have been at one time. I've asked but he's not talking, nor does it bear pushing the issue because his teeth are sharper than mine and his temper is arguably worse. To be fair, though, he does have some sterling qualities, although they escape me right now.

Marlowe had insinuated himself into my life some three years ago, right after I first opened my agency. I was at my desk at the time, so bored that I was drawing family trees linking the royal families of the seven kingdoms (yes, we're all related) as I waited for potential clients to realize that I was their last best hope for finding what had been lost or hidden. And I waited...and waited...and waited, idly wondering at times if I should just give it up and be a princess.

Then the door opened, and my life changed forever. In swaggered a two-foot-tall (yes, walking upright) ferret. He wasn't dressed nearly as nattily as Puss in Boots, but clothes don't necessarily make the man...or the ferret, I suppose.

"Nice joint, babe," he commented as he looked around. "Needs just one thing. Me."

"What?" Hmmm. Not exactly the wittiest of responses. I started again. "What makes you think you're qualified to work for me?"

"Ya got it all wrong, doll. I'm not going to be working for you. I'm going to be your partner. Marlowe and Goslin, Private Dicks. Silk so far?"

"What?!" Apart from being dumbstruck by what the ferret—Marlowe, I surmised—had proposed (and with his name first, the little weasel), he was talking gibberish.

"Shut the door, will ya, babe?"

That struck me as a good idea, but when I turned to walk back to my desk, there he was, perched on my chair.

"Get. Out. Of. My. Chair. NOW!" I shouted, baring my teeth in my most fearsome smile. Would have made Daddy proud, except that all Marlowe did in response was bare his teeth at me. Maybe he thought his was a smile. Mine certainly wasn't.

"Get out of my chair right now!" I could have been shouting into the wind for all the ferret cared. I had to admit he was kind of cute, in a weaselly way, with a little triangular head and no shoulders and a humpy lower body. His face looked a little clownish, with a dirty pink nose and two dark patches under the eyes of a predominantly white face.

"Now where were we, babe?"

"*We* were not anywhere. *You*, on the other hand, are leaving."

"Don't blow your wig, doll. You need me, *capiche?* Can you talk to animals? Charm birds out of trees? Sneak through tight spaces? Make princesses talk baby talk and reveal their innermost secrets to you because you're just so cute? I thought not. Well, you need someone who can, and I'm your number."

And thus I gained as a partner a creature with a brain the size of a walnut, an ego the size of a mountain, and the propensity to talk in some kind of arcane slang.

I had set up shop during an epidemic of stolen magic rings, rampaging giants with riddles, and misplaced princesses in the kingdom of Arkady and the six neighbouring realms. The upshot of this crime wave was a desperate shortage of princes, shepherds, and simpletons for the sore-pressed monarchs to call upon to find the rings, answer the riddles, and rescue the princesses.

Enter Marlowe and me to deal with the problem. The catch, however, in dealing with kings is that they are nowhere near as generous with professional locators like me as they are with the aforementioned princes, shepherds, and simpletons. No half-of-my-kingdom, no pile of gold equivalent to your weight, no priceless gems or magic birds. In particular, no hand-of-my-daughter/son-in-marriage. No, only a regal "You have Our Royal Thanks, Mistress Goslin, for locating Our Precious Daughter" or some other lofty but empty expression of gratitude, as opposed to cold hard cash. Thank goodness for commoners and their coin, paltry though it is.

But right now for some reason, neither commoners nor kings needed the services of Goslin's Location Agency (aka Goslin and Marlowe, Private Investigators). What to do, what to do?

A particularly colorful burst of cursing came from Marlowe's corner.

"Shut up, Marlowe," I snarled. "You take the desk. I'm going out to see Dilnavaz to see if she has any jobs for us." I tell you, things had to be really desperate if I was contemplating throwing myself on the mercy of my fairy godmother. She's one of the good fairies (as opposed to Carabosse and her evil fairy crew who specialize in cursing newborn royals). She always means well; it's just that bad things tend to happen in my life when she's involved.

But the universe had other plans for me. As I stood to leave, the door burst open and in poured a crowd headed by the Royal Chamberlain, looking more officious than usual, followed closely by the Royal Nanny, puffy-eyed, wringing her hands; half a dozen guards, hands firmly attached to sword hilts, trying not to look nervous; and two maidservants, who gave me the distinct impression that they would rather be in the scullery or perhaps even in the frog pond, rather than here as part of the august company in my office.

"My pretty baby, she's—" blurted the Royal Nanny.

"Her Royal Highness, she's—" snapped the Royal Chamberlain at the same time.

They glared at each other. The guardsmen stood stiffly at attention, one of them appearing to develop a nasty facial tic. The two maidservants just looked scared.

They tried again...

"This lackwit woman let—"

"The Royal Chamberpot doesn't know—"

...with as little success. Their faces reddened, and they appeared on the verge of either a screaming argument or apoplexy. My turn now.

"Sir, Madam," I said pointedly, giving them the benefit of the doubt and making allowance for their stress. "Princess Snow White has disappeared, and you require my services to find her."

Blessed silence in the room as everyone stared at me pop-eyed. "But...but how did you know?" asked the Royal Chamberlain, agog.

"Come now, Sir Chamberlain, your princess disappears and you don't think the news will get out?" In fact, I had heard some rumors, which was another reason I had been in a bad mood: I couldn't understand why the palace hadn't come to me immediately, considering that I had done work for them before. "Now, Mistress Nanny, if you would be so kind, tell me precisely what happened yesterday afternoon."

Nanny swiped at her tear-filled eyes, then lunged at one of the maidservants. The maid tried to dodge out of the way, but Nanny, being well-practiced in the art of catching small children and servants, grabbed her ear and hauled her before me. Glaring at her hapless victim but relinquishing the ear, Nanny started her story in a voice brimming with venom.

"This ne'er-do-well was supposed to be watching over my poor wee lambkin while she was playing, but she probably fell asleep, lazy useless cow that she is, and my poor wee mite has vanished."

I raised an eyebrow inquisitively at the maid. "So you were with the princess when she disappeared?"

"Aye, mistress. Her Highness and I were playing at the ball under that huge old oak at the edge of the woods. We oft-times play there together; the princess likes to believe there are fey folk dwelling in that tree. But suddenly...well, out comes this strange little hairy creature from the woods and flings me to the ground. And then he grabs my little lady and runs back into the trees with her. So I starts screaming for help, but they just completely disappear..."

She babbled on. She was lying. At the same time, she was telling the truth. It gave me a queasy feeling, almost like looking at something that is under a glamor, but partially seeing through the enchantment. It reminded me of the time I'd been hired to find a little boy who had disappeared. A truly nasty child, he had sassed the wrong old woman and had been turned into a pig. But she hadn't actually turned him into a pig; she had just cast a glamor over him to make people believe he was a pig; it was just as effective as a transformation, and took far less out of her. When I finally realized what the old woman had done, and looked at the pig, I could see the pig and boy images overlaying each other, shifting back and forth in and out of focus.

This is what listening to someone telling a story is like. Unless they are wholly telling the truth or wholly telling a lie, I can hear truth and falsehood shifting back and forth in my head.

"What's your name, child?"

"Alys, mistress," the maid mumbled.

"So, Alys, you were playing ball with the princess?"

"Yes." The truth.

"And then a 'strange little hairy creature' came out of the trees?"

"Yes." A lie. Sort of.

"No! Now what really happened?"

She had been fidgeting with the ties on her bodice, but now looked up at me fearfully. Suddenly, her eyes filling with tears, she blurted out, "I was tired of playing, so I tells the princess that it's quiet time. So she sits down and is weaving a chain of clover. What with the birds singing and the leaves rustling, and me being so tired, I shuts my eyes..."

She stopped talking momentarily at the hissed intake of breath from Nanny. But she was telling the truth.

"It was only for a moment, Nanny, truly it was," she whined. "And then my princess was gone. She just vanished. And now the king will have my head, and I deserve it!" With this, she began to bawl in earnest.

Not much point in questioning her further. This second time around, she had been telling the truth, although I was still puzzled about the mixed feeling I got when she referred to the "strange hairy creature."

Both the Royal Chamberlain and Nanny looked as if they might save His Majesty the trouble of executing the maidservant by doing it themselves right here in my office. Scrubbing out bloodstains being somewhere near the bottom of my list of favorite things to do, I quickly sought further details from the guardsmen, who had not yet spoken.

Four of the six guardsmen had accompanied the princess and her maid to the oak tree at the edge of the wood. I had encountered Big Iain, the bear-like one, a few months ago when I was last in the palace. He was off duty at the time and playing pinochle in the barracks, and we had chatted.

"Aye, lass, I would guard the little princess with my life."

Unless you were playing cards or dicing, I thought then. Otherwise, I knew he meant it.

Now, in my office, I didn't even listen to the guards' protestations that they had seen nothing. They weren't lying: One look at Big Iain's guilty face told me they had indeed been gaming.

Inwardly, I groaned. All I had to go on—the only scrap of information that might be even remotely useful in my search for Snow White—was Alys's reference to the strange little hairy creature, which could mean anything. But smiling brightly, I assured the Royal Chamberlain and Royal Nanny that I would do my best, and could they please set me up with an audience with the king as soon as possible.

Blissful silence descended as the royal party stormed out of my office. Massaging my aching brain, I pondered my next move. It had been at least 24 hours since the princess had vanished. The clearing under the old oak tree had probably been thoroughly trampled by now; not much hope of finding any clues there. What worried me more was the thought of who or what might be lurking in the woods, awaiting a tender little princess.

Why had King Orfeo waited so long to call me in? I did have my suspicions. After more than two years of deep mourning for his dead Queen Meroudyce, he had fallen in love once again—to the great joy of both the court and the people of Arkady, who had suffered while he had been distracted from ruling the kingdom.

The word was that during those years of grief, Orfeo had lavished any remnants of his ability to love on his young daughter, Snow White. But the king has always been an all-or-nothing man, and with his newfound lady love now occupying his time, did he even realize that his daughter was missing? Was the chamberlain loath to break into the king's happiness? Did he figure that it would be easy to find the princess, so no one had bothered informing the king?

If so, what did that mean? Had Snow White been kidnapped—perhaps by the "strange little hairy creature" the maidservant claimed to have seen—or did she wander off, perhaps deliberately, to wrench her daddy's attention away from his new wife?

So many questions, so few answers. But at least I was no longer bored and grumpy.

The door slowly opened and in sauntered Marlowe. I hadn't even seen him leave, but ferrets are built for slinking away. "Nice of you to drop in," I observed. "Where did you disappear to? And by the way, we have a job."

"Too noisy in here for me, doll. I couldn't hear myself think. So have you figured out where the kid is?"

"Figured out where she is? Mab's tits, I haven't even figured out whether she was kidnapped or wandered off on her own. And how much did you hear anyway?"

"I took a powder when you started questioning the soldier boys. So what do we have?"

I hate when Marlowe does that—trying to out-organize me, that is. He knows it, too, the little weasel.

"First, was the princess kidnapped or did she wander off?"

"You're repeating yourself, doll."

"Thank you, Marlowe, for your clever observation. Moving right along: If she was kidnapped, who would have done it? Arkady has been at peace for decades. King Orfeo has no enemies that I know of. The only clue we have is what the princess's maidservant, Alys, said: that a 'strange little hairy creature' came out from the woods and snatched Snow White. But I think she's telling only half the truth."

"Oh yeah? But why would someone want to snatch the kid anyway?"

"Good question. Now what if she just wandered off? Why? And where did she go? And why did the chamberlain wait for a day before coming to us? In fact, does the king even know that his daughter is gone?"

"Does he even care?" Marlowe mumbled, albeit loud enough that I could make out the words.

"Let's assume he does," I said, but I wasn't so sure.

***

The messenger from the Royal Chamberlain showed up the next morning with a summons to meet with the king. Snow White had been missing for over a day.

I met with King Orfeo and his new queen, Nistala, by myself. Marlowe was off at the edge of the woods to see if anyone or anything had witnessed the disappearance or kidnapping of Snow White.

The king came across as his usual very sweet self, a man with a heart of gold but not exactly the brightest scepter in the royal treasury. To give him credit, he's at least clever enough to surround himself with smart advisors. His old queen, Meroudyce, had been one of them; his brother, Roland, seneschal and the supreme military commander, was another. Would Nistala fill in as a third? Certainly if she proved to be as wise and insightful as she was stunningly beautiful, Orfeo would be well served by his new love.

"I don't understand, Goslin. Who would want to hurt my little girl? She's the sweetest, most loving little girl in the Seven Kingdoms, isn't she, my precious?" He turned his puppy-dog eyes towards his new queen, as if willing her to agree with him.

She patted his hand and smiled, but the smile never reached her eyes. "Of course, my love. I'm so blessed that not only do I have your love but also the love of your—our—precious child."

Interesting reaction on Nistala's part, I thought.

"But if no one wanted to hurt the child—"

"Who would?" Orfeo interrupted. "I have no enemies. Our kingdom is at peace with all our neighbors. My people are happy."

"Then the only other option is that Snow White either wandered off by accident—perhaps she saw something in the woods that intrigued her—or she deliberately ran away."

"No, my daughter would never run away. I give her everything she wants." Again, he turned to Nistala. "Is this not so, my precious?" The queen looked down at her feet.

"Your Majesties, perhaps I could speak with the queen in private?"

Orfeo leaned over to kiss Nistala's cheek, then stood, nodded politely to me, and left the room.

"I'm not a very good liar, am I, Princess?" Nistala finally broke the silence that had fallen after Orfeo closed the door.

"Your Majesty, it's just Goslin when I'm on the job. And no, I'm afraid you're not."

"I really do want to love Snow White, but sometimes she makes it so difficult. Yes, I can understand that she still misses her real mother, but..."

I waited.

"She resents me. And it's not so much that she misses her mother. It's that she misses her father. Orfeo built his life around Snow White when Meroudyce died, and now..."

Again silence.

"She hates me, and I fear her. That's stupid, isn't it?" She laughed bitterly. "Me, an adult, fearing a child?" She shot me a challenging look, then dropped her eyes.

Not much I could say here. No reassurances. No there-theres. I had to ask one more thing, though. "Your Majesty..." At this, the queen looked up. "Would you hurt the child?"

"Never."

She was telling the truth.

"So what do you think happened to her?"

"Perhaps she just saw something in the woods and wandered off. I just don't know. Forgive me for saying this, but I think she may have run away to teach her daddy a lesson."

There was nothing to add, so I thanked the queen and moved on.

My next interview was with Roland, King Orfeo's half-brother, palace seneschal, commander of the Arkadian army, and my usual contact at the palace when my professional services were required. Roland and I had an "interesting" relationship. Where Orfeo was gentle and easygoing, Roland was a definite by-the-book kind of guy. Good for a seneschal and, I suppose, a military commander, but it meant he had a problem with my parentage—such mixed marriages as my parents had didn't fit into his world view—and with the fact that I was a princess working just like common folk.

On the other hand, he never denied that I got results, so we got along, at least on a professional, albeit very formal, level.

"Princess." Roland stood and bowed as I stepped into his office at the palace. "I gather you're here about my niece's disappearance."

"Correct, Your Highness," I said, resisting the temptation to bob a curtsey and instead seating myself across from him. "What's your take on the situation? Was the princess kidnapped? Or do you think she just wandered off?"

"I notice you haven't suggested option three: that she willfully disappeared. I'm fond of my niece, but she can be an obstinate child who's determined to get her own way. And Orfeo has spoiled her, especially since Meroudyce died. I've advised him several times that he's doing neither himself nor her any favor, but he refuses to listen. And now that he's found a new lady to love..."

"Are you saying, then, that you think your niece disappeared deliberately? She's only six; where would she go?"

"All I'm saying is that it's a possibility. As to where she would go, I don't know. I've ordered all the household guards to comb the area. We just have to hope that they find her before—"

I didn't want to think of what "before" might mean, so I interrupted. "Alys, the princess's companion, initially said a strange little hairy creature came out of the woods, knocked her down, and made off with the princess. Then she changed her mind and said she had fallen asleep and the princess must have wandered off. Have you any idea what she might have meant by 'strange little hairy creature'?"

"Is that all the girl said? A strange little hairy creature? Not much of a description. Could be anything, even an animal she'd never seen before." He shrugged, then suddenly snapped his fingers. "There's another possibility. It might have been a dwarf. We've always found them to be a hardworking, peaceable group, although there was bit of unrest a few months ago, mostly over a faction among them wanting to be paid more for their iron and gold. But we came up with what both sides agreed was a reasonable deal, and everything's been quiet since then."

Hmm, interesting. Dwarves were a new twist, although why they'd want to kidnap Snow White was beyond me. So I thanked Roland for his help and moved on to question the servants.

As I neared Snow White's rooms, I could hear the high-pitched whining of my next subject and the lower threatening voice of her tormentor: not a good thing, because it meant that I would have to forcibly separate Nanny from Alys if I wanted to get any kind of useful insight into the princess.

Sure enough, Nanny was there and immediately jumped in with the official line: Of course, her little lambkin was a charming, loving, beloved, obedient... (at this point, I stopped listening) ...an all-around angel. Nanny took a deep breath, priming herself to continue with her paean. Me, I took the pause as a gift from Above to pull Alys out of the room.

"Nanny," I tossed over my shoulder, "thank you. You've been very helpful. Now Alys and I are going for a walk to look at where the princess disappeared." Nanny puffed out her chest and drew herself up to her full height (much shorter than me), preparing to object, but I glared at her in my best princessy/ogre-ish fashion, and she deflated rapidly. I did feel a slight twinge of guilt, knowing that Nanny would vent her spleen later on poor Alys.

Alys and I walked for a bit in silence, heading towards the oak tree at the edge of the wood where she had last seen Snow White. I ignored the pairs of guardsmen scouring the grounds looking for any evidence that Snow White had been there.

"So, Alys, is the princess good to you?"

"Oh, my lady, she's so sweet and kind. She's always laughing, and we have such fun together. We're such good friends, we are."

"And what about the other servants?"

"Same with them, my lady."

Considering that Alys was looking everywhere except at me, even Marlowe could have figured out she was lying.

"Alys, do you want to find your princess?"

"Of course, my lady. How can you even ask me that?"

"Because I overheard you and Nanny arguing, and Nanny was threatening you. Alys, you're a good girl..." she nodded vigorously in agreement "...and good girls don't tell lies or bad things happen to them."

A rather tentative nod this time. I swung her around to look at me, and the waterworks started. "I hate her! She's mean to me and she always tries to gets me into trouble. She says I hits her, but I never did. And she's mean to everybody, and she hits and pinches us but if we does anything to her, she screams to Nanny and then we all gets punished." She took a deep breath and a panicked expression crossed her face. "You won't tell Nanny what I said, will you, my lady?"

I was just about to reassure her I wouldn't breathe a word when a voice piped up behind me.

"Babe, tell your little girlie friend to take a powder. I know where Snow is."

Marlowe had returned, his signature fedora pulled down low over his forehead as he half carried, half dragged a wriggling sack behind him.

"What is *that*, my lady?" Alys cried, clutching at my arm in terror. She blanched when she realized that she had grabbed me (well, I suppose I am her better) and just as hastily unhanded me.

"That's Marlowe, Alys. My partner. Now be a good girl and go back to the palace and tell them I'll be there shortly."

Alys turned and hitching up her skirts, ran for dear life. Marlowe just snickered at Alys's reaction. He likes to shock people.

I nodded at the wriggling sack. "What's in the bag, Marlowe?" I wasn't sure I wanted to know, but I had learned that Marlowe works in strange and wondrous ways that usually get results.

Saying not a word, he opened the sack, stuck in his head, and pulled out a small white rabbit by the scruff with his teeth. "Take it before it escapes," or words to that effect, he mumbled out of the corner of his mouth. We didn't really have to worry about the rabbit making a break for it; it was almost paralyzed with fear (or possibly from the smell of ferret breath).

I cradled the tiny creature in my hands and stroked its trembling head until I felt it calm down. "Yes, Marlowe?"

"While you were bumping gums with the king-hombre and his lads about who would want to snatch the princess, I'm thinking that maybe she just wandered off. Now why would she do that, I asked myself. I mean, she has everything she wants, right?"

"Marlowe, just get on with it. Why did you drag this rabbit here?"

"I'm just getting there, babe. Hold your horses."

"Marlowe!"

"Hold your horses, babe. I snuck into the woods where the kid disappeared and listened to the talk. I heard some rabbits chinwagging about the princess and how they got her to follow them into the woods."

"Why would they do that? And you said you know where Snow White is now. Where?"

"Getting there, babe. Let's let bunny-boy explain." He pulled himself up to his full height and bared his teeth at the formerly calm bunny in my arms. The creature squeaked and went into full panic mode, leaping out of my arms and trying to make a run for it. Marlowe, however, was faster and caught the little guy again by the scruff. The rabbit flopped down dead.

"Nice going, Marlowe. You've killed it."

"No, I haven't. Pick it up."

Sure enough, the rabbit was still alive, although from the wild beating of its little heart, I wasn't too sure how long that state would continue.

"Marlowe, if the rabbit has information for us, how about letting me do the questioning?"

"You don't speak its lingo," he pointed out.

"Then you stand there and talk, and I'll hold the rabbit here and protect it."

The bunny finally woke up, Marlowe emitted some squeaks and grunts that I assume were rabbit talk, the rabbit gave him what I assume were answers, and the three of us headed into the woods. It turned out that a small hairy creature had asked a number of cute little forest creatures to lure Snow White to a small house in the woods. Said creature had told them that it (he? she?) had a wonderful surprise for the princess that would make her very happy.

Cute little forest creatures live to make little girls happy; our little bunny captive was the first to find the princess and entice her into the woods. And now the three of us—Marlowe, the bunny fastened to a rope that Marlowe pulled from his sack, and I—hied off to find her.

I had no doubt that we'd find Snow White, and perhaps I would even meet my first dwarf. From what I had learned about the princess, I was less certain that we'd find out what was really behind her disappearance. Fortunately, that wasn't my problem.

Marlowe was back to muttering to himself and I was contemplating how much Orfeo would pay us when suddenly there was a most unrabbit-like squeal from the bunny, who started pulling at the rope. I looked up to see a little girl skipping towards us. She was alone, but out of the corner of my eye, I thought I saw a small, no more than two feet tall, humanoid melt into the deeper woods.

We had found Snow White. She was carrying something in her left hand.

I had last seen the princess at her christening, and she had definitely grown into an adorable and charming child—physically, at least. But appearances can be deceiving, even without a glamor being cast. As we met, I introduced myself and told her I'd been asked by her royal father to find her.

"Find me? Was I lost?" she said, eyes wide with feigned concern. She smiled, but the smile was lips only. It was obvious that we would never be bosom buddies. As a matter of fact, we bristled at each other on sight, and I felt an overwhelming sorrow for Queen Nistala who, I now realized, was justifiably afraid of her stepdaughter.

"Your father thinks you were, Princess, and both he and your mother (I used "mother" instead of "stepmother" deliberately to gauge the child's reaction—a study in neutrality) were frantic with worry. Where were you?"

"Oh, some little bunnies danced for me and I followed them into the woods and got lost. But they watched over me when I fell asleep, and then some bluebirds came and led me back here. And I found this mirror. See, isn't it pretty?" She held out her left hand.

"It's lovely, Princess. I'm sure it will look very pretty on your wall."

"Oh no, it's not for me. It's for my darling stepmama. Do you think she'll like it?"

Mesdames of Mayhem

About Cheryl Freedman

Cheryl Freedman was executive director of Crime Writers of Canada for 10 years until she resigned in 2009, partly to write her own mystery series.

Except she decided that it was way more fun – and far more profitable – to edit other people's work.

In "real" life a freelance editor, Cheryl's editing ranges from religious books to academic articles to memoirs, but she holds a special fondness and expertise for editing mystery and crime manuscripts.

An honorary lifetime member of the CWC, she's also the chair of the board of directors of Bloody Words, Canada's original mystery conference. Bloody Words is no more, but the annual BW literary award – the Bony Blithe Award for Light Mysteries – is still going strong.

"Mirror, Mirror" combines Cheryl's fondness for ferrets, fairy tales, and the 40s in a pseudo-historical mystery. Goslin and Marlowe will be back in *Mirror, Mirror*, the novel.

Crime Writers of Canada
Mesdames of Mayhem

AFTERWORD

By Joan O'Callaghan

There are no secrets that time does not reveal. The 17th century French playwright Jean Racine may well have had crime fiction on his mind when he spoke these words, for in the pages of *13 O'Clock*, every evil deed is eventually found out and justice is done, be it through due process of law or the machinations of fate.

The human impulse to do evil is part of the human condition ranging back through history, beginning with the biblical tale of Cain and Abel to speculative fiction in a future world that we can only imagine. And from biblical days through the ancient Greeks, Shakespeare, to the present day and beyond, one thing remains constant. The need to believe that evil cannot flourish and that good will ultimately prevail.

And so *13 O'Clock* has taken you from mediaeval times through the twentieth century into the twenty-first, to futuristic and fantasy worlds that exist only in the imagination. We hope you enjoyed your journey through time and that you leave the book satisfied, confident that all's well with the world.

Mesdames of Mayhem

ACKNOWLEDGMENTS

By Donna Carrick

In *13 O'Clock*, the Mesdames of Mayhem bring you a unique and diverse representation of our current work.

An anthology of this scope and quality relies upon the quiet dedication of numerous individuals.

Our first measure of gratitude goes to author and founder M.H. (Madeleine) Callway (*Windigo Fire*, Seraphim Editions, 2014).

Without her inspiration and untiring motivation, this work would not have come together. The Mesdames are her brainchild, and she remains the fulcrum upon which our efforts turn.

Our boundless thanks go out to copy-editor and contributing author Ed Piwowarczyk. True, he did have helpers, but the vast burden of polishing our work and lifting it to the high standard you see here fell upon his shoulders.

A veteran journalist; copy editor and editor (*National Post*, *Toronto Sun*, *The Sault Star* and Harlequin novels), Ed lent us his wealth of experience in the industry of words.

Our gratitude must also extend to our energetic and contagiously enthusiastic *ideas* person, Joan O'Callaghan. Joan coined the phrase Mesdames of Mayhem, and what a ride that sent us on! Her knowledge and passion for writing and reading are matched by her understanding of marketing in today's strange literary landscape. Without her, our collective's work may well have died in infancy.

On behalf of Carrick Publishing, I'd like to thank each of the contributing authors who created *13 O'Clock*. Your devotion to your craft is clear in every drop of ink, and it has been our tremendous pleasure and pride to work with each of you.

Readers are the life-blood of this industry. Without you, beloved readers, we are nothing. Above all, we thank you for your friendship throughout these pages.

May you always find joy, fun, entertainment and sometimes wisdom in our words, and may we keep our covenant with you: to offer only our very best in every endeavor.

Yours in literary excellence, now and forever...

Donna Carrick
Carrick Publishing

http://mesdamesofmayhem.com/.

Mesdames of Mayhem
founder M.H. Callway (centre) with
Donna Carrick (left)
and Joan O'Callaghan (right)
raising a glass to celebrate the completion of
13 O'Clock,
An anthology of crime stories
(Carrick Publishing 2015)

26501683R00191

Made in the USA
Middletown, DE
01 December 2015